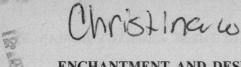

ENCHANTMENT AND DESIRE

"You must leave now," she whispered urgently.

"What is this place?" he asked.

" 'Tis only a dream," she replied. "It does not exist."

His fingers tightened about her wrist. Again he felt that unusual tingling of warmth that he'd felt when she'd touched him in the great hall outside William's court, just before the world seemed to explode around him.

"It does exist. Tell me!" He pulled her against him. Her full, high breasts pressed against him and her slender hips were molded to his. At the intimate contact, she gasped and in that shuddering sound he sensed a sudden, fierce passion.

Then, beyond the castle's crumbling walls he heard distinct sounds as familiar to him as breathing. The sounds of battle.

She stood with him at the window opening. As her hand closed once more over his arm, he turned. Even if it was a dream, even if as she said, he would not remember it, he knew what this place was.

Camelot. The legendary kingdom.

As the storm broke around them, lightning exploded near the window. He felt her pulling him toward the light. Once again, he experienced that intense burst of light and chaos of sight and sound that exploded around him. Then he was falling and her hand slipped from his. . . .

* * *

"Sorcery, enchantment, mystery and romance blend together perfectly in Quinn Taylor Evans' MERLIN'S LEGACY. Like Mary Stewart and Marion Zim̄̄̄̄̄̄ that enchants . . . truly memora

WATCH FOR THESE REGENCY ROMANCES

MERLIN'S LEGACY:
DAUGHTER OF LIGHT

Quinn Taylor Evans

ZEBRA BOOKS
Kensington Publishing Corp.
http://www.zebrabooks.com

ZEBRA BOOKS are published by

Kensington Publishing Corp.
850 Third Avenue
New York, NY 10022

First Printing: January, 1997
10 9 8 7 6 5 4 3 2 1

Printed in the United States of America

What once was, can be again.
A dream of love,
to hold against the dying of the Light,
the waiting Darkness of the night . . .

One

London, 1067

"Tell me, daughter," the thought came to Vivian, as easily as if her father stood beside her in the great hall of London Tower, and spoke them. *"Tell me what they speak of."*

There was an odd urgency in his tone as those thoughts connected with hers, as if he sensed something more but would not speak of it. For though he knew her thoughts in that special way that bound them together, he had closed his own thoughts to her.

Vivian stood in the shadows of the main hall of the newly built London Tower, the fortress where William of Normandy, now king of England, held court.

A year of bloodshed and conquest had brought a new king to the throne. She looked for her husband, for she had come late to court after attending to her son, who now slept soundly with a full stomach.

He was a sweet baby with her fiery red hair and his father's eyes, and the curious spirit of a changeling. With the blood of both a warrior and a sorcerer flowing through his veins, she was going to have her hands full. But for now, he was sleeping soundly under the watchful eye of Ninian, her mother.

Vivian was now the king's counselor as her father, Merlin, had once been counselor to another king. But of late the baby demanded more of her attention than even King William. Tonight, however, she had been drawn to court by reasons she did not understand, but sensed along every nerve ending like a prescience of warning that hung like a heavy presence in the air and appeared in disquieting visions in a woven tapestry.

"Much has changed, Father, in the year since William took the English throne," she murmured aloud, knowing her thoughts would connect with his even though he was not there to hear her words.

"And at the same time very little has changed. The Saxon barons are secretive and mistrustful. There are constant rumors of plots against the king. William's barons and knights grow restless and quarrelsome. The king grows restless and wishes to return to Normandy. Rorke wishes for us to leave this place, but I cannot. I am needed here. I sense it."

"What word is there?" he asked anxiously, and she knew the reason for she had seen it as well in the glossy silken threads woven into the tapestry.

"There is no word. The men he sent to the western lands are long overdue. The worst is feared."

Even as she spoke, argument broke out once more among William's knights. Many were in favor of sending additional men into the western lands, while an equal number were against it and spoke openly of their desire to return to Normandy, for many had left families there—families they had not seen in more than two years. It was dangerous talk with the Saxon barons listening attentively and plotting their own schemes should William withdraw from England.

Much had changed. The heralds and emblems of the Saxon nobility that once adorned the walls had been replaced by elaborate tapestries and the brightly colored standards of the House of Normandy, Anjou, Portiers, and a half dozen other noble European families whose knights now held titled lands in England as payment for services to William.

Torches burned at the walls, the acrid smell of animal fat blending with the pungence of woodsmoke, cold sweat, and the heated flesh of so many bodies crowded into the main hall as other arguments broke out.

William the Conqueror, now self-proclaimed king of England, sat at the table on the raised dais a full level above those who argued so vehemently on the main floor.

He was a robust man of ample height, the width of his shoulders enhanced even more by the layers of rich satin and velvet at his tunic. His russet hair was slightly graying at the temples, his eyes a fierce dark amber that burned with the fire of ambition that had won him the throne of England. Beside him, Queen Mathilde, recovered now after the birth of her third child, a son, sat in watchful silence.

To his other side, sat his friend and loyal knight, Rorke FitzWarren. At seeing her husband's fierce, handsome profile Vivian felt a welling of pride and desire. There had been no private moments between them of late since the birth of their son and with matters so difficult in the western lands.

Long hours each night he counseled with William about matters of state. It was widely rumored that if William decided to return to Normandy he would make Rorke FitzWarren chancellor in his absence, with complete authority in all matters.

Vivian never intervened with her powers in matters that concerned Rorke's position with William, but she was not about to let him be drawn into political intrigues. She had worked long and hard to make certain it would not happen, using her own very special powers of persuasion. But Rorke had found out her scheme and he was furious with her. Even now, she knew he was still furious that she dared interfere by using her immortal powers.

Even now as she watched, his lean hawkish features were deceptively calm, eyes hooded as he sat back in the high-backed chair to William's right, his fingers loosely wrapped about the handle of a tankard.

She alone sensed his wariness and alertness to everything that was said, each change of expression and movement among those who attended court.

She sensed, too, the danger that was suddenly very near, and approached silently to stand beside his chair. She laid a hand at his shoulder, both a warning and the instinct to protect, only moments before the doors to the great hall were violently thrown open.

Rorke immediately came out of the chair, pulling her behind him as his hand went to his broadsword. About the great hall other weapons were seized and drawn, as several warriors strode into court without waiting to be announced.

Their battle armor was caked with mud. They wore no colors. If they had once carried a standard that might identify them, it was not visible. They were a ragged, tattered and bloodstained lot, their faces smudged with filth as they came to a halt before the steps to the king's dais. Only their battle swords gleamed bright and true, catching the light from dozens of torches.

One warrior strode among them. The others parted to let him pass by. His mail coif was pushed back to his shoulders. The fine metal mesh was twisted and torn, several tears bloodstained and gaping open where he had been wounded. His dark hair was plastered to his head, his features barely discernible beneath the mask of sweat, grime, and blood. Only his eyes were recognizable, kind eyes once filled with gentleness and friendship when Vivian had needed a friend, but which had seen such tragic loss in the death of a beloved brother.

Gavin de Marte stood silently before his king, his men fanned out behind him. His mantle was stained and torn, his crest unrecognizable. They had obviously ridden for days and under the most horrible conditions to reach London. The blood stained across mantle and armor told of the terrible conflict in the western lands.

Across the hall, Vivian saw the bright golden cap of her sister's hair, like a radiant beacon. But even had she not seen her, their thoughts would have connected in that ancient way that they shared with their father.

There was far more that had not yet been revealed. Something far more dreadful than the sight of these beleaguered warriors and the tales of battle she sensed they had brought back to their king.

"Something dreadful has happened," Brianna's thoughts were filled with apprehension. *"Just as you saw in the tapestry."*

"Yes," Vivian answered. *"I feel it as well."* All their attention focused on Gavin de Marte as he strode wearily forward and approached his king.

"I bring a gift from the western lands, milord," he said, his voice taut with weariness and pain from those myriad injuries couldn't disguise the undercurrent of rage that she sensed in him, like a bowstring drawn to the breaking point.

"Sent by the Welsh rebels." From beneath his mantle he produced a basket. Holding it before him, he walked forward. Going down on one knee he presented it to the king.

More than danger now, Vivian sensed a dreadful horror. It came to her as clearly as if the top of the basket had already been removed and the contents revealed.

"Rorke . . ." she whispered, her voice part caution, part trepidation, her gaze fastened on the basket.

He turned, for a moment allowing his attention to be distracted. His gray gaze narrowed on her.

"What is it? Is it some danger to the king?"

Her fingers closed tightly over his arm, as if seeking his mortal strength.

" 'Tis dangerous for us all."

Her vivid blue gaze met his. And in that moment before the lid to the basket was drawn away and the contents revealed for all to see, she said with certainty, "You will have no need of your sword, my husband."

His gaze narrowed, then he turned and stared at the basket. William rose and walked down the steps of the dais to the main floor of the hall. He stared intently at his knight, then down at the basket. He reached inside and retrieved the gift that had been sent.

It was round, thickly wrapped in cloth, and about the size of a bee hive. The cloth was badly stained. As he unwrapped it, the contents fell and rolled across the stone floor.

Across the hall, from Saxon and Norman alike, were gasps of horror and revulsion as everyone stared at the ghastly severed head of John Curthose, William's trusted knight and emissary sent to negotiate peace with Prince John.

Ladies who attended the court gasped in horror. Poladouras the monk, who had raised Vivian from a babe, uttered a hasty prayer as all around the court there were reactions of shock, revulsion, and horror.

The queen let out a startled, strangled sound, but it was drowned out by the infuriated reaction of Stephen of Valois, William's bastard son.

John Curthose had practically raised Stephen until he was old enough to sit astride a horse and ride at his father's side.

Rorke FitzWarren had taught him everything he knew about being a knight. John taught him about the world beyond the battlefield—a world of cultures far older than his own; of languages, history, and philosophy.

Rorke had taken the young boy and made a warrior of him. John had taken the young warrior's mind and filled it with knowledge. Now, that dear friend and mentor had been brutally slain.

"By God!" Stephen exploded, shock turning to pain, then rage as he stepped from amidst William's other knights. "These rebels will pay for what they have done!" He turned to Gavin de Marte.

"How many men were lost?"

"Ten of my own," Gavin replied, glancing from Stephen to the king. "All of Sir John's men are dead. He had been hung in a tree for the birds to pick at his bones. This," he gestured to the ghastly gift that had been sent for the king, "was delivered to our encampment the morning we found them massacred."

Stephen was of an even height with his father, but with that lean, animal intensity of youth in every rigid muscle and taut feature at his face. His eyes were that same deep color of amber, his hair the richer, dark color William's had once been.

There were more than mere traces of the father in the son, in the same strong jaw and sharply angled brows. But there the resemblance ended. He had the wide cheekbones and sensual mouth of his mother— that beautiful, guileless creature whose only sin was that she was of common birth with no land or titles to bring to a marriage.

Though William had loved her wildly and deeply, with that first passion of youth from which a son was conceived when William was only fifteen years of age, he was forbidden to wed her by the very father who had also made him a bastard by birth but who claimed him as his rightful heir—Robert of Normandy.

Vivian knew that William saw himself as he had once

been in the son who stood before him. Father and son were bonded by the circumstance of their birth. He was William's firstborn son and was loved as none of William's other sons. Stephen of Valois, more than any of his other children, was the son of his passion and desire, the son in whom he saw the pain of the past and glimpsed the hope for the future.

"This cannot be allowed," Stephen spoke aloud what every knight and warrior in the great hall was thinking. "You must send an army into the western lands."

"We will discuss this at another time."

"Another time?" Stephen replied, aghast. "Another time, the next heads that roll may be within these very walls. You must act now."

"We will not speak of this now!" William replied, his voice going low with unspoken warning for his son's foolishness in speaking so openly before the entire court, which included the Saxon barons who would like nothing better than to see William cast from England once and for all. It would make no difference if the lawless Welsh rebels to the west were the cause of it.

But Stephen would not be put off. For months there had been rumors of trouble in those lands that bordered England at a not remote distance. The western lands were only several days ride from London.

First the king had sent John of Curthose, and then Gavin de Marte. Now, many men were dead. What more proof did his father need? Frustration and anger goaded him to speak perhaps more unwisely than he should have—frustration that he alone among his father's knights was constantly overlooked in matters of military strategy even though he had earned his knight's spurs five years before at an earlier age than any of William's other knights, including Rorke FitzWarren; and anger that every word, each gesture, each decision that was made was a reminder of his low birth. That he was not considered as worthy as the king's other knights and noblemen whom he entrusted with his entire kingdom. That anger made him reckless.

"I demand that you send me to the western lands!" Stephen told the king, standing before him with unbowed head, eyes narrowed in silent challenge to his father. His fists were tightly clenched, every muscle taut with anger as if ready to charge into battle.

"You have made me commander of your army. It is my duty to protect the king and avenge the death of your knight."

William perhaps saw too much of himself in his son—that reckless passion, the finely honed warrior's skills, and the anger. The son was what the father had once been. And the boot did not fit particularly well.

"You are commander by my leave," William replied, low under his breath, his words meant only for his son. He was not particularly pleased to be reminded that his generosity had now placed him in a difficult situation.

"You may demand nothing. And you would do well to remember that what you have, you have by my generosity." It was said with the hope of dissuading Stephen from such haste, but it had the opposite effect.

"What I have," Stephen replied loud and clear for all to hear, "is mine by right of blood spilled over countless battlefields fighting at your side, milord. No less than the blood of others who have served you, and by which you now hold the throne of England."

A sudden silence fell across the great hall. The king was not pleased to be so reminded.

"By God! You forget yourself!" William slammed his fist down on the table before him, rattling the metal tankards. "The knights who serve you, do so by the grace of my purse."

"I forget nothing!" Stephen replied. " 'Tis you who have forgotten!" Beside him, through the gathering of knights a warrior appeared. Tarek al Sharif, the mercenary who had also fought beside William and who was wed to Vivian's sister Brianna, cautiously stepped forward and laid a warning hand on the young warrior's arm.

Stephen jerked away, ignoring the warning as he boldly approached his father, the king. He furiously stripped off his gauntlets and the tunic with the crest of Valois, which William had bestowed upon him when he first earned his knight's spurs and sword.

He threw both to the floor at the foot of William's throne. Then he spun on his heel and strode from the hall, hand clamped over the handle of his broadsword and with a sweeping glance silently daring any of William's knights to stop him. They did not, but instead, at a sharp glance from the king, let him pass.

Tarek's gaze sought that of his wife. They had traveled from the north country to bring word to the king that Mardigan and his raiders threatened the north coast no longer.

A look passed between them as Brianna joined her thoughts with his. The image in the tapestry—a portent of an uncertain future—had already begun to unfold.

Stephen strode angrily from the hall. If he could have slammed the stout oaken doors, he would have. Instead he had to be content with frightening a young woman he found in the hallway just outside the royal court.

They collided. Muttering an oath, Stephen reached to steady her. Beneath the sleeve of her gown he felt the sudden tension of slender muscles and tendons, and then surprising strength as she attempted to twist free.

For a moment his anger with his father was forgotten. He frowned for the young woman was not dressed as other women at William's court, in their rich brocades and satins, with the heavy spicy fragrances of sandalwood and frangipani imported from the middle empires by the Normans and bestowed upon their new Saxon brides who had brought them riches in land and titles.

Beneath his hand, the sleeve of her gown was brilliant blue and soft as velvet, the rest of it hidden beneath the soft gray mantle that swirled about her slender body as she pulled away.

The mantle was made of the lightest fabric that glittered with hidden light, and shimmered across the stones of the floor where it puddled at her feet.

As she struggled, the hood fell to her shoulders, revealing the thick midnight satin of glistening long dark hair that fell in shimmering waves past her shoulders, beautiful features beneath satin ivory skin, and the most extraordinary eyes he had ever seen. They were violet, brilliant as rare gemstones, and filled with alarm.

"Who are you?" Stephen demanded. "What are you doing here?"

"Let me go!" she whispered frantically, trying to twist free of his grasp. But Stephen refused to release her. He tightened his grasp, preventing any hope of escape. Beneath his fingers he felt slender, delicate bones, tendons, and pliant muscle.

"Please!" she implored, that violet gaze once more returning to his. "You must release me at once!"

As she spoke a blinding flash of light exploded in the darkened hall as if the torches had exploded at the walls. The intensity of the light sliced painfully through his brain and burned at his eyes. Then it expanded, surrounding the young woman.

Stephen tried to pull her back from that circle of light certain she would be burned by the intense heat. Instead, he felt himself being drawn forward, pulled toward the light.

There was nothing to hold onto except the slender wrist clasped in his hand. Then the light surrounded them both. It shimmered and pulsed as it grew brighter and hotter. It burned at his skin and seemed to suck the air from his lungs.

Even though he still held onto the young woman, he could no longer see her. In the intense light she had become a slender golden shadow. Then, the light exploded inward, collapsing in on itself.

Stephen felt as if he'd taken a blow that dropped him to the floor. Except the floor no longer existed. It was as if he'd fallen through some sort of opening and was being hurtled through a passage of blinding light.

He was tumbled end over end, rolling, slipping and sliding, through a vortex of light and sound. Everything whipped past him in an vivid blur of color and intense sensation. Myriad sounds roared past him as if a million voices cried out all at once.

He felt like a piece of wood caught in a powerful current, being sucked through the chaos of light, unable to free himself, unable to stop what was happening, capable only of holding on to that slender hand clasped like a lifeline.

Then, as suddenly as it began, the whirling vortex of light, color, and sound suddenly ceased. He was hurtled down onto a rough, hard surface, the sharp edges of stones cutting into his hands and scraping his face.

It hurt to breathe, and he felt cold. His muscles hurt as if they'd been torn apart, and his bones ached as if he'd just taken a brutal beating in the practice yard.

He had heard death described by knights and warriors who had encountered it on the battlefield. If not for the intense pain that pulsed through him with every beat of his heart, he would have thought himself dead.

Where was he? Had the king's fortress been attacked?

Gradually those chaotic images ceased spinning about him. Eventually he was able to drag air back into his lungs. He attempted to move his arms and legs, and immediately regretted it as pain throbbed in every muscle and joint. He was weak as a newborn babe.

When the world seemed to have settled around him once more, he attempted the much simpler task of flexing his hand, and discovered he no longer held on to the young woman. He slowly opened his eyes.

Sight and sound focused painfully. He again felt those cold stones beneath him, not coarse and rough, but smooth and polished.

Was he in the great hall in London? It seemed greatly changed. No torches burned at the walls. There was no sound of warriors and knights at William's court. All was dark and silent.

As he slowly turned over onto his back, he felt something light as goose-down brush against his face. Then he felt it again. As he stared overhead, his gaze slowly focused on the white snow flakes that slowly drifted down through the broken opening in the roof overhead. Gradually he felt strong enough to push slowly to his feet.

White and silent, snow drifted down through that opening and blanketed crumbling stone walls with a glistening white mantle that hid the scars of ruin and decay. This was not the king's tower in London.

What had happened? Where was he? What was this place?

As his strength gradually returned, Stephen slowly walked through the crumbling ruins. It was an ancient place, cold and silent, shadows steeping the walls at the edges of pale light that spilled through the gaping roof. But even in that meager light he could discern that it had once been a large and grand castle.

The stones were all pale, smooth, and gleaming beneath the bracken and debris that had accumulated through the centuries. Panels of window openings opened out onto a large courtyard bordered by more long, low buildings. And surrounding all was a wall linked by stone towers made of that same pale stone.

The towers gleamed in the silent falling snow, like ghostly sentries that still guarded this ancient place. But he sensed far more in what could not be easily seen but lay hidden beneath that mantle of snow and debris.

With the instinct of all warriors who have ever stood on a battlefield and smelled death, he knew that once a fierce battle had been fought within these walls.

Beneath the debris and rubble of ages and gathering snow he found the telltale signs—the blackened edges of pale stones where fire had swept through the castle; scattered metal flagons and crushed pottery; and in the large main chamber, the tattered remnants of some long lost king's standards and the crumbling skeletal remains of the last defenders who bravely made one last stand against impossible odds.

Their ancient battle armor lay where they had fallen about the crumbling and decayed ruins of what appeared to be a large round table. Twelve breastplates and twelve battle swords lay upon the stones as if the weary warriors had merely laid down to rest for a time before taking up the battle once more.

He slowly approached the table. The surface was badly scarred and stained from the elements that had claimed the castle in the centuries after that final battle. But like the stone walls and those ancient warriors who somehow refused to give up the battle, ancient carvings set into the surface of the stone could still be seen.

Stephen ran his fingers lightly across the surface of the table. There were figures of warriors in carved panels that rimmed the edge. Within the ring of panels was another ring of letters forming words written in latin but indecipherable.

He brushed more debris aside, but they were in poor condition and in the meager light he could not read them clearly. Then, he suddenly jerked his hand back. Though it was unbearably cold inside the crumbling castle, his fingers tingled as if he had touched something warm and alive.

Snow had turned to icy rain. The wind came up and he heard the distant rumble of thunder. Overhead, through the gaping opening in the roof, lightening flashed. The afterglow flared across charred walls.

Yet, within the fortress, there was a strange, expectant silence as in those moments often experienced just before a battle when it seemed every warrior's heart ceased its frantic beating. When he turned, he saw the young woman he had encountered outside the main hall.

In the sudden flare of light through the roof overhead, her skin was pale as fine marble, as if she had stepped from one of those ancient stones. Her eyes were an extraordinary shade of violet above high cheekbones, and her hair was the color of the night sky. About her neck, she wore a necklace with stones etched with unusual markings. She seemed not a creature of this world. But when he reached for her, the slender arm beneath his hand was flesh and blood, warm and very real.

"You must leave this place now," she whispered urgently. "It is dangerous for you to be here."

Her other hand closed over his and again he felt that unusual tingling of warmth. Where their hands joined he again experienced that sudden light-headedness and confusion as he had in the great hall outside William's court, just before the world seemed to explode around him. Again, he was surprised by the unusual strength he felt in that slender wrist, almost as if she chose it she could pull free of his grasp. But she did not.

"Please," she implored him again. "You must not be here."

"But I am here. Who are you?" he demanded. "What is this place?"

" 'Tis only a dream," she replied. "It does not exist."

His fingers tightened. "It does exist. Tell me!" He pulled her against him. She was no dream. She was very real, warm, and flesh and blood.

The mantle shimmered about her shoulders and seemed to whisper about her slender body. Beneath that pale, glistening fabric her full, high breasts pressed against him and her slender hips were molded to his.

At the intimate contact, her head came up, violet eyes going several shades darker until they seemed as dark and fathomless as the night sky, the sweet warmth of her breath startled past her softly parted lips. In that shuddering sound he sensed a sudden, fierce passion.

Then, beyond those crumbing walls and towers with the crest of some long lost king, he heard distinct sounds as familiar to him as breathing. They were the sounds of battle. He pulled her with him to the gaping window opening of the great chamber.

Beyond the storm, he heard the clash of steel, the thunder of horses, and the cries of the dying carried on the fury of the rising storm. The stench of battle rose up from the valley beyond the castle walls, carried on a cold, dark wind. War.

He had experienced it many times across the whole of Europe and most recently at the battle of Hastings— enemies met on a large flat plain in a fight to the death.

The castle of some long lost king . . .

She stood with him at the window opening. As her hand closed once more over his arm, he turned. Even if it was a dream, he knew what this place was as he felt the warmth of her touch burning through him.

Camelot, the kingdom of the legendary king who had once ruled all of Britain.

As the storm broke around them, lightning exploded at the window opening. Instead of trying to free herself, he felt her slender hand close over his. She was pulling him toward the light.

Once again, he experienced that intense burst of light and chaos of sight and sound that exploded around him. Then he was falling, and her hand slipped from his.

Stephen felt the cold hard stones that scraped his hands and cheek. Slowly, he pushed himself up from the floor. The light at the torches in the hall smoldered feebly, then steadily burned brighter.

As his senses cleared, he heard familiar voices raised in argument from the main hall nearby. He recognized the guards who stood at the entrance to the hall. Everything was a rich texture of familiar sight and sound, exactly as it had been when he first walked from William's court. But this time the young woman was nowhere to be seen.

Was she real? Or had he only imagined her?

He slowly opened his fingers. Clutched in his hand, so tight that it had made an impression at his palm, was one of the gleaming rune stones from the necklace she had worn.

As he reached for her in that ancient place the necklace must have broken. The stone he held in his hand was proof that he had not imagined her! But if he had not imagined her, then what had happened to her?

He looked down at the smooth pale stone. The image carved in the surface of the stone was the figure of a man holding a weapon. To those who believed in the ancient runes and the destiny they foretold, he was known as the warrior.

Two

Streamers of mist, like the gray veils of bent old women, draped the trees of the king's forest at the edge of London in the gray predawn.

There was a chill in the air that had not been there days before and warned of the coming autumn with winter fast on its heels. The leaves in the trees had lost their green, tinged with yellow at the edges, fading to shades of gold and orange, yet still clinging to the branches overhead like tiny fluttering gold banners.

Leather creaked and harness jangled as horses snorted and stamped their feet impatiently, blowing clouds of steam in the frosty morning air. They sensed the coming journey and were restless at their tethers, eager to escape the confines of the stables.

Battle swords gleamed dully in the predawn gray. Bedrolls were secured at saddles. Two carts carried provisions of food. When the provisions ran out, they would live off the land.

"You go against the king's orders," Rorke FitzWarren cautioned Stephen as they stood together among the warriors who had gathered to join him, the eagerness for the coming journey hot in their blood.

He had followed his young friend from the fortress walls of London Tower. One by one throughout the night the other warriors and knights who followed him had also left the fortress, sleeping in the forest. The food and cart had been provisioned from within the city, for there was always an eager merchant willing to earn gold coins for his purse no matter the hour of the night.

The night before he had infuriated William by throwing down the gauntlets and tunic with the emblem of Valois, the estate and title in Normandy William had bestowed upon his son a year earlier for valor of service.

He had not taken up the emblem but instead wore a black tunic and leggings. His kite-shaped shield which hung at his saddle was also black with a single bloodred mark slashed diagonally across the face of the shield and written below it the latin word—*Desdicado*. A word that proudly proclaimed his bastard birth.

"I go against no orders," Stephen retorted, tying down the scabbard to his broadsword with furious, taut movements. Then he slanted Rorke a look and slowly smiled. It was a fierce, cunning smile, very much like his father's when William was confronted with insurmountable odds on a field of battle.

"The king said only that I could *'demand nothing.'* Very well, I demand nothing." He finished tying the last leather cord that secured his weapons within easy reach when astride his warhorse.

"As commander of the king's army, I am sworn to protect him against any threat or danger." His smile shifted, reaching his eyes with a glint of pure pleasure that his father would have appreciated.

"I sense a threat to the kingdom. Therefore, it is my duty to pursue them and put down the threat."

"Your own interpretation of the king's words," Rorke muttered, knowing full well that such an interpretation would do Stephen no good if William chose to interpret his actions otherwise.

"The king's exact words the day he bestowed the honor upon me."

"And if, as the king's chancellor, I forbid you to go to the west country?" Rorke asked, prepared to do just that if it might preclude a dangerous confrontation between father and son, yet already knowing the answer he would get, for he knew this young man as well as if he was his own son.

Stephen's smile vanished, replaced by another expression Rorke had come to know well in the father— that ruthless, resolute expression when a decision was made and would not be changed.

"Do not forbid it," Stephen warned, his hand resting on the handle of his broadsword. "I would not choose to lose a father and my best friend all in the same day. But if it must be, then so be it." Leaving no doubt he repeated, "I am going to the west country. Do not try to stop me." Then his fierceness eased. "Surely you above all people, understand why I must go."

"I do understand. All I ask is that you wait for a time."

"For what?" Stephen demanded. "For my father to find a dozen reasons to keep me at his side in London, while he sends his other knights far afield to secure his kingdom? What of John of Curthose? He was an honorable man. He did not deserve to die as he did." Stephen shook his head, his mouth set in a rigid line as he secured his blanket roll behind his saddle.

"William will not claim me as his son, nor will he allow me to seek my own destiny." He jerked the leather ties savagely. "I have done his bidding in everything he has asked. I have asked for nothing in return but the chance to prove myself a worthy knight, yet he denies me the opportunity when it is at hand. Just as he denies my existence."

Stephen finished tying off the bedroll. He looked across the saddle at his friend and mentor. "I must do this," he said, his voice suddenly quiet but with equal passion as he remembered his encounter in the hall

the night before. It was an encounter he did not understand, but somehow sensed was part of this journey.

The smooth stone with the figure of the warrior etched
in the surface was tied to the pommel of his saddle, a
token of that encounter. He held it between thumb and
forefinger, feeling the warmth of the stone, as if it still
held some of the girl's warmth. Then his expression was
closed, his thoughts carefully hidden away.

"I must do this," he repeated. "Just as I know that
my father would try to prevent it if he knew of it."

"There are some who would call your actions trea-
sonous," Rorke reasoned. "In the very least, it is foolhardy. You take only a score of men with you."

"Almost the exact same number of men you took with
you, when you first ventured into the north country,"
Stephen pointed out, his mouth curving into a smile.
Then the smile faded, and Stephen was most serious.

"The men who ride with me are the finest warriors.
You helped train them. We travel fast and light, like the
rebels we seek."

Rorke knew this young man as he knew himself. He
knew also the inner demons he struggled with, for he
had confronted much the same struggle over his own
bastard birth. But his father had not been a king, who
could not make choices of the heart; Rorke's father had
no heart. There was nothing he could say, and they
both knew it.

He clasped Stephen at the arms, wishing he was riding with him, to protect him as the younger knight had
protected him against an enemy blow many times.

"Go with God, my friend, and watch your back. I will
protect it here in London, as much as I can."

Stephen clasped Rorke's arms in strong hands. In his
expression was a depth of gratitude that could never
be repaid. "Thank you."

As Rorke left to speak with the other knights who

rode with him, a slender figure appeared on a shifting current of mist. Then as the mist shifted once more in the opposite direction on some unseen current of air, Stephen saw that it was Lady Brianna, the wife of his friend Tarek al Sharif.

Her hair was like sunlight in mist, her eyes the color of a forest glade. The gray predawn seemed to wrap around her as if she was part of it, and not a creature of this earth. As she approached, her steps were tentative, her gaze measuring.

She said nothing at first, but slowly approached the warhorse. The animal was nervous, moving restlessly at the tether and could easily have crushed her with a single misstep. But Brianna seemed not to notice or be concerned. As she approached the beast, she reached out and laid a slender hand along the heavily muscled neck. Almost immediately, the animal calmed, slowly blowing out a cloud of steam as if sighing contentedly.

It never failed to amaze Stephen, the effect all the women in her family seemed to have on animals. As if they were kindred spirits who sensed that in these special ladies they need fear nothing.

She stroked a hand down the length of velvety nose, whispering soft, unintelligible words. Almost as if it could understand her, the stallion lowered its large head and seemed to listen. She smiled faintly, her gaze meeting Stephen's.

"It is a gift of all those of my blood. We have a oneness with nature and all those who are part of it." She slowly rounded the tall steed, until she was standing beside Stephen. Yet she continued to stroke the stallion's neck, as if completely absorbed in only that.

She continued to speak softly in that strange language. Eventually, she spoke words he understood.

"Rorke could not dissuade you from going," she said softly, not a question but a statement of fact, as if she had heard every word spoken, or knew it before it was spoken.

"I knew that you must go. I saw it in the threads woven in the tapestry." There was a sadness in her voice "You are part of it now, as she is."

Stephen's gaze narrowed, but he revealed nothing either by word or gesture. He had seen the tapestry once, when it was barely begun. Then, his friend Tarek al Sharif had spoken of it more recently when retelling the story of his own battle against the forces of Darkness.

In the tapestry were the images of war, great battles, and danger, the struggle against evil for the sword Excalibur, the search for the legendary Grail, and the image of a warrior interwoven with that of a beautiful, dark-haired young girl with exceptional eyes the color of violets.

Stephen had told no one of his encounter outside the king's court—of the unusual young woman with midnight black hair and extraordinary violet eyes, dressed in a shimmering mantle; nor of his experience when he had touched her, as if he had stepped into another world.

Brianna's gaze met his. In those velvety, green eyes and in the soft curve of her smile, he saw the resemblance to the Lady Vivian.

"The resemblance is strong in my family," she said, with a faint, secretive smile as if she knew his thoughts. "Her name is Cassandra," she said, the smile becoming a sad expression.

"She is my sister." As if she had read his thoughts and the question that kept repeating itself over and over.

Stephen's gaze narrowed. If the young woman was her sister, then she was also Merlin's daughter.

He knew the legend, as did almost every living man— of the great wise counselor to the English king who was supposedly imprisoned and later died, after the death of King Arthur. Some said Merlin was merely a very learned man, but there were others who said he was far more. A man of unusual talents and powers, drawn from the forces of the universe.

Stephen had seen those powers firsthand in Merlin's daughters. Vivian of Amesbury possessed unusual healing skills that could mend torn flesh and shattered bones. She had the ability to see events before they happened, and the power of fire like a life force that lived within her.

Brianna had only recently discovered the full extent of her own powers—that of knowing another's thoughts without the necessity of speaking them, and most extraordinary of all—the power of transformation. Drawing on the powers of the Light that flowed through her blood as with her sister, she was capable of assuming many different forms.

Their mother was Ninian, the Lady of the Lake, who had carried the sword Excalibur to the world between the worlds and given it to Merlin after Arthur's death. Ninian had joined Merlin in his world, because he could not live in hers.

Though it had been over five hundred years since Arthur was slain and his kingdom destroyed by the powers of the Darkness, far less time passed in the world between the worlds. As if it was somehow suspended.

There, in that magical prison, trapped in a place that was neither one world or another, but a place in between, Merlin was only marginally older than when he had served at Arthur's side. And in that place where time moved out of time, he had fathered three daughters, who were sent far away to live in anonymity in the mortal world so that they might be kept safe from the powers of the Darkness.

Brianna sensed his unspoken thought. Her gaze followed his then widened as she saw the rune stone tied to the pommel of his saddle.

"It is the sign of a great warrior," Brianna explained, answering his unspoken question. She frowned slightly, her delicate brows drawn together. "A warrior who wears no crest upon his shield."

Or perhaps, Stephen thought, the mark of a bastard who may not rightfully wear any shield because of his bastardy.

"Where did you get this stone?" But before he replied, she sensed the answer.

"Cassandra," she whispered, her gaze fastened on the rune stone as she held it between her fingers. "We have not heard from her in many years."

At his surprise, she explained, "Cassandra believed our parents had abandoned her. When Merlin refused to allow her to return she was hurt and angry. Afterward, she refused to accept her heritage. She never returned to the world in the mist."

She stroked the stone's glossy smooth surface as if seeing far more than the simple image etched there. "We do not even know what powers she possesses."

"I have seen her. She is here," Stephen replied, seeing no reason why he should not reveal it to her. For she would believe what he had seen while others might not.

"The rune stone is hers."

Brianna nodded, still holding the stone between her fingers. "Aye," she said softly. "I sensed her presence the moment I saw the stone."

"Perhaps now she has chosen to return."

She lifted her head slightly. She had a very far away look in her eyes, as if seeing something that others could not.

"I would know if she was here." She shook her head sadly. "Whatever reason brought her here, she has gone, and without a word even to our mother."

"Where has she gone?"

Her gaze came back to his then, beautiful, soft green, as young as springtime and as old as time with the immortal powers that she possessed.

"She has returned to the west country."

"How is that possible? I saw her two nights ago outside the royal hall, and yet it is many days ride over difficult terrain and through dangerous countryside to the western lands. If," he added, "what I saw was real."

He had learned in previous encounters with the powers of the Light and the Darkness that all was not what it seemed. One could not always trust what one saw, the forces took many forms and wore disguises. The most recent scars he carried were proof of the power of those forces.

Brianna sensed the frustration and confusion he had felt those two days since. His thoughts revealed his encounter with Cassandra, the incredible journey he had made, and the images of the ruined castle fortress.

"It was very real. I sense her life force lingering about the stone. If your encounter had only been an illusion, I would not sense her presence." She frowned, wondering what had brought Cassandra to London after all these years. So near to her family, yet refusing any contact. One thing she knew for certain, Cassandra's contact with him was all part of what was woven into the tapestry.

"Your journey has already begun," she whispered.

She shivered as if she had felt something that could not yet be seen, but could only be sensed. A disturbance in the forces of Light that balanced their world and protected the mortal world from danger.

The Darkness was growing, just as her sister, Vivian, had seen in the tapestry. But one thing she still had no sense of—the immortal powers Cassandra possessed.

Had her sister turned from the powers of the Light

to the side of Darkness? No matter how hard she concentrated on the essence that lingered about the stone, like an afterglow of warmth that was part of Cassandra's presence, she sensed nothing about her sister's powers. She realized it was part of the journey that awaited Stephen of Valois.

"There will be great danger," Brianna told him with a troubled frown, unable to sense exactly where the danger would come from. She had hoped at least to give him that much—a warning that might help protect him when the danger came.

"I do not know whom you may trust. But the danger comes from far more than avenging the death of your companions and securing William's throne against rebel attack."

From within the folds of her mantle she retrieved a small roll of cloth. It was narrow, no more than a ribbon of fabric and the color of gray mist. It glistened as dawn slanted through the trees in the forest. The color on the other side of the ribbon was deep blue. Brianna seized his wrist and tied the ribbon about it.

"It is a spellcast," she explained. "The threads are the same as those woven into the tapestry. But if it is placed around Cassandra's wrist, she will be left powerless the same as any mortal." At his doubtful expression, she warned, "Do not doubt me, warrior. For I speak the truth. It will protect you. It may well be the only protection you will have, for what lays ahead your sword will be of no use to you."

Stephen stared down at the narrow strip of ribbon. It seemed delicate and fragile, like a talisman given by a fair maiden before a tournament. Yet it was strong as the steel of the finest sword to be found in the middle empires. The color had changed. It was no longer gray on one side, blue on the other, but changed constantly, shimmering to shades in between. "Do you know what danger it may protect me from?"

In her eyes, he saw his answer—Cassandra, her own sister.

She nodded. "You must find the ancient Oracle. It was stolen by the powers of the Darkness five hundred years ago when Merlin was banished from the kingdom. Cassandra is the only one who may seek the stone. She alone possesses the ability to find it. Only she may use its power.

"But there is more. Not even Merlin can sense Cassandra's true heart. It is possible she has turned to the powers of the Darkness. The spellcast ribbon will give you strength for what must be done for it possesses Merlin's power combined with that of my sister and I."

She did not need to explain what must be done.

Stephen nodded gravely. He understood what she spoke of for only recently his friend Tarek al Sharif, now a chieftain in the northern lands and Brianna's husband, had faced that same dreadful possibility.

"What is the Oracle? How will I know it?"

She smiled faintly. "You will know it when you see it, if you are fortunate enough and strong enough to prevail. It is the ancient crystal which possesses the knowledge of the universe. Whoever possesses the Oracle, possesses that knowledge and will have the power to alter the future of mankind. Once the crystal belonged to Merlin. But it was stolen and hidden away during the great cataclysm when Arthur, the ancient king, was betrayed and killed."

"What can you tell me of the threat in the western lands?"

"It is real. The Welsh prince has joined the rebels together with the Saxons who fled after King Harold's death on the field of Hastings. He has no intention of surrendering the western lands to your father."

"Can there be peace?"

"I do not know. The powers of Darkness grow strong in the western lands, for it was there that it all began in that long ago time. Now the future will be set in motion, and not even Merlin can see the outcome."

"What of John of Tregaron?" he asked, for it was at the edge of Tregaron's lands that his fellow knights had been attacked and died.

"He is ambitious. He looks only to protect the fortunes of Tregaron. He will do whatever is necessary to protect what is his." She sensed, however, that Tregaron was not the greatest threat.

"If you are strong and cunning, he can be dealt with."

Stephen heard the hesitance in her voice, and asked, "Do you sense something else?"

She nodded. "Something I cannot clearly discern. But there is another much more dangerous threat—the danger of the Darkness. Not from Tregaron, but from one close to him. More than that I cannot tell you for it does not reveal itself to me."

Stephen snorted. "At least you bring no bad news."

Her soft green eyes flashed with anger. "This is no matter to be taken lightly."

With no small amount of irony he said solemnly, "I defy my own king in what I do. The father may forgive, but the king cannot. If I succeed in this, he may well order me hanged. I am damned if I do, and most certainly damned if I do not." All trace of humor was now gone.

"I assure you," he said, not unkindly. "I do not take this lightly. I take it most seriously."

"You will need someone to guide you through the western lands," she added. "I can guide you there, for I can see what you cannot."

He shook his head, his answer adamant. "I cannot allow it. And even if I did, your husband would never allow it. I will have enough enemies in the western lands, I do not need to make an enemy of one of my closest friends and him at my back."

"But you have only the directions of Sir Gavin and the men who returned with him. They may not correctly remember everything. It is dangerous to travel unguided in foreign lands . . ."

He gently but firmly refused. "No, Lady Brianna, I forbid it. If the danger is as you say, I will not endanger you as well. Besides," he added, a handsome smile curving his mouth, hinting that there was more than a little truth in the rumors of his liaisons with the women at William's court though he steadfastly refused to be wed with any of them, "Your image was not woven into the panel of the tapestry."

She could not deny the truth of his words. This was his destiny, and Cassandra's. Though her own powers were strong, she could not interfere with what was already woven in the tapestry. As for what lay ahead in those murky, magical unwoven images that had not clearly defined themselves, it could only be discovered by Stephen of Valois and her sister.

"Very well," she reluctantly agreed, though her brows knit together with unspoken thoughts

Across the clearing the call went out for all to mount their warhorses. It was already dawn and the mist slowly lifted from the forest. They must leave while there was still time—before they were seen by the king's guards from the fortress walls. Stephen swung astride his warhorse.

The spellcast gleamed deep violet once more about his wrist. It was warm to the touch, as though it were alive. His thoughtful gaze met hers.

"What will happen to this fortress and those within, if I should fail?"

Without saying it in so many words, she knew his

thoughts were of the father whom he loved even though he defied him. He might show anger and resentment, even defiance, to the world, but within his heart was a deep love for the man who had sired him.

She shook her head, and said solemnly, "You must not fail."

With battle armor and weapons concealed, wearing only plain breeches and tunics and carrying hunting gear with nothing to identify them as soldiers and knights of the king's army, Stephen and his men emerged from the forest just as the mist lifted and rode through London.

William's soldiers regularly patrolled London, so they rode in small, inconspicuous groups of no more than two or three with the hoods of their tunics drawn low over their faces. A score of fierce men astride horses riding together, whether plainly dressed or in full battle armor, would have drawn attention.

Sir Kay, newly arrived from Normandy, was a young knight whom Stephen had trained and earned his spurs with. He was the last to follow, with soot-stained fade to hide his features and badly stained clothes that reeked of some disgusting smell. He might have been an accomplished thief if not for his noble birth. He could scavenge a fortune from a pauper. He drove the provision cart, his horse trailing behind.

At his fellow knights' complaints about the stench that seemed to hang over him like a cloud, Sir Kay merely grinned.

"It will keep anyone in the city from coming too near the cart."

It took nearly two hours for all of them to make their way through the city. They met in a small secluded wood outside the city near the old Roman road that linked

London with smaller towns and cities to the west. Sir Kay was the last to arrive, that devilish grin appearing amidst the soot on his face.

"Was there trouble?" Stephen asked as he rode back to the cart.

The grin deepened. "I stopped along the way to acquire a few more provisions."

Sir Kay seized the edge of the heavy canvas covering the cart and pulled it back, revealing two hogsheads of mead which hadn't been there before. There was a movement from beneath the other end of the canvas and he shrugged. "I bought a few chickens from an old hag. The hunting might be lean with winter coming on."

The noise coming from the back of the cart was enough to wake the dead. Stephen frowned. In addition to his abilities for acquiring almost anything anyone might need, the second thing Sir Kay was known for was his appetite.

"Perhaps," Stephen said, displeased by the delay that could have gotten them all caught, "we should send word to the king of our departure for surely it is no secret now. Every merchant in London will know of it."

Sir Kay shrugged, undaunted by Stephen's anger. "You will thank me when it comes time to make camp, besides what harm can a few chickens and a sow cause."

"Did you pay for them?" Stephen asked. "Or will we have the king's revenuers following us as well."

"I paid for them," Sir Kay said indignantly as though he'd been insulted at the suggestion he might have stolen them. "And a fine bargain it was too. The old hag was easily duped. I practically stole the lot from her."

With a dubious look at his friend, Stephen whirled his warhorse around and gave the order for them to ride. They still had several hours light left and he wanted to put as much distance between them and London as possible, before their absence was discovered.

As an extra precaution against being followed by the king's men, they kept to the forest and rolling countryside rather than using the old Roman road. If they were followed, their pursuers would expect them to use the road. Stephen had no intention of making it any easier for them to be followed.

They continued riding long after nightfall, the ribbon of road guiding them in the distance below a three-quarter moon that played hide and seek among the clouds. They made no fire that night but ate crusts of bread, cheese, and strips of dried meat each carried in a pouch on his saddle. The following morning, even before the mist had lifted and while the sky was barely starting to lighten, they continued their journey.

They avoided villages, hamlets, and farms so that no one could provide any information that they had passed this way. The second night was passed as the first one, with no fire to signal any who might follow as to their location.

The third day, Stephen pushed riders and horses to the point of exhaustion before halting just before sundown beside a small stream at the edge of the woods. Tonight he allowed cook fires as several men slipped into the surrounding forest to hunt. Sir Kay unpacked the provision cart. No man had complained, but the promise of a warm meal appealed to all.

Then from across the encampment came a piercing scream. Weapons were seized, swords drawn. Several of Stephen's men returned from their hunting, weapons also drawn. An equal number did not immediately return but remained hidden in the forest, yet watchful of the encampment.

"Take your hands off the girl, you filthy troll," a voice shrieked. "Or I'll gullet you like a cod."

From all around the camp, Stephen's men converged

on the provision cart and Sir Kay. But it was not Sir Kay's threat they'd heard.

He stood at the back of the cart, crates of chickens littering the ground along with the two hogsheads of mead, and various cloth sacks of grain, wrapped loaves of bread, a wheel of cheese, and dried fruit. As torches were brought and light flooded the clearing, they saw the source of the threat.

An old hag faced Sir Kay down. She was barely more than half his height and reed thin. Long white hair framed her face in a silvery nimbus. One bony, heavily veined hand clutched a walking stick which she leaned on. Her shoulders were rounded and frail beneath ragged garments. In her other hand was clutched a long, slender knife aimed with deadly accuracy to the vulnerable area just below Sir Kay's belt as though she had every intention of carrying out her threat.

Sir Kay stood planted firmly in one place, as if he'd taken root, not even daring to breathe as he hung onto a slender, young girl.

She was small and dressed equally as plainly as the old hag, but there the resemblance ended. She looked to be no more than fourteen or fifteen years of age, her heart-shaped face just beginning to take on the sculpted angles that would mark her a beauty. Her skin was pale and luminous, almost translucent and pale as a pearl in the light from the torches. But it was her eyes, wide and filled with emotion, that drew attention for they were the color of aquamarines, neither blue nor green, but an unusual shade in between.

Wordlessly, she struggled to free herself from Sir Kay's grasp, and as she struggled the hood of her mantle fell to her shoulders. Her hair tumbled loose over her shoulders and caught the light of the torches. It was thick, a rich, warm honey color filled with pale shimmering golden light, and the more she struggled the more in peril Sir Kay found himself at the deadly end of the old hag's blade.

To Sir Kay's further discomfort, Stephen ordered his men to lower their weapons.

"It is my gullet the old witch intends to slice open," he reminded Stephen, from between clenched teeth.

Stephen muttered an oath. "I should help her do it." Kay looked at him as if he'd lost his mind, or at the very least taken leave of a good portion of his senses.

"Who is easily duped?" Stephen remarked, reminding his friend of the claim he'd made days earlier as they left London. "I would say you are the one who has been duped, my friend. And because of it, I should let the old witch have her way with you." Then he ordered Sir Kay, "Release the girl."

"But the old woman came at me with a knife. God knows what she's capable of."

"Far more than you can imagine or would care to experience," Stephen assured him. And repeated, "Release the girl."

Completely bewildered, Sir Kay released the girl. She immediately fled behind the cart. Eventually the old woman lowered the blade. Her fierce expression eased, replaced by a faint smile as she turned to Stephen and his men saw for the first time that her eyes were almost milky white, the once-blue color almost completely obscured in her blindness.

"I suppose there is no need to ask how you came to be in the cart," Stephen remarked.

The old woman cackled. "Only if you are a fool, Stephen of Valois, and you are not that. Perhaps headstrong and impetuous, but not a fool."

Sir Kay stared from one to the other incredulously as around them the other men returned to their places around the encampment.

"Do you know this old woman?"

"Aye," Stephen nodded with equal parts anger and frustration. "I know her. She is called Meg."

"Meg? The Lady Vivian's guardian?"

"I was once her guardian," Meg announced proudly, turning toward his voice as easily as if she saw him, and then stared him down.

"Now that she has fulfilled her destiny, I am no longer needed."

"You are not needed here," Stephen cut across their conversation. "You will return to London."

"Ah, warrior . . ." She sighed. "You cannot do that for it would require you to send one of your men with me and that you cannot do for you will have need of every man in the western lands. You also have need of someone to guide you there."

Sir Kay snorted with laughter. "You, old hag? A guide?"

She turned on him, finding vulnerable flesh with the tip of her blade with unerring accuracy, as though she was not blinded at all but as sighted as he.

"I was born in the west country. I know every valley, river, and rock. And I do not need these eyes to see what I must see."

Stephen gently restrained her. "I do not need to ask who sent you."

She slanted him a knowing smile. "It was not the destiny of either Vivian or her sister to venture to the west country. But there is nothing woven in the tapestry which says an old woman cannot accompany you."

"Tapestry?" Sir Kay looked from old Meg to Stephen. "What is this nonsense."

" 'Tis no nonsense," Meg told him. "And for what lays ahead, you would be wise to believe."

"What of the girl?" Sir Kay asked.

"She will be no trouble," Meg assured them both. "She will be my eyes, my hands and feet. For there are times the stiffness settles into my bones that I cannot move as easily as I used to."

"Can she not speak for herself?" Sir Kay demanded, a little more boldly than he should have.

Meg's pale gaze narrowed. "Her name is Amber. She has not spoken for several years past, since her village was attacked and her family slain." Then her gaze narrowed even further as though she had sensed a thought he had chosen not to speak aloud.

"Have a care, warrior," she warned. "I can still get around well enough to find you in your bedroll and slip this blade between your ribs before you know it is done if you so much as touch the girl again. She is not for you."

"Leave well enough alone," Stephen added his voice to her caution. "The girl will not be treated like a camp follower."

"I'll finish unpacking the cart later," Sir Kay hastily announced, picking up two crates of squawking chickens and retreating to the campfire a safe distance away.

Stephen turned back to old Meg, "He will not trouble the girl," he assured her. "In the morning, you will return to London. One of my men will escort you as far as the edge of the city."

Meg shrugged. "We will escape and follow. You cannot prevent it. And you will have one less man whom you will desperately need in the weeks that lay ahead."

He knew she was speaking the truth. And if he tried to bind her hand and foot, she would escape that as well for old Meg was descended from a changeling and a mortal. Though her powers were limited, she could still find ways to outwit him and his men, and he had no time for such things.

"We will leave you and the girl at the next village," Stephen informed her, not about to be encumbered by the old woman and the girl. "You will be safe there.

Until then you may have the cart for your own use."
He cast a glance toward the sky where clouds obscured
the stars that had come out. "It will protect you against
the weather." Then he turned on his heel and returned
to camp.

Meg snorted. "We will see, warrior. We will see."

Three

The cottage was at the end of the tree-lined path and surrounded by forest where it had stood for longer than anyone could remember. Over the sound of the wind in the trees, the thunderous sound of the ocean roared as it hurled itself onto ancient cliffs where the forest met the sea.

The angry sea it was called, like a caldron that seethed and boiled below cliffs dripping with green moss, while above, perched on a high promontory like some snaggle-toothed old crone whose bones bleached in the sun, were the ruins of Tintagel, an ancient fortress whose origins were lost in myth.

Some said the legendary king, Arthur, had been born there. It looked out across the western sea, which some called the great lake, toward an island visible only occasionally through the mist and clouds. The ancient name for the island was Avalon.

But the ruins of Tintagel stood empty, inhabited now only by seabirds. They guarded Tintagel's secrets, clumped like sentries along the top of crumbling walls, calling to one another before swooping from their perches to the rocky shoals and tide pools below in search of fish and shell creatures left behind by the retreating tide.

A spiral of smoke curled from the smoke hole in the

thatched roof of the cottage that stood in the shadow of Tintagel, carrying with it the strange pungent odors of some ancient brew.

It was here farmers, villagers, fishermen, and the forest-dwellers came, seeking the healing potions and tisanes of the Old One to ease some illness or crippling injury. There were others who came for far different reasons. They slipped silently through the forest, appearing at her door singly or in groups of two or three, in search of help and guidance in the old ways—the ways of their ancestors who believed in the powers of the earth, wind, and sky.

Their requests were always answered in one way or another. Elora turned no one away. But there were some she refused to see, those whom she did not trust.

Many had seen her in the forest, leaning heavily on a walking stick, picking at moss and lichens, gathering an array of dead and molding things into a cloth bag that hung suspended from the belt tied at her waist. But there were others who claimed the creature they saw was no crippled old hag but a young woman of uncommon beauty who quickly vanished when she saw them.

Inside the hut, a large, white wolf suddenly raised its head from its paws, ears cocked toward the stout door made of animal skins stretched over a wood frame.

"Aye," a voice responded from near the hearth. "I heard it was as well, my friend. We have a visitor."

It was not an old voice nor a young one, but an ageless voice that sighed like the sound of the wind.

"The girl, Lodi, from Castle Tregaron. She comes begging more powders for her mistress."

The white wolf rose to its feet, the thick ruff of fur at its neck bristling.

"She is harmless," the disembodied voice near the hearth finally took form as the one who lived there stepped from the shadows.

"It is her mistress who fancies herself a conjuror of the lost arts." She made an impatient sound. "Spell-casting with mixtures of herbs, spider's webs, and earth from unhallowed graves. Lady Margeaux believes it is only a matter of finding the right potion to give her the power she seeks."

It began with healing potions to dispense among the villagers of Tregaron. Then it was powders to ease the black moods of Lord John of Tregaron, her brother. More recently, she had come to the forest cottage herself, seeking other potions that might give her the power of insight.

The gifted one had returned to the hut one afternoon not long ago to find Margeaux of Tregaron already there, poking among the pottery jars and flagons that contained medicinal herbs and powders. Though the lady pretended innocence, the gifted one sensed some of the precious herbs and powders had been stolen.

It was not the loss that concerned her, but the woman's increased fixation on the powers she was certain the mixtures held.

"We must find something to send back with the girl," the gifted one said aloud to the white wolf. "Something that will amuse the Lady of Tregaron for a while."

She turned from the shelf of jars and vials at the light rapping at the threshold. As the white wolf took a protective position between her and the door, she called out in a voice that seemed as old as time, "Come in, child. What do you seek?"

But with wise eyes the color of deepest violet, she already knew what the girl had come asking for.

Lodi entered the hut hesitantly. It took a moment for her eyes to adjust to the soft shadows inside the hut. It always surprised her that it was such a pleasant place. Not dark and damp, nor reeking of foul, vile odors, but warm and welcoming, the pungence of pleasant fragrances wafting past her through the door opening. But the assortment of creatures that dwelled in the cottage with the Old One always gave her a start.

Now, as she closed the door of the hut behind her and her eyes grew accustomed to the meager light within, she drew up suddenly at the sight of the large shrewmouse that scuttled about from the old woman to hide in the corner beside the hearth.

She had seen rats before in the granary and store rooms at Tregaron, but the size of this creature always startled her. It had the pointy features of a mouse but it was the size of a large cat. It did not flee out of fear, but watched her from the shadows. It almost seemed as if its eyes glowed, a silvery gray color that burned through her. She approached the old woman hesitantly.

"Come forward, girl. Do not be shy." With a faint smile, the old woman added, "I won't eat you." She saw the watchful look that sprang into the girl's eyes.

"You must not believe everything you hear. Tell me, now. What brings you to the forest?"

"My mistress seeks a restorative," Lodi explained in a rush of words, retrieving a pouch from the folds of her mantle.

The Old One's eyes sharpened for she knew the pouch contained gold pieces, payment for the powders and potions that were anticipated. Gold pieces that would be given to those who needed them, after the girl left, for Margeaux of Tregaron was stingy, taxing the farmers of Tregaron into poverty.

"What sort of restorative?" the Old One asked as she returned to the pot that bubbled and simmered at the hearth, sprinkling sweet lavender over the top of the steaming brew. "What ails your mistress?"

But even before the girl spoke, the Old One sensed her words and frowned.

" 'Tis not an ailment," Lodi replied. "She wishes a

physical restorative—a potion that will give the appearance of youth." She hesitantly laid the pouch of coins on the nearby table.

"What of her powers?" the Old One asked. "I have heard it said your mistress considers herself a great conjuror. What need has she of an old woman?"

"Every day my mistress looks in the mirror and sees a new line or mark. And she is most distressed, especially now."

The Old One frowned, for she had sensed nothing in the girl's manner to hint at the reason for her mistress's unusual distress.

"Why is she so gravely concerned now?"

The girl looked around as if she expected the walls to have grown ears. "Because she is not yet wed. She is most anxious about it. Even now she prods Lord John to join his army with that of the other Welsh princes against them. They have planned an attack. But if King William invades the western lands with his entire army as he invaded England, she is determined to be prepared to make an advantageous alliance."

The Old One frowned deeply. Only that morning she had seen a most unusual vision. She had accidentally cut her hand while harvesting rare herbs in the forest. It had bled badly. Returning to the hut, some of the blood had dripped into the small bowl of water as she cleaned the wound.

In the crimson cloud that formed from her blood swirling in the water she had seen a vision—a vision of armed warriors who wore no crests, astride great warhorses, and bathed in blood. But she had not seen Margeaux's ambitious plans. For the first time, her own powers had failed her.

"Where will this attack be?" the Old One asked, curling her fingers over the palm of her hand, where even now the cut was all but healed.

"On the Brodmir Plain at the mouth of the valley. Lord John's advisors say it is the perfect place to trap them. They will all be slaughtered of course, as the first ones were."

With set mouth, the Old One thrust two pouches of powder into the girl's hand. "Take this to your mistress," she instructed.

"Will it restore her youth and beauty? For if not, I fear she will be most angry."

The Old One nodded. "Tell your mistress, it must be mixed precisely—two parts of the blue powder with one part of the white powder and simmered slowly until it becomes a liquid. Then it must be allowed to cool."

"Will it work?" Lodi asked with incredulous expression.

"Aye, it will," the Old One replied with a distracted wave of her hand. "Now go."

She heard the girl turn to leave, sensed, too, when she hesitated and would have grabbed the pouch of coins back as her mistress had instructed her to do.

"Leave the pouch, and go now," the Old One said, lowering her voice to a growl. "It grows dark. You wouldn't want to be caught in the forest alone."

With that warning, Lodi rushed out of the cottage, the pouch left on the table. The Old One ceased her stirring and turned to stare after the girl, the door left standing open in her haste to leave.

The large shrewmouse had disappeared. In its place, transformed, was the large white wolf. It growled low in its throat.

"Aye, Fallon," its mistress said with a new urgency in her voice. The wolf looked up at her with wise, silver eyes. The Old One had also transformed, once more taking her true form, that of a slender young woman of uncommon beauty, with raven black hair and violet eyes.

"You must go," she commanded the wolf. Though

she knew it was a betrayal, she sensed a far greater urgency in the air that quivered around her with its dark secrets.

"The soldiers of King William must be warned of the attack."

In her thoughts she again saw the vision of that morning, the warriors covered in blood, and the one who led them with no crest upon his tunic or shield, only the black colors he wore and the single word that dripped blood upon his shield—*Desdicado*.

Stephen and his men had made camp just inside the narrow mouth of the valley. There was fresh water and plenty of forage for the horses. The hunting had been plentiful in the forest they had just left.

Still, he felt restless, as before a battle, with that inexplicable rush of energy that seemed to burn beneath the surface of his skin, making it impossible to sit by the fire with his men. Instead, he rode the perimeter of the encampment.

Sir Kay and John de Lacey rode up, informing him, "We have not been able to find the girl or the old woman."

Stephen's jaw tightened. "When were they last seen?"

"Just before we made camp. I thought the old woman needed a moment of privacy. I didn't take my eyes off them for more than a moment."

"A moment is all she needs," Stephen said grimly, for over the past several days he and Meg had struck an uneasy alliance—he didn't attempt to send her back to England, and she didn't attempt to turn his men into standing stones, which he thoroughly believed her capable of doing.

"Which direction were they last seen?"

"Near the large cluster of rocks we passed. She stepped around behind a large rock."

"A rock you couldn't see around," Stephen speculated. He could guess the woman's cleverness, blind as she was, eluding her guardians.

"I'm sorry," Sir Kay replied.

"Lady Vivian is very fond of that old woman. You will be more than sorry, if any harm comes to her."

"I give my sympathies to anyone who crosses her path," John de Lacey replied. "I still have not recovered from the bees she placed in my blanket roll."

"She warned you to stay away from the girl," Stephen pointed out.

"I could have been killed."

"Before this is done, you may wish it." Then he whirled his horse about. "I will be back before the moon is high overhead."

"I will ride with you," John de Lacey announced turning his own horse around to follow. "The countryside is unknown and dangerous."

"Stay with the others," Stephen ordered. "One alone is less of a target than two. Find the old woman and the girl. I will not be gone long." Then he guided the warhorse away from the encampment.

The moon offered scant light on its slow ascent. He marked the way by memorizing unusual rock formations or a peculiar curve of the land in the pale silvery light. The west country seemed filled with such peculiarities. Then he broke through a copse of trees and saw a peculiar sight.

He had grown accustomed to seeing the large rocks on their ride into the west country, but it was the unusual placement and configuration of these rocks that made him rein in the warhorse. Instead of clumped or laying piled on top of each other as if some giant had rolled them all to the bottom of a hill, these stones stood upright.

They were huge, at least the height of two men, dark and gleaming in the moonlight. Equally large stones were braced across the top of several pairs of upright stones, forming a large open circle on the flat valley floor.

He saw the girl, Amber, first standing outside the stone circle in the shelter of one of the huge stones. Meg stood within the circle, head thrown back, arms spread wide.

His horse would go no farther, snorting and digging in when Stephen tried to force him onward. He finally dismounted and tethered the stallion. He continued the rest of the way afoot. As he drew closer to the standing stones, he heard old Meg's voice as she spoke unintelligible words that had an odd rhyming cadence.

Stephen approached where the girl stood, calling out softly so as not to frighten her. Wordlessly, she turned to him. Her vivid blue eyes were pale as moonstones, her hair like dark, spun gold in the moonlight. She was shivering violently for the night was cold and neither she nor old Meg had worn their mantles. Stephen sent Amber back to wait with his horse. Then he slowly approached the circle of stones.

"I know you are there, warrior," Meg said softly. "Approach very carefully or you will frighten him."

She sensed his unspoken question and explained, "The magnificent creature on the other side of the stone circle."

It was surprisingly warm inside the circle as he slowly stepped inside, as if the wind did not reach here although there were gaps in the upright stones the span of several feet. As Stephen slowly approached near the old woman he finally saw the creature she spoke of.

It was a magnificent white wolf, larger than any he had ever seen. It stood on the far side of the stone circle, just inside the two, northernmost blue slate stones. As he moved beside old Meg, the wolf's silver gray gaze swung to him.

He had seen that very same look in an animal's eyes before, just before it attacked. He had not expected to find the old woman confronting a wild beast. Wishing he had brought the broadsword from his saddle, he drew his hunting knife from the sheath at his belt. Meg reached out and clamped a hand over his wrist as easily and accurately as if she were sighted.

"It would do no good," she whispered. "For the creature is protected within the circle of standing stones and cannot be killed."

"And I am not protected within the circle of stones," Stephen replied sarcastically.

Meg slanted him a look. "You need have no fear of the creature. It has come to warn you."

The hairs stood up at the back of his neck in instinctive alarm. Old scars at his shoulder, inflicted in an encounter with a creature of the Darkness tingled as though only recently healed. Every muscle tightened.

"What warning?"

"Of grave danger," Meg replied. "Not more than two days ride from here. There will be an attack. You and your men will be greatly outnumbered—at least ten to one—as were the knights who came here before you."

"The wolf told you this?" he asked, recalling a previous encounter with a wild boar that had very nearly killed the Lady Vivian.

The boar had been a creature of the Darkness. How were they then to know this creature was not also sent by the Darkness?

"The wolf is the messenger," Meg explained. "He brings the message from another."

Stephen's eyes narrowed on the old woman, wondering what conjuror's trick this was. "What game is this?"

"No game, warrior, but deadly serious. You and your

men are in grave danger. Many will die unless you heed the warning and take precautions?"

"Precautions?" He asked incredulously. "Against an army ten times greater? Perhaps," he suggested, with equal amounts sarcasm and consternation, "you should ask the wolf how it is to be done?"

Meg shrugged. "You are the warrior. That is for you to determine." Then a slow smile curved her mouth. "But there is no rule that says you must meet this enemy on the open battlefield."

"Who sent the creature?" Stephen demanded. She smiled slowly for she knew that in asking the question, he accepted that the message was true.

"You have met her, warrior, in the lost kingdom. My young mistress, Lady Cassandra."

"Where will this happen?" Stephen demanded, but when he looked back, the white wolf was gone as though it had disappeared in the mist that slowly rose around the standing stones, mixing with moonlight until a pale, shimmering cloud enveloped the entire circle of stones.

"You have been warned," Meg reminded him, calling to the girl, Amber, as she turned and walked out of the ring of stones. "Make the most of it."

Stephen did not immediately leave the ring of stones, but remained, aware of that unusual sensation as if he had once again stepped from the real world, where his men were encamped only a short distance away, into some other world that existed very nearby. It was exactly as it had been the night he left his father's court and encountered the young woman in the shimmering blue mantle.

His fingers closed over the smooth rune stone with its strange marking tied at his belt, and felt the unusual warmth in the stone in spite of the cold night air that now filled the ring of stones. It was the same warmth he had experienced when first stepping inside the ring, as if her essence lingered in the stone.

He glanced back as he left the stone circle. The smooth blue upright stones seemed to glow with an unnatural light below the arc of the moon overhead. When he looked again the silver light that engulfed it was gone The stones stood like silent, unmoving giants in the night, guarding their secrets.

Near midday, two days later, Sir Kay and de Lacey returned with word that rebel warriors had been seen less than an hour's ride ahead. It left them precious little time to prepare a defense, still with the memory of Curthose's death he took the old woman's words to heart.

It was not necessary for them to fight on an open field. There were other ways to fight, which he had learned from his friend, Tarek al Sharif, whose idea of a good fight was to strike without warning, flee, then strike again like the desert warrior tribes he was descended from.

Stephen chose his own ground to fight upon. If the rebels knew of their presence then let them come to him and his men, he rationalized. Throughout the rest of the morning he had his men prepare snares and deadly traps for the rebel warriors in the forest.

Ropes were strung across clearings. Sapling trees were stripped of all leaves, ends sharpened into deadly spikes, which were then embedded along trails and paths, awaiting the headlong rush of their attackers. The forest became a deadly trap for the unwary. Then he gave his men strike and run positions, heavy battle armor stripped away in favor of freedom of movement. All were given orders to meet on the other side of the small forest.

He left Meg and the girl with the horses at the far

side of the forest with instructions that if the rebels reached this far they were to take two horses, scatter the rest, and flee. Then he returned to a forward position with his men to await the dawn.

"You have prepared well, warrior," a voice called out from the cover of the trees.

"But you have less than fifty men. And Malagraine sends near five hundred mercenaries and Saxon rebels against you."

Stephen drew his battle sword and spun to meet the attack. But instead of confronting a warrior slipping through the trees and brush, he saw no one. Instead, a figure clad all in green and brown dropped from an overhanging branch above to the ground before him.

"You will have need of far more than fifty men." A steel blade carved the air, wielded by two strong hands and slicing the air before a handsome, bearded face. "I offer my sword in your service."

Stephen stared incredulously at the apparition that seemed to have dropped from the sky. "Aye, far more," he agreed, bringing his sword up, uncertain whether to laugh or slay the fool where he stood.

"But we'll manage. Perhaps we'll start with you," he suggested.

"Perhaps," the stranger conceded, the grin that curved his mouth, reaching his cobalt blue eyes, features framed by midnight black hair, his mouth and chin wreathed by an equally dark beard.

"But you've need of every man who can raise a sword. Let me live, and that makes fifty and one against Malagraine."

"You are either an idiot or a fool," Stephen remarked.

The stranger threw back his head and laughed. Then he plunged the tip of his sword into the soft, loamy earth, either a very brave move or a very foolish one when confronted by a broadsword.

"Aye, well perhaps a bit of both. I am Truan Monroe," he said. "I offer you my service. You would be wise to take it. You may slay me if you choose," he added as if he read Stephen's thoughts, "but then you will be short one sword and a very good warrior."

With a lightening quick movement that made a lie of the fool's grin on his face, he seized the sword by the handle, extracting it from the ground as if it weighed no more than a feather and wielded it with deadly accuracy, the tip resting only inches from Stephen's throat.

"Or you may let me fight beside you and take my chances against the rebel army."

Showing no outward sign of fear, Stephen asked, "How do I know you are not one of the rebels sent by Tregaron? You might turn on me in battle."

Monroe shrugged. "If I wanted you dead, English, you would already be dead. You walk through this forest like a wild boar, rooting around, stomping for all to hear, announcing your presence to everyone. I have already had too many opportunities."

"And I suppose you move more quietly!" Stephen retorted.

Truan Monroe grinned. "I came upon you before you could draw your weapon."

Stephen watched him through narrowed eyes. From Rorke FitzWarren he had learned that a man's true heart would be revealed in his eyes. An honest man met your gaze straight and true, a deceiver or coward could not.

"Why do you make this offer?" he asked bluntly.

"You know why I make this offer."

Stephen wondered if it was the fool who answered now, or if there was some greater meaning hidden in the words.

"We have only just met. How would I know your reasons?"

Then the grin reappeared, making Stephen certain it was the fool who answered.

"Because we are both warriors. It is our destiny. You may not deny my destiny."

Stephen could not explain it any more than he could explain the warrior's strange words, but there was something in the fool's demeanor which lacked the believability of a fool, as if he played at some deadly serious game. The man was greatly skilled with a blade and the truth was that he could easily have slain Stephen before he ever knew of it.

Through the trees, Stephen heard his men approaching. They burst into the small clearing with swords drawn. Monroe was completely outnumbered and yet seemed unconcerned.

"I do not make the offer lightly, English," Truan reminded him, sensing the choices he contemplated. Then he shrugged again. " 'Tis only blood. Mine will spill very nearly as easily as yours if that is the choice you make."

"Hold!" Stephen ordered his men as they advanced, though he could not understand why and feared he might live to regret it.

"This man has come to join us," he told his men.

"Join us?" Kay remarked with more than a little surprise. "With sword drawn against you? Give the order and we will slay him where he stands."

"Stand away," Stephen told his men, then added with a bemused expression, "he was making a point. If he wanted me dead, I would already be dead.

"You may join us," he told Truan. "But if you betray me, I will separate your head from your shoulders."

Truan smiled devilishly and bowed low from the waist.

"A fair bargain, but you will forgive me if I try my best to hold onto my head. I've grown quite fond of it."

"I would advise it," Stephen warned, resheathing his broadsword. "You are not from the western lands," he commented as they walked back through the forest to the encampment.

"I am from west of the western lands, from a place across the sea," Truan answered obliquely, grinning his charming smile.

"West of west?" John de Lacey murmured in lowered voice, at Stephen's other side. "The man is an idiot. There is nothing west of the western lands but open sea."

Truan grinned. "A fool only when I need be," he responded, surprising both men that he had overheard their conversation. "And there is far more west of the western lands than you could ever possibly imagine."

Then he went off to give Stephen's men suggestions on other traps which might be made in the forest and how they might better reinforce their positions, as if he had been one of them and fought at their sides for years instead of a recent threat who must still prove himself.

The battle came at sundown as Truan Monroe predicted it would. While the rest of the rebel army rimmed the hills, two hundred warriors charged the encampment of tents and smoldering campfires at the edge of the forest only to discover that it was completely deserted. Then, they plunged into the forest beyond following the clues that had been deliberately left behind to guide them. It was a mistake that cost them dearly.

Many died in the traps that had been set, impaled on stakes, trapped in snares, cut down by an enemy they could neither see nor hear until it was too late. Then the next wave of warriors followed. The fighting became fierce as they were lured deeper into the forest.

Stephen's men fought and fled, then turned and fought again from a score of directions. Always luring

the enemy deeper into the forest until they were hopelessly scattered throughout. Then, emerging at a prede-
termined point, Stephen ordered the forest set afire.
The rebel army had little choice but to retreat or be
burned alive.

Stephen and his men fled ahead of the flames to the
river's edge where Meg and Amber waited with Sir Kay
and the tethered horses. Truan Monroe emerged from
another part of the forest, with soot-stained face and
smudged clothes. He had proved his loyalty several times
over, but did not wait for Stephen's words of gratitude.

"Many will escape the flames. And it will not take
them long to ride around the forest and give chase,"
he warned. "We must flee while we can."

"Flee where?" Sir Kay asked. "The forest is at our
back and the river before us." And night fast descended, along with the threat of a storm which would help
extinguish the fire and slow their own progress over
slippery, uneven terrain.

"There is a place of safety nearby," Truan told them.
"I will lead the way." He saw the doubtful expressions
in their faces. "Or stay and greet the rebels as they follow."

Stephen hesitated. Beside him, old Meg laid a hand
on his arm. In that way of hers that always stunned him,
as though she knew his thoughts, she said, "Do not
doubt now, warrior. You must follow the way of the white
wolf."

With an enemy army at his back and unknown terri-
tory ahead of them, Stephen hesitated. Then as the
clouds parted briefly overhead, he saw a streak of silver
white light at the horizon. It must be lightning, he
thought. But in the way that you see something in the
dark of night best without looking directly at it, he saw
the white wolf standing on the far horizon, in exactly

the same direction Truan Monroe said they must take. He made his decision quickly.

"Lead the way," he told Truan, and even as he spoke, hundreds of yards away and beyond hearing, the white wolf leapt ahead as though leading them.

The place Truan led them to was on a rise of land at the convergence of two rivers. The old fortress was surrounded by water on three sides that gleamed like dark, silvery ribbons beneath a leaden sky, with high stone walls facing out across the valley below.

It was dark and abandoned, appearing to be little more than a pile of rocks with its uppermost walls crumbling down onto thicker walls below. But in the shadow play of moonlight through clouds, the inner walls shown pale and luminous, a ghostly image of what had once been in another time.

"I know this place," Stephen said as they entered through the crumbling wood gate, the walls and inner courtyard revealing its Roman influence beneath the debris and destruction that had take place over several centuries.

"I have been here before."

His men fanned out through the fortress, seeking ways to barricade and fortify the entrance and a dozen other places that could be easily breached while he took a torch and walked through silent, abandoned halls following the path the white wolf had taken as it loped through the ruins ahead of them.

He had glimpsed the wolf several times as they rode, always in the distance. Now there was no sign of the creature as he searched the fortress.

The columns, wide stone steps, and smooth pale stone walls were reminiscent of similar fortresses in the middle empires, a convergence of influences but most strongly that of Roman architecture with its open verandas overgrown with vines and moss, tall columns that were scarred and smoke-stained beneath layers of filth that had accumulated over the years. But beneath the layers of dirt and destruction, pale walls gleamed, many painted with vivid murals whose images peered out from soot-blackened plaster.

There had been a great fire here as if someone had tried to burn it down after ransacking it. But the stone and plaster remained, a silent, ghostly skeleton of what had once been. In size alone it had been most grand, a castle fortress built for a king and easily protecting the population of a small city within its gates. But that was before the cataclysm that had befallen it, and most quickly by the appearance of things.

Tables had been turned over, ornate carved chairs smashed to splinters. The floors of most chambers were littered with smashed pottery, rotting tapestries that had once adorned the walls now reduced to mere threads, and the skeletal remains of the last inhabitants who had died trying to defend it.

They were strewn throughout the fortress, a much smaller number that he would have expected to defend such a large fortress. Unless the army had been called away and the fortress left defenseless. Then he discovered the starchamber.

The large double doors sagged at their iron moorings. The light from the torch, thrust through the gaping, broken entrance, gleamed off pale blue walls. Overhead, the ceiling—most of it still miraculously intact and made of thick, clear resin panels—gleamed with the light of a thousand stars that looked down on the center of the room. He kicked aside broken timbers and crawled through the broken doors. Light from the torch gleamed off hundreds more stars set into the walls.

He heard the scurrying sound of mice fleeing from the light, along with the faint stirring of the wind through some broken window opening. Then the light from the torch fell across the large round table in the center of the starchamber.

It was at least fifteen feet in diameter, the surface badly scarred and etched. It had been burned in several places as the invaders tried and failed to destroy it. But what the invaders hadn't accomplished, time had.

The table sagged where one stout leg had rotted and given way. The surface was covered with dust and dirt, but the filth and destruction couldn't disguise the beauty of the table or the colorful, ornate panels that had been carefully carved into its surface.

There were twelve panels in all rimming the table, each carved with an emblem or crest. Inside the rim of panels were Latin words etched into the wood. Stephen leaned closer, holding the torch high overhead as he peered intently at each panel. They told a story of bravery, courage, and sacrifice. Of noble knighthood pledged to a common cause.

The panels contained crests that were familiar, centuries old, others seen on the battle shields of warriors he had fought in other campaigns. Still others were obscure, their meaning lost in antiquity.

"Twelve panels, twelve crests, twelve knights." Exactly the same as he had seen before.

As he leaned closer and ran his fingers over the carved symbols and crests, light shimmered from a darkened corner across the chamber.

"Who is there?" he demanded, holding the torch aloft in one hand illuminating the starchamber in pale golden light, his sword held before him in the other.

"Declare yourself. Do not, and you will die." There was no answer.

She watched from the shadows behind a column, her hand on the coarse ruff of fur at Fallon's neck, communicating her thoughts through her touch, and restraining him.

Light from the torch overhead played across the warrior's features—high cheekbones, the sharp angle of his nose over a firm, full mouth, and dark amber eyes. He wore no battle armor, but the plain clothes of a warrior who pledged his allegiance to no king.

His dark hair fell to his shoulders, the light from the torch finding the hidden auburn light in thick, silken waves. Strong brows drew together in a fierce expression. He was tall, his shadow long in the light from the torch, reaching across the chamber to touch her where she stood in the darkness. Around his neck he wore a length of leather and the rune stone she had lost the night she encountered him outside the king's hall.

She remembered the touch of his hand at her wrist, strong yet gentle and his fearlessness as that contact had pulled him through the portal of light with her. And just like before, she experienced a mixture of fascination and terrifying uncertainty. She wanted to escape at the same time she found it impossible to do so.

"Who is there?" he demanded again, rounding the table and approaching several steps closer.

Terrified that she would be discovered, Cassandra took several steps back into the shadows behind the column. As she did, her mantle whispered softly about her ankles, the silver threads woven through the pale blue fabric reflecting the light of the torch he held.

She was certain that he had seen her. Yet she was unable to leave, as though drawn to this warrior who had mistakenly made a journey with her through time to this very place and now stood before her again.

It would be daylight in a few hours. Word of the disaster in the forest would spread quickly to Tregaron. In saving one man she had betrayed the man who was like a brother to her.

She sensed the movement before Fallon's silent warning as the warrior discovered her hiding place. Light from the torch drove back the shadows, exposing her for a brief moment. Recognition flashed across his face.

Just like before, she felt a connection to this warrior, as if he reached out and touched her. She turned and fled through the portal of light with Fallon, leaving the warrior to wonder if he had only imagined her.

Stephen slowly circled the large chamber with drawn sword, the torch he held aloft illuminating the shadows. His search brought him back around to the large round table in the center of the room with those twelve crumbling chairs set before twelve panels into the wood.

Slowly, he rounded the table, the Latin words turning over and over in his thoughts—the words translated meant honor, duty, loyalty, trust, bravery—ancient words written hundreds of years ago in another time. A code of rules that formed the lines of a pledge.

He ran his fingers over the carvings, painstakingly translating them from the ancient Latin text. He could only make out the first few words, the others destroyed by time and decay. Yet the words seemed to quiver in the still air as though other voices repeated them—twelve voices that pledged their sword, blood, and sacred honor over five hundred years ago. Stephen knew this place.

It had lain buried and lost in ancient myth so long that most doubted it had ever really existed. Camelot— the ancient kingdom of the legendary King Arthur and his brave and loyal knights of the round table.

He heard the creak of a sagging timber. Light from a second torch appeared at the shattered doorway and spread across the floor of the chamber. Truan Monroe pushed aside debris and crawled through the shattered doorway.

He held the torch aloft. Light pooled into the chamber, illuminating the table with its ancient carvings and those twelve places spaced evenly around the edge.

"To my brethren, I pledge my sword, my blood, and my sacred honor . . ."

His expression was intense as he repeated the ancient vow word for word surrounded by the once magnificent chamber of the ancient king.

"You know these words?" Stephen asked, watching the young warrior who had joined them so recently.

For once there was no witty comment or affable grin. The fool who could wield a battle sword with the skill of the finest warrior was gone, replaced by someone Stephen did not know.

"Aye, I know them," Truan replied, his voice low as though momentarily lost in some memory, all traces of humor gone from his handsome face and teasing eyes.

". . . beyond this life, beyond death, until my soul's final journey into the light . . ."

The words seemed to echo from the charred walls, the domed star ceiling overhead, and sigh across the stone floor, like some ancient litany that reached across the centuries. As though the men who had first spoken those vows whispered them from their graves as a reminder.

Then the spell was broken as several of Stephen's men also found the chamber and crawled through the crumbling doorway.

"We have secured the fortress, and await your orders," Sir Kay announced, his usually boisterous voice lowered as he gazed in amazement about the unusual round chamber with its domed ceiling encased with stars.

Gavin and John de Lacey were equally in awe of the chamber as they stepped carefully through the rubble and debris. De Lacey found an ancient sword, fallen from a crumbling hand as bones of the warrior who had once wielded it finally turned to dust.

Gavin had heard stories of the legendary round table and frowned in disbelief at the crumbling ruins of the table that had lain undisturbed as though waiting for the warriors who had once joined there to take up their places once more.

"What will you do?" Truan asked, his intense blue gaze fastened on Stephen. "Now that you have twisted the lion's tail."

Stephen felt the scrutiny of his own men, the same question on all their faces.

"There is a deep well, with more than enough water," Gavin finally spoke up. "Now that we know their numbers, we could rest and then return to England."

"The king will support you once he knows of their great numbers and the Saxons who have joined them," Sir Kay added his voice to the argument.

Clearly, they both felt that they should retreat to England in the face of such overwhelming numbers. It was the logical thing to do. But Tregaron, and the Welsh prince he served, had no way of knowing their true strength.

Stephen turned to de Lacey, with whom he had trained as an apprentice knight and earned his spurs, and trusted like a brother. Like himself, John de Lacey was also born a bastard. He understood as those of legitimate birth could not the demons that had driven Stephen to defy his father and come to the western lands.

"You have not spoken yet," he told John. "What say you?"

John looked up, his expression startled. Though their friendship ran deep, Stephen had always made his own decisions, including the one to leave England. Through his veins ran the royal blood of Normandy. He had no need of any man's council. Still, he asked it as he would have asked it of any of his other knights.

"We have come far to avenge the deaths of our fellow knights," de Lancey replied. "Malagraine still lives. We have not done what we came to do."

"We are only two score and ten," Stephen replied,

speaking aloud what he knew was in every man's thoughts. "Even with their losses in the Brodmir forest, they outnumber us at least eight to one. We are in a foreign land where no one will give us aid."

"They do not know our true numbers," de Lancey replied. "We might be fifty in number or five hundred. And we have these walls to protect us."

"Aye," Stephen replied thoughtfully. "We have these walls." Walls which had survived a dreadful battle that had reached within, and yet stood another five hundred years. But it was not a decision he could make for them.

His other knights had joined them and stood inside the doorway. Among them was the old woman, Meg, and beside her the girl, Amber. They were few in number. Twelve to be exact—the same number of loyal men who had served the ancient king unto death.

"Each man must be free to make his own decision," he told them. "I cannot make it for you. But as for myself," he turned toward the decaying table with those ancient words of loyalty and honor, and laid the sword down on the table so that the blade pointed toward the center, "I will stay and avenge those who died here."

In that ancient place, filled with dust, debris, and cobwebs, it was like they became a part of some ancient ritual. De Lacey was the first to next lay his sword upon the table. Then, one by one the rest of his knights came forward and also laid their swords down in exactly the same way, until eleven swords rimmed the round table.

"What of him?" Gavin asked, his gaze narrowing on Truan Monroe. "Where lies your loyalty, stranger?"

" 'Tis written in the stars," Truan replied enigmatically with a gesture toward the star-filled dome overhead.

"A foolish answer from a fool. How do we know he will not betray us?"

Aware that the girl, Amber, the silent one, watched

him intently from beside the old woman, Truan smiled, white teeth flashing in the wreath of his dark beard.

"If I wished to betray you, your blood would soak the earth in the Brodmir forest." He took his sword and laid it upon the last vacant place at the table, the blade gleaming with blue light in the glow of the torches.

"I will stay," he told them all. Then the smile widened and the look of the fool returned. "I wish to see how fifty in number intend to defeat Malagraine."

"Fifty-one," Stephen reminded him, his sharp gaze fastened on the young man who seemed to transform from simpleton to cunning warrior with the simple act of drawing a breath.

"Aye," Truan said through laughter. "Fifty-one." Then he retrieved his sword and resheathed it. Stepping through the debris, his grin deepened as he approached the old woman.

"Do not frown so, old hag. It will cause more wrinkles."

Meg sniffed indignantly, her expression thoughtful as she stared up in his direction in spite of her blindness, as though trying to see something beyond the boundaries of normal sight.

"Who are you?"

"Just a fool with some skill with a sword."

"Too much the fool, I think," she replied, a puzzled expression on her face. Then he turned to Amber.

Quicker than the eye could see, far too quick for her to be forewarned and shyly retreat as she normally would have, Truan's hand shot out. With the dexterity of an accomplished warrior, he sliced the air and from behind her ear, retrieved a small white flower.

She had not spoken a word the entire time she and Meg had traveled with them. Yet, now, her delicately curved mouth formed a startled O, a surprised sound coming out in a rush of air as her eyes widened with instinctive, unguarded pleasure.

"Come," Truan told her, not touching her for he knew the girl would only have shied away, but extending a hand to let her pass before him. " 'Tis a simple trick. I will show you how it is done. Then I will show you how to make things disappear."

He followed Amber from the chamber. When he was no longer within hearing, de Lacey commented tightly, "As easily as he will disappear when he has betrayed us."

"If he wished to betray us, he would have already done so in the forest. Instead he killed many rebels, fighting at your side, and preventing more than one blade from separating your head from your shoulders. I have no more reason to doubt his loyalty than to doubt yours." He turned back to the round table, surrounded by the rest of his knights.

"This will be our stronghold. Here we will make our stand." And as he spoke the words, he felt the cool, still air in the chamber quiver as though someone unseen listened.

Four

A slender ribbon of light glowed in the corner of the chamber at Tregaron. It expanded, growing brighter until it opened and Cassandra stepped through the opening, followed by the white wolf.

A quick glance about assured her that the chamber was just as it had been when she left it hours earlier. But before she could even light the coals at the brazier against the chill that had settled into the chamber during her absence, there was a light rapping at the chamber door.

Lodi, she thought, with that certainty of knowledge that she'd possessed since a small child. There were no latches to bar the doors at Tregaron, except Margeaux's chamber. Her adopted sister insisted upon her privacy but thought nothing of invading the privacy of others at whatever time of the day or night she deemed necessary.

Only Lodi, the poor sweet girl who had the misfortune to be Margeaux's maid servant, knocked before entering. Or possibly she had been there before and received no answer. Anyone who would have lifted the latch would have found their way barred as though locked, even Margeaux. With a wave of her hand Cassandra released the spell that barred the door.

"You may come in, Lodi," she called out softly.

The door was pushed open hesitantly, Lodi's timid

face appearing at the narrow opening. Relief flooded her features.

"Praise be you're here at last, mistress," she said, pushing the door open a scant few inches further.

"What is it? What has happened?" Cassandra asked as she lit the brazier behind her with but a simple thought of fire. The flames burst to life, framing her as she turned back toward the girl.

Lodi was completely loyal. She glanced at the sudden flare of flame that had not been there a moment before and now burned brightly, but said nothing.

"The nobles are to arrive at Tregaron," she said with great urgency. "They are expected any time and the mistress is in a dreadful mood." Her voice hitched faintly and she would come no farther into the room.

"Please, come closer, and tell me," Cass said gently already suspecting what she would see. The girl shook her head adamantly.

"She asks for you, mistress," she went on insistently, and in the shadows, Cassandra saw her bite anxiously at her lower lip.

"Nothing pleases her when she's in these moods. Perhaps you could see her." The girl sounded close to tears.

Cass crossed the chamber and pulled the door open further, light from candles and the brazier spread about the room, falling on Lodi's features. The girl cringed back into the shadows but Cass stopped her.

Lodi's left cheek was swollen, a purplish bruise rimming her eye, which was almost swollen shut. There was really no need to ask.

"Margeaux," she whispered angrily.

"Please, mistress," Lodi begged her. "Say nothing. 'Tis bad enough as it is with her in such a high temper. If you could see her now. Please."

Unfortunately, Cassandra knew it was true. Margeaux

had an unpredictable temper, usually aimed at the servants. But no one was immune to her anger.

"Where is she?"

"In her chambers." Then Lodi added, "Prince Malagraine comes as well. 'Tis said they have sent a misery of peace to the army of King William."

"Misery?" Cassandra replied. "Do you mean emissary?"

"Yes, mistress. That is it. Emissary."

Cass frowned, for she had sensed nothing of these things when she left earlier that morning. But if Prince Malagraine traveled to Tregaron, that at least explained Margeaux's fit of temper.

"Very well, Lodi," she said thoughtfully, wondering how the knowledge of this had escaped her, for she usually sensed such things. "I will see what may be done."

"Do you wish me to go with you?" In the girl's quiet, trembling voice, she heard the fear and reluctance.

"If I need you I will send for you," Cass told her, laying a soothing hand on the girl's shoulder.

"Thank you, mistress," Lodi said, her voice catching with gratitude.

"Go, now," Cass said gently. "Learn what you can of these visitors and bring word to me. There is much that must be done before their arrival." Lodi went to do as she asked, grateful to escape a return to Margeaux's chamber.

"What are you looking at?" Cass asked Fallon, who looked back at her with wise, knowing eyes.

"Yes, I know," she answered. "A visit to her chamber is like jumping from the stew pot into the fire, but if I do not go she may bring all of Tregaron down about our ears. And there are things I would know about this visit of the nobles," she added thoughtfully. Her mouth curved into a soft frown.

"I should have sensed it."

Fallon whimpered slightly, giving voice to his own opinion of Margeaux as he lay down with a disgusted sigh, the large head planted on crossed paws.

"Coward!" Cass accused. He rolled over on his back, looking up at her with upside-down affection, large tongue lolling out the side of his mouth, those lethal fangs appearing quite harmless when he was in such a playful mood that one could almost think him domesticated. But he made no effort to go with her.

"Then stay if you will. I am not afraid of her. Margeaux's bark is truly worse than her bite." Under her breath she muttered, "I hope."

Margeaux's chamber was in another part of the fortress at Tregaron, occupied by all those who had gone by the title, Lady of Tregaron. It was a title she claimed for herself by right of blood not marriage, for she was sister to Lord John who still had not taken a wife, although he had fathered several children among the servants and unfortunate girls from the village.

Lodi might well have been one of his conquests had she not sought out Cass's help.

"You know the Old One in the forest," Lodi had whispered desperately one day when she was barely past the age of fourteen. " 'Tis said the Old One can prevent a man getting a babe upon a girl."

Cass was reluctant to speak of the Old One for it was many years since she had lived in the forest with Elora, as the Old One was called, in the time before she came to Tregaron.

"I know you go there," Lodi told her. "I followed once."

"What did you see?" Cass had demanded, fear knifing through her heart that old secrets may have been discovered.

"Nothing!" the girl blurted out, and Cass knew it to be true. "I saw only the Old One at the cottage in the forest, after you had gone there. And I've heard stories, that you lived there as a wee child. You must speak to her for me. She can help me."

"What has happened?" Cass asked, for even at the tender age of twelve she was wise beyond her years and knew of the servant girls sent nightly to her adopted brother's chambers.

"Has he touched you?"

"Not yet. But 'tis only a matter of time. Please, help me mistress."

Cassandra could not refuse even though she knew she took a great risk. "I will do what I can," she told Lodi. "But you must speak of this to no one. Do you understand?"

Lodi vowed she would say nothing. In the days that followed, Cassandra provided an herbal mixture which she explained had come from the Old One in the forest.

"Will it prevent a child in my belly?" Lodi asked anxiously.

"It will do far more than that," Cass told her, for she wished to spare the gentle girl the act that had delivered the others to such a fate. "It will cause warts in certain places for any man you do not wish the attentions of."

"Will it work the same for the other girls?"

"Aye, for all who drink it as a tea, but you must say nothing to them. You have promised."

"It will be our secret," Lodi assured her, expressing her heartfelt gratitude for all knew the fate of girls who found themselves with child by the lord of Tregaron. They were shipped off to some remote village far from their families and never heard from again.

Soon after Lodi began drinking the special tea, Lord John approached her again. Not long after, he became violently ill. The recovery was slow and painful, though not life-threatening. He became surly and ill-tempered, certain that he was dying. It was rumored he had ceased sending for the young girls at Tregaron to visit his chambers late at night.

Then, with wide-eyed wonder, Lodi revealed that one of the young male servants told her Lord John was covered with ugly painful warts on a certain appendage, and feared it might rot and drop off.

The malady of course, disappeared eventually. But whenever Lord John returned to his previous nightly habits, the condition returned. He never bothered Lodi again.

Cass hesitated outside Margeaux's chamber at the sound of breaking pottery.

"The pot into the fire," she muttered to herself. "I think I'd rather jump into the fire."

As she raised her hand to knock at the stout door, she felt a solid presence beside her. Through the shadows that steeped the darkened hallway she saw silver gray eyes looking up at her and smiled. With a hand resting at the ruff of Fallon's neck, she opened the door.

"Do not bring that beast in here!" Margeaux snapped as Cassandra appeared at her doorway. She ignored Margeaux's churlish temper as did Fallon. He lay down inside the doorway looking as if he'd like to wrap his paws over his ears. He rolled those great silver eyes at her and then pretended to sleep.

"The place is acrawl with vermin and you bring that creature in here. We shall all be infested."

"You asked for me?" Cass reminded her, experiencing a vague uneasiness within the chamber. It seemed unusually dark within the chamber as though the light of the candles and brazier struggled. Almost like a veil of darkness that lay over everything in the room. Then it was gone.

"I asked for you hours ago. Where have you been? The nobles are to arrive this eventide. It is said Prince Malagraine arrives with them. There are hundreds of things which must be attended to and I cannot find you when I need your help."

Her help? Cassandra almost laughed aloud, for it was well known that while Margeaux claimed the title of lady of Tregaron with all the responsibilities that included, it was Cass who saw to the myriad day-to-day details of running the household at Tregaron.

"All is in order," she assured Margeaux as she cast her thoughts to the far corners of Tregaron, from the kitchens to the stables, and assured herself that it was so.

It was an efficiently run household. Cass had seen to that when the responsibility had passed to her upon the death of old Lord John's second wife Anne, for although Margeaux was rightfully lady of the lands until young Lord John married, she showed no ambition for those responsibilities. She was far too consumed with her own ambitious plans.

Margeaux had inherited her father's handsome features, dark brown hair, and cool gray eyes. She had also inherited his ruthlessness and ambition, and the bitter disappointment that she had not been born a son of Tregaron. But what the fates had denied her, Margeaux intended to seize for herself.

She persuaded her brother to turn down proposals of marriage to lesser nobles, in favor of the title of princess, which she coveted. It mattered little that Prince Malagraine had already taken a wife.

"She is sickly and will not live long," Margeaux had spoken dismissively and with little concern. "The prince has spoken of his desire for many fine sons. He will plow nothing but barren soil between her pale, pathetic thighs.

"In time he will seek rich, fertile ground where his seed will take root and grow strong."

She had watched as Margeaux sat before the polished steel looking panel in the rich velvet sleeping gown, lost in her own thoughts as she cupped her small breasts through the soft fabric, stroking herself until her nipples hardened with arousal beneath the fabric.

But the princess lived longer than most expected. Long enough to bear a daughter who lived only a short time. Then, weakened by childbirth and a series of unknown maladies, she had died the previous year.

Margeaux journeyed to Pendragon with Lord John and the other nobles. Afterward, when they returned to Tregaron it was rumored Prince Malagraine had already taken another to his bed. Margeaux did not seem distressed by the thought.

John of Tregaron was neither a warrior nor a politician. He had none of the cunning required for the one or the cold ambition required of the other. He was of average intelligence with his mother's slack gray features, black stringy hair, and pale blue eyes. But one trait bound brother and sister together—a cruel ruthlessness.

It had not always been so. Their mother died when they were very young and Lord Tregaron had taken a much younger second wife. Anne of Aberswyth was a kind and gentle young woman, who became both wife and mother to two young children upon her marriage. But she longed for a child of her own.

Unable to conceive a child, she sought the help of the Old One who lived in the forest. It was there she formed a deep attachment with the sensitive, introspective child the old woman had fostered since a baby—Cassandra.

Cass went to live with Elora when she was only an infant. Of her family, Cassandra knew very little.

She was haunted by dreams. Elora tried to explain the dreams and the parents who loved her but had sent her away. All Cass understood was the loneliness. When the time came for her to return to her family, Cassandra angrily refused.

"You and Fallon are my family," she told the old woman. "I have no need of anyone else."

The Old One could not force her to return, for even at that young age Cassandra's powers were far greater than her own.

Eventually, the Lady Anne persuaded the Old One to allow Cassandra to live at Tregaron. Though no words were spoken, Cassandra sensed in that special way that she knew all things before they happened, that Elora's time was very short.

She was only six at the time and Elora took her deep into the forest as she had countless times before to gather herbs and leaves of plants that only grew in the secret shaded places.

"It is time that you went out into the world," Elora explained. Then warned, "But you must be careful whom you trust. Not everyone will understand your powers. Some will try to use them for their own personal gain. You must guard against such people for they do not understand such things. Only those of your blood understand the powers you were born with—your true family."

The same family that had abandoned her.

Then, Elora had explained that arrangements had been made for her to go Tregaron, for Lady Anne would help her learn things of the known world. They spoke of many more things that day, of the time before the cataclysm and the last known days of the old kingdom. Of kings, knights, sorcerers, and changelings. A magical world of light that had been plunged into a void of evil and darkness five hundred years earlier.

They returned to the forest cottage as the sun was setting through the trees. Elora moved very slowly, pausing often as though to see her way clearly. She smiled at Cassandra, the wisdom of centuries burning in her old eyes, for it was said she had lived in the time before the cataclysm, the last survivor of the ancient kingdom.

She leaned heavily on Cassandra as they reached the cottage, taking the chair beside the opened doorway, with the last rays of the setting sun bathing her worn, wrinkled face.

As Cassandra knelt beside the chair, Elora spoke in a soft voice that seemed to whisper from some far away place as though she was not really there in the cottage at all, but some distance away and had turned back at the last moment to tell Cassandra something that she must know.

"You were a cherished gift, entrusted to my care," she told Cassandra. "I will always be with you, my child. But you must not turn away from the Power of the Light."

"You must fulfill your destiny," she whispered feebly, struggling for each breath. "It is in your blood and grows more powerful with each passing day. Protect the knowledge of your powers and do not hold anger in your heart. Anger is the weapon of the Darkness. It will use it against you if it can."

Then she gave Cassandra a gift, the necklace she had always worn made of pale polished stones, each embossed with a strange carved figure.

Cassandra refused to take the necklace as tears filled her eyes, for the old woman had worn it always and she knew its importance.

Elora smiled softly. "I give it to you, my child. For those with the power to read them, the runes tell the future that awaits." She gently closed Cassandra's small hand around the cool stones with her own fingers.

" 'Tis your legacy, child. The one you were born to fulfill." Then her eyes slowly closed, as if she only rested. The same way Cassandra had seen a thousand times. But this time she did not awaken when Cassandra called to her. Nothing she could do could rouse her beloved guardian.

Then, the old woman began to fade away, slowly, at first so that it was barely noticeable. But when Cassandra kissed her withered old cheek, it seemed she touched only air, a soft presence of warmth that bathed her face and comforted her like the gentle touch of a hand. Eventually, Elora was gone. Yet her presence lingered everywhere.

The following morning Cassandra wrapped her few precious belongings, including the rune stone necklace, in a square of cloth and waited for the mistress of Tregaron. When she arrived, Cassandra explained that Elora had gone into the forest, refusing to think of the old woman as dead.

Her life at Tregaron was not unpleasant. Anne was sweet-natured and kind, and spent many hours teaching her of the known world, as Elora had called it. Though Margeaux and John were some years older and had studied far longer, Cassandra excelled far beyond their abilities.

She had a natural gift for languages, mathematics, and sciences, and soon had read every book at Tregaron. Often, when she wished to escape John's dark moods or Margeaux's petulance, she took a book and returned to the forest cottage to read in peace and quiet.

There she felt once more the special bond with the Old One, formed as a child, and where rumors persisted that Elora still dwelled in the forest cottage. For when the sick and injured came seeking the Old One's healing potions, Cassandra could not turn them away.

Yet she was mindful of Elora's warning that others must not know she possessed such powers. Therefore she took on the appearance of the Old One, using the power of transformation first discovered when she was a very small child. Late one afternoon, she returned to

Tregaron to find the entire household in tears. Lady Anne was gravely ill.

Weeks earlier it was announced that the lady of Tregaron had at last conceived a much longed for child, but she was ill almost from the beginning. Then, that morning the bleeding began.

Cassandra tried to go to the forest for a healing herb that would stop the bleeding but Margeaux, older by eight years and reveling in her temporary position as lady of the house, forbade it. Just before first light, Cassandra finally escaped Margeaux's watchful eye.

She was gone only a short while but when she returned, she knew it was too late. Lady Anne and her unborn child were dead.

She had never experienced the loss of someone she loved before. She did not consider Elora's transformation from the physical to the spiritual world to be the same, for she sensed the Old One's presence with her constantly. But this was different. This was something she was not prepared for.

The loss was deep and wrenching, for Lady Anne had been much more than her guardian. She had been like a mother to her. Following the loss of his pretty, young wife Lord John retreated more and more from the duties of Tregaron, leaving them to his son who was ill-prepared at twenty to assume such duties.

At eighteen the responsibilities of the household fell to Margeaux who assumed them all too willingly with an appreciation for the power it gave her.

Not long after, Lord John died, from a wound received while hunting that had festered when he refused to seek proper care. Young John became Lord Tregaron, and at twenty-three Margeaux became Lady of Tregaron.

Life changed little for Cassandra. Younger than Margeaux by almost eight years, she was paid little attention by either, except for her abilities to efficiently run a large household, a talent that Margeaux neither possessed nor cared to acquire.

"Now I have this cursed rash," Margeaux wailed. "I swear that foolish girl gave me the wrong portions!"

Cassandra glanced at the table and saw the scattered contents among the broken pottery. In a glance she sensed that it had been mixed exactly according to the instructions she had placed within the pouch and given to Lodi at the forest cottage.

She smothered back a smile as she saw the rash that quickly spread up Margeaux's neck, giving her the mottled appearance of a sow that had been wallowing in a mud bath. She could not let Lodi take the blame for this malady.

"You mixed it yourself?"

"Of course!" Margeaux snapped. "You do not think I would trust that foolish girl to get the measurements right."

"Two parts blue powder to one part lavender?" Cassandra held aloft the instructions, precisely written just as she'd told Lodi at the forest cottage. But as she spoke, the letters faded, revealing the true mixture beneath. It was a small deception and not a harmful one. But one which perhaps might teach Margeaux a badly needed lesson.

"Of course not!" she snapped. "One part blue to two parts lavender. I followed the instructions exactly." Margeaux snatched the parchment from her hand. She read the instructions and grew visibly pale.

"Oh, dear," Cass murmured. "It seems you did not read it correctly."

The parchment fell from Margeaux's stunned fingers as she turned and flew to the looking plate. The reflection was not perfect, but revealed enough to send her into fits of wails that started Fallon to howling.

"What will I do?" she cried, scratching furiously as

the rash spread. "Tonight must be perfect. Everything is in readiness. I have planned everything."

And with those words, Cassandra sensed the unspoken as clearly as if Margeaux had blurted it out. With the nobles, particularly Malagraine, due to arrive at Tregaron, Cassandra sensed the reason for her high temper.

"Try not to scratch," she told her.

The nobles and Prince Malagraine did not arrive until the following day, much to Margeaux's relief. By then most of the rash had subsided although she was still given to occasional scratching.

All was in readiness. A lavish feast was prepared. Margeaux appeared at the very last moment, taking her place as lady of Tregaron beside her brother. She was pale, but otherwise there was no other outward sign of the malady that had previously plagued her.

" 'Tis a pity," Lodi commented discreetly. "But I'll wager was no match for the itch between her legs. She acts foolish before the prince."

But this was no fool's game and Cassandra sensed that Margeaux was deadly serious. She understood Margeaux's ambition, it was no secret. But Cass could not understand how she could offer herself so willingly to Prince Malagraine.

He was not an unpleasant man in appearance, powerfully built and carried himself like a warrior. Nor was he old like the other nobles who had offered Margeaux proposals of marriage with an eye toward the wealthy dowry John would settle upon her. But there was a coldness about him, that hinted at a cruel nature.

For the most part his expression was closed and unreadable. Unlike the other nobles his thoughts were not easily known to Cassandra. But there were unguarded moments when he thought no one was looking and she saw the cunning that gleamed in his eyes. And more than once as he spoke with Margeaux, his responses whispered low like that of a lover, she felt his gaze on her watching her from across Tregaron hall.

In those moments, his expression was open, completely unguarded, predatory and dangerous. She shivered, for in his eyes she glimpsed something she had never seen before. An evil so pervasive that it closed like a fist around her heart so that she found it difficult to breathe.

Fallon seemed to sense it as well, pacing the hall restlessly, reluctant to let her enter the hall, then following her with a fierce protectiveness that for the first time made her fearful of what the white wolf might do if provoked.

She left Tregaron, drawing on the power within to make the journey with a single step through a prism of light, emerging in the space of a heartbeat at the small forest cottage. Fallon leapt through the portal behind her.

She lit no fire nor candle but instead threw open the door. A canopy of stars glittered above in the cold night air while a full moon rose fat and pale above the spires of trees. She sat in the chair Elora had sat in that last time, drawing the Old One's thick woolen shawl about her shoulders as though trying to wrap herself in the woman's gentle presence.

"I do not understand what is happening," she whispered. "I sense a powerful presence. Speak to me. Tell me what to do."

But there were no answers that moved in reply to connect with her own thoughts, no comforting thoughts to calm her fears and uncertainty. It was strangely silent. Not even the wind moved through the trees. No forest creatures made their night sounds. As if everything waited in hushed silence.

She had no idea how long she sat there. Eventually she felt Fallon's nudge at her hand. The moon was no longer high overhead, but had begun its descent, peeking through the lowering branches of the trees.

"Aye," she said softly as though in answer to the wolf. "It is late."

She did not return through the portal of light, but chose instead to return through the comforting, earthy, fragrant darkness of the forest. She closed the cottage door and set the latch, then turned down the familiar path she had traveled so many times as a child beside the Old One.

"You must fulfill your destiny."

She heard it as clearly as if someone had spoken to her, but when she turned around to see who had spoken, no one was there.

Five

Except for weary servants who cleared the remnants of supper of the night before from the tables, the great hall at Tregaron was silent when she returned with Fallon.

"Master John went late to his chamber," Lodi informed her, weary-eyed from lack of sleep, and eager to seek her own bed. Still the girl grinned.

"But he'll not bother none of the girls. Had to be carried, he did. Too deep in his brew. The other nobles are spread out in the rooms above."

"And Lady Margeaux?" Cassandra asked.

"She left early. She said I was to send you to her, but that was hours ago."

Cass frowned. The past two nights she had brewed a sleeping draught for Margeaux, for she could not sleep for all the itching from the *youth* potion she'd smeared all over her body. But she had seemed far better today. Still, if she failed to provide the draught, Margeaux would be displeased.

Fallon padded up the long, winding stairs ahead of her. She passed several chambers where the nobles slept, their servants slumped in the hallway outside if they should be needed during the night. She passed her own chamber, confident that none had entered there.

Torches had burned low, others smoldering in the

darkness along the wall. Yet she moved easily in the shadows of Tregaron, her eyesight as keen as an animal's. Fallon loped ahead of her, yet as they approached Margeaux's chamber the wolf suddenly held back.

His eyes glowed intently, head angling from side to side. Then his lips curled back over fierce teeth and he growled low in his throat. Cassandra frowned, for he had sensed something she had not been able to sense.

Then she saw the guard outside the door. He did not see her as he stepped out of the shadows and rapped at the door. Instinctively, she pulled Fallon back into the shadows and on a single, hasty thought warned the beast to silence.

There was a grunted command from within the chamber and the guard pushed the door open. Light from the torch he carried fell across the bed and the two people entwined there.

Margeaux was sprawled across the bed, her dark hair unraveled from its coil of braid and fanned out loosely about her head. She was completely naked, her pale body gleaming against the layers of dark furs at the bed, the thatch of dark feminine hair exposed above parted flesh. Prince Malagraine stood over her at the side of the bed, facing toward the doorway.

He looked up as his man entered and nodded a hasty command, unconcerned that someone else watched his coupling with Margeaux.

"Send him away!" she said huskily as she reached for Malagraine, slender nails raking the flesh where the front of his tunic gaped open exposing bloodied marks that streaked his heavily muscled chest. The laces of his breeches hung open, engorged purplish flesh jutting up against his belly.

With a slow smile, Margeaux arched her back as Malagraine guided her legs about his waist and made hungry, begging sounds at the back of her throat.

He wet his fingers, then cradling her bottom, thrust them inside her. Her body spasmed with pleasure. Then, lifting her hips, Malagraine pressed the engorged tip of bulging flesh between the pale folds at the opening of her body.

There was no pretense of tenderness as he thrust violently inside Margeaux. She cried out, a sound of both pain and pleasure, back arched, fingers clawing at the furs at the bed, head thrashing back and forth.

The sounds she made were not human, but that of an animal in heat. Then the sounds changed, joined by Malagraine's as he grunted and thrust against her, building to a feverish pitch, the shaft of flesh stabbing her again and again until she was certain Margeaux would die from it. But she did not.

Sweat beaded across Malagraine's chest and shoulders as their joining became frenzied. Still, Margeaux begged for more, twisting and writhing beneath him, her eyes glazed with feverish pleasure. Then the sounds became labored, almost anguished, and from where he bent over the bed, his body thrusting inside Margeaux's, Malagraine slowly looked up.

He looked past his guard, through the opened doorway, as if he saw Cassandra hiding in the shadows, unable to leave lest she be seen, unable to look away. And the look in his eyes as he continued to thrust inside Margeaux was only for her as a smile of evil pleasure spread across his face.

Beneath him, Margeaux's movements became more frenzied, but he seemed unaware. He looked only into those shadows beyond the doorway, his smile only for Cassandra.

Then, his gaze still fastened on those shadows, he thrust inside Margeaux twice more, his body going suddenly rigid. Margeaux cried out beneath him, as her pale body spasmed with her own release.

She heard Margeaux's husky whisper, thick with spent desire, then Malagraine's murmured response. His tone changed and the guard entered the room. With the guard blocking the doorway, Cassandra seized her opportunity and fled to her own chamber. For she had seen something in Malagraine's eyes that terrified her.

When she reached her own chamber she slammed the door. All about the portal a thin ribbon of light glowed—the protective spell beyond which no mortal could pass. Then she heard footsteps in the passage beyond the door, heard, too, when someone paused outside her door, and knew it was Malagraine.

The ribbon of light quivered and grew faint, then she heard a hand at the latch. The hackles went up along Fallon's back as he moved between her and the door, lips pulled back over bared fangs. She ceased breathing altogether.

She no longer felt what mortals felt, but experienced an intensity of wild, turbulent energy unlike anything she had ever experienced before as every part of her reacted violently to a danger she had never known before.

Then it passed. The intense energy slowly faded. Fallon, too, sensed that the danger had passed. His ears angled forward as he listened for any sound. There was only silence from the other side of the door. Malagraine was gone.

Cassandra stayed away from the main hall as much as possible the next day as the nobles and Prince Malagraine met with John of Tregaron. But Margeaux saw to it that she was constantly at Malagraine's side.

She smiled frequently, startling the servants with her light-hearted banter and laughter, a feverish glow at her eyes, her gaze fastened on Malagraine with an open, lustful hunger.

Just after midday word came that the knights of the

English king would reach Tregaron by nightfall to discuss terms for peace. Yet, Cassandra felt uneasy.

John, Prince Malagraine, and the nobles were in unusually high spirits. The losses at the Brodmir forest were hardly spoken of, as if they did not matter. And over all was an expectant tension as impenetrable and pervasive as the evil of Darkness Elora had spoken of with fear.

Then the call went out that King William's knights had arrived. The gates of Tregaron were thrown open. A lavish feast had been spread. Only a few guards appeared at the top of the walls, far fewer than John usually ordered to protect the fortress. Only a handful of his personal guard were in the hall. Something was not right.

As honored guest, Prince Malagraine sat at the center of the large table near the hearth. Margeaux sat beside him, John as host and lord of Tregaron sat at her other side. Cassandra would have preferred to watch from the shadows, but John insisted she join them, sitting at his other side.

His request surprised her until she saw the expression on Malagraine's face. A slow smile curved his mouth as he bent to listen to something Margeaux whispered. But his gaze was fastened on Cassandra.

Tension filled the air as the knights of the English king slowly entered the main hall, each with several warriors. They did not wear lavish colors or crests. Nor did they carry any banners. Instead they were all dressed in dark tunics worn over dark leggings and boots. Chain mail glinted beneath their tunics. Beneath their mantles blades of pale, cold steel reflected the light from dozens of torches.

She searched among them for the warrior she had first encountered in that darkened hallway in London. After her second encounter with him only days ago at the ancient fortress, she knew him to be the leader of these men.

A warrior strode forward among the others. Like the warrior she'd encountered, he was tall and wide of shoulder. He was dressed all in black including the leather boots that encased his long, well muscled legs. His mantle swirled around him as he led his men into the hall with a lean agile strength, his gloved hand propped at the handle of his sword. The edge of the hood was angled low over his face, preventing her seeing his features clearly.

Cass frowned thoughtfully, for she sensed none of the fierce, passionate emotions she had sensed on their previous encounters. But more disturbing, try as she might, expanding her own senses for some essence of the man, she could sense nothing at all about him. It was most unusual, for as Elora, the Old One, had taught her, mortals were easily known to her with her special powers of intellect and intuition.

"You carry battle swords into Tregaron," John remarked, a frown creasing his gray features. "Those were not the terms agreed upon."

All along the wall and from corners, John's men made their presence known as they stepped forward, hands clasped over sword handles and lances.

"As you have already demonstrated," the leader of King William's men replied, his hooded head angling toward that line of warriors who threatened from the shadows.

John's lip curled with contempt. Beside him, Margeaux sat up with renewed interest, her attention drawn away from Malagraine for the first time. The prince sat back in his chair, his dark gaze fastened on the hooded warrior. He said nothing, but raised his hand a few scant inches from the arm of his chair, a gesture that immediately silenced John's reply.

Cassandra sensed John's anger. For the first time, she sensed who truly ruled Tregaron. Not John. Not even

Margeaux whose ambitions hungered for far more than those stone walls and verdant fields.

She felt a cold ribbon of fear for the portent of the dark future that lay ahead, for already Prince Malagraine made his authority known in the simple lifting of his hand that immediately silenced John's protest.

"An oversight," Malagraine explained as if it was a mere triviality. "These are dangerous times. Many have died. Precautions are to be expected." With a wave of his hand, John's men stepped back into the shadows.

Cassandra was not deceived and she suspected the warrior who stood before them was not deceived either. Though they relaxed their weapons, the soldiers remained. And she now sensed several more, unseen, among them. She frowned though, for they were neither Prince Malagraine's warriors, nor John's.

She could not see them, but she sensed their presence, their fierce emotions, and their dangerous thoughts. She became uneasy. At her feet, she sensed Fallon's uneasiness as well.

Stephen watched from the shadows, hidden among the peasants of Tregaron with the rest of his men, dressed as they were with weapons concealed beneath their coarse clothes.

His narrowed gaze swept the hall, mentally counting the enemy. They had used disguises to gain entry to Tregaron, they would have to use cunning to escape, for he was now certain of the outcome of these *negotiations*.

He and his men had accepted Tregaron's invitation, but he was no fool. Having narrowly escaped one trap, he suspected another. For that reason he had another lead but a handful of his men directly into Tregaron Hall.

Truan Monroe insisted that he be allowed to lead those men, even though the danger was great. They were surrounded by Tregaron's warriors, cut off from any possible escape unless Stephen and the rest of his men were able to open a means of escape. In spite of the odds against all of them surviving, Monroe insisted.

"They won't kill me," he said, with incredible confidence in the face of such overwhelming odds.

"You are reckless, my friend," Stephen told him. "This will be very dangerous."

"There is much danger in the world," Monroe replied. "If we hide from it, it will surely find us."

Now, he stood in the center of the hall with a handful of men, surrounded by Tregaron's warriors.

Then Stephen saw the young woman who sat on Tregaron's right behind the long table, the same young woman he'd encountered outside the royal hall in London and again only days earlier in the ancient fortress. Cassandra of Tregaron.

She was as beautiful as he remembered . . . as beautiful as the silken image woven in the tapestry. But whom did she serve?

She sat, unmoving, her face expressionless. Except for her eyes. They were bright as sun-drenched violets with the turmoil of countless emotions. Her face was pale in the shifting light from the torches. Hair the color of black satin swept over one shoulder and tumbled past her waist. She rose from her chair once, but Tregaron stopped her. Yet, watching her, Stephen saw what few others saw when she broke Tregaron's hold as easily as if she had brushed a speck of dust from her skirt.

He saw Tregaron's embarrassment, then the dangerous rage that glistened in his cruel eyes.

"These are the terms by which you and your men may live," John of Tregaron repeated, reveling in his powerful role, as he laid down the conditions. But Stephen knew where the real power came from—Prince Malagraine.

"You will surrender your horse and weapons, "Tregaron went on to demand of Monroe. "Your men will also surrender their horses and weapons.

"Your king will pay restitution for the lives lost in the western lands. In addition, he will pay a ransom fee for his knights' lives.

"If he does not do this, then his warriors will die. These," he repeated with a smile void of any humor, "are our only terms."

Cassandra was stunned. These were supposed to be negotiations for peace to end the killing after the brutal deaths of the warriors first sent by the English king, and the recent unprovoked attack at the Brodmir forest.

His terms were insulting. He must be mad. Then her gaze met Malagraine's and she saw the dark evil that gleamed in his eyes. She saw the truth in those cold eyes that had watched her, trapped in the shadows as he and Margeaux came together. And she knew he had no intention of negotiating for peace.

It was all a lie. But as she watched him, she realized it was far more. He was deliberately provoking a confrontation. He had to be stopped, before more men died. She started up out of her chair.

John clamped a hand over her arm, pulling her back down into the chair.

"Do you seek to betray me again, sister?" he whispered viciously. "By warning them as you did at the Brodmir forest? You forget who you are dealing with."

She stared at him incredulously. He could not possibly have known that she had warned the English for he was ignorant of her powers. Yet, somehow he did know. Then, she felt another watching her—Malagraine. His dark eyes were intense.

She slowly sat down in the chair. She could not allow this to happen. Whatever Malagraine planned she vowed she would stop him. She concentrated her power. Then, meeting John's confident gaze, she easily broke his grasp on her wrist as if she did no more than brush at a bothersome insect. She would not let him do this.

"You do not know what *you* deal with, brother," she warned him. "Be careful."

But John no longer listened. "What say you?" he demanded of the warrior.

"I am no knight of the English king," the warrior assured him, taking several steps closer. He removed his gauntlets and pushed back the hood of his mantle.

Cassandra stared at him with surprise, for he was not the warrior she'd encountered at King William's court in London nor again in the castle ruins. He was a complete stranger to her. She could not sense his thoughts as she so easily sensed the thoughts of others, and yet she sensed that she must know him.

His features were difficult to discern for the dark beard that covered his face. But it could not disguise the strength in the angle of his jaw, the sensual mouth curved with a hint of a smile, and cobalt blue eyes that glinted with humor and cunning.

"I owe obedience to no man."

"Yet, you lead the warriors of King William."

"I do not lead them. I fight *with* them. There is a difference."

"You have our terms," John reminded him, his hand curling into a fist on the top of the table as his patience wore thin.

"Aye, well, there is the problem," the warrior replied amicably. "We cannot surrender our horses," he said, chuckling softly. "For how then are we to leave the western lands? And we will keep our weapons as well, for there are dangerous Saxon rebels about."

His smile deepened. "As I am certain a man of your position is well aware. Surely you would not want to leave these men unprotected, for then they might fall under attack from some unseen enemy."

Cass's interest sharpened at the subtle play on words. This man was not the affable fool he pretended. He knew exactly what John was up to. Nor, she sensed, had he and these men simply walked into Tregaron assuming they would be greeted with welcoming arms of peace.

Who was he? Why did he appear to lead these men when she knew different? What was it about him that seemed somehow familiar at the same time she was certain she did not know him.

"King William would not look favorably upon such things and might find it necessary to send the whole of his army into the western lands," the warrior speculated. Then, he shrugged good-naturedly as if they discussed horse trading and merely haggled the price. "As for restitution from the king, I fear there will be none."

Then Cass heard the subtle change in the warrior's voice. This was no game they played.

"Now, you will hear _our_ terms."

John's brows drew together sharply at something he had not anticipated. Malagraine gave no outward appearance of surprise, except for the narrowing of those dark watchful eyes.

"If your men surrender their weapons, you will be allowed to live."

John stared at the warrior incredulously. Then he laughed. "You have barely a score of warriors. I do not think you are in a position to make such demands when there are so few of you."

"Appearances can be deceiving," the warrior replied, his handsome mouth wreathed by dark beard curving upward at the corners in a thoroughly charming, yet thoroughly predatory smile. Though she could not sense his thoughts, Cassandra sensed the danger in this man. Like the fool, John laughed again.

"You have barely a score of warriors."

The warrior laughed. Then his voice became cold as

death, a transformation so sudden and terrifying that Cass shivered.

"Your men made the same mistake at the Brodmir forest," he reminded John.

She saw the movement from the shadows where John's men stood, lined against the wall. In less than a heartbeat a dozen of them toppled forward, dead where they fell. Then she saw the warrior who stepped over the nearest guard at the same time at least another two score warriors suddenly appeared among John's men.

The hood of the peasant costume he wore was thrown back, dark sable hair glinting in the light of the torches as the warrior drew his sword.

Now she realized the deception as he led the rest of his men out of the shadows where they had been hiding among the servants and villagers who had entered the gates of Tregaron.

The gaze that met hers was like molten amber. A fierce expression hardened the handsome features. His thoughts were as clear, and dangerous as the first time they met.

John bolted out of his chair, sending it over backward. Through the chaos, she heard Margeaux's scream and saw Malagraine draw his sword. King William's warriors swarmed through the hall.

One of the warriors vaulted over the table and seized Margeaux. Cassandra tried to get to her, but could not as the table was overturned and a half-dozen more warriors charged the dais upon which the table sat.

John drew his sword as he backed away from the table, then turned and fled abandoning them all. Surrounded by several of his men, Malagraine fought his way out into the hall. Cassandra could easily have fled using her powers, but she did not.

John had lured the warriors of King William to Tregaron with promises of peaceful negotiations. Now they were trapped inside Tregaron. For if she knew her adopted brother at all, he no doubt summoned more men waiting at that very moment.

With Fallon at her side, she whirled around in search of the warrior she had first seen in London. There might still be a chance to save his men. She was cut off by one of John's men who found himself confronted with a hundred and twenty pounds of snarling wolf. He was flattened to the floor, his sword spinning from his fingers. When another tried to grab her, he was thrown backward by the wolf as it attacked.

She saw the tall, bearded warrior embattled at the center of the great hall. He gradually fought his way out, cutting through men with great skill. More of King William's warriors swarmed around the overturned table.

If she could reach them, she would be able to protect them and lead them to safety. But she found her way blocked by the warrior she'd first encountered outside the king's hall in London.

"Good eventide, Cassandra. We meet again." Anger glittered in his golden amber eyes as he greeted her with drawn sword.

"Is this the welcome you planned for me and my men?"

Startled by the question and that he knew her name, Cassandra stepped back hesitantly. Her need to reach his men and lead them to safety had been mortal instinct. Now, she reached out with her other senses and the powers she'd been born with and sensed his thoughts. She immediately connected with his memory of her from those other encounters, but anything more than that eluded her.

"There is no time," she warned. "You and your men must leave now."

"Aye," he agreed, "we shall just walk out, and two

hundred Saxon rebels waiting beyond these walls to cut us down will let us pass through."

She frowned at his cold sarcasm. "There is another way," she explained. "Through the caverns below the fortress. But you must go now, and quickly. Or you will all die."

"And you would not care for that to happen?"

"No, of course not."

The handsome bearded warrior had joined them, along with several other warriors.

"Tregaron and his men have fled," he informed them. Even as he spoke the fighting was reduced to no more than a few last skirmishes between his warriors and the last of Tregaron's men who had not yet fled.

"Summon the rest of the men," Stephen ordered. "We leave this place now." He grabbed Cassandra by the wrist. "And you will show us the way."

She sensed a strange warning of danger from this warrior that she had not sensed before. Instinctively, she tried to twist free, but could not. When he would not release her, she tried to escape him by drawing on her powers.

"Not this time," he said as he drew a length of blue ribbon from the front of his tunic and quickly bound it around her wrist.

Light as goose-down, soft as satin, it shimmered in the light of the torches as though alive and bound her wrist as surely as if it was made of steel.

With growing alarm, she again tried to draw on her powers but found she could not. She tried again to twist free of his grasp without success. Next, she tried to summon Fallon, but discovered she could no longer communicate with him by just a simple thought. Confused, wary of these strangers and the fear he no doubt sensed in her, the white wolf slunk into the shadows.

Panic welled inside her. Her heart hammered wildly.

For the first time in her life, she experienced an emotion she'd never known before. Fear.

What was happening? Who was this strange warrior she'd first encountered by accident as she stepped through the portal of light outside the king's hall in London.

What power did he possess that she now possessed none? Elora had told her stories of the old days and the time of the great cataclysm. She had warned about the powers of the Darkness.

Was he a warrior of the Darkness?

Though she no longer possessed the power to know another's thoughts, she remembered everything the Old One had taught her.

The Darkness is an evil so pervasive that it consumes the light of truth, honor, and love. Beware child, for it will come again. It is there now, waiting in the shadows. You must destroy it, or be destroyed.

Stephen pulled her against him, dragging her arms back and binding her wrists together behind her like a guinea fowl trussed for market. The light from the torches gleamed in the depths of her wide violet eyes, filled with dark, haunted shadows.

What did he see there? Fear? Betrayal? Anger? Or the shadows of Darkness that may already have claimed her powers?

Cassandra felt the raw power of his warrior's strength down the entire length of her body pressed against his. The light of the torches played across the hard angles of his face. His amber eyes narrowed as though trying to see inside her. Terror built inside her unlike anything she'd ever known. She felt stripped naked, completely powerless, with only her mortal strength to protect her and no match for his.

"What have you done?" she whispered.

"I've just taken you prisoner."

"There is no need. Release me. I will help you escape."

"You will help us escape, and I will not release you."

When she started to protest, he gave the signal to his men to follow. Then he turned back to her.

"Where is this passage below the fortress?"

She led them to the entrance, a series of stone steps that led down through the warren of rock passages and caverns that the fortress had been built over in anticipation of invasion by previous lords of Tregaron. She had no idea if John knew of the caverns.

His men followed, stringing out behind them, taking up positions along the way with weapons drawn lest she lead them into a trap. She caught a glimpse of Margeaux, escorted by two of his men. When she began cursing their captors, they silenced her with a cloth tied over her mouth. She had been similarly bound and glared at her captors, yet went along easily enough.

The walls were damp, seeping with centuries of moisture that leached the walls, dripping from the ceiling, the air foul and fetid smelling. Cass had discovered the passages long ago when she first came to live at Tregaron. Though her unusual powers allowed her to leave Tregaron at will, there were times when she might have been seen returning and she had used the passages as a precaution against anyone discovering her powers.

Crisp sea air washed over her face and filled her lungs as they reached the end of the passage which opened at the sea cliffs.

"These cliffs are at the edge of the forest. You may escape without being seen." In the pale silvery light that slanted across the cliffs, her eyes were dark in the pale oval of her face. Though her voice trembled, she said defiantly, "Your men are safe. I demand that you release me."

"I cannot do that," the warrior replied. "You're coming with us."

Fear tightened her throat. She twisted her wrists, trying to free them from the coarse rope. She took a step back, trying to rely on her senses, attempting to summon the power she had always relied upon. She could sense nothing of their thoughts. She did not know whom she could trust and whom she could not. She took another step back, approaching dangerously close to the edge of the cliff.

"I will not go with you. You cannot force me." Brave words, when terror clutched at her heart.

The wind whipped at her hair and molded her gown against her body. Her feet slipped over the wet stones as seaspray plumed up from below. She unwisely took another step back.

As she did, she was suddenly grabbed by one of his men—the blue-eyed warrior who had led his men into Tregaron. In the stark white of the moonlit night, his eyes glittered brilliant blue. She screamed as he swung her away from the edge of the cliff. When he set her on firmer footing, she jerked away and tried to escape.

One hand closed over her shoulder, the other lightly stroked the back of her neck. It was the last thing she remembered as darkness engulfed her.

She collapsed, her head nodding forward against Truan's shoulder as he swung her up into his arms.

"What happened?" Stephen demanded.

Truan shrugged. "She must have fainted." Then he grinned, teeth flashing. "At least this way, she will cause no more trouble."

Frowning, Stephen nodded. "Aye, bring her. We must find the horses and leave this place." He glanced up at the fortress of Tregaron, perched on the rocks above. Lights glowed throughout the fortress. It would not be long before their escape was discovered.

"We must reach Camelot before dawn."

Six

Cassandra awakened slowly, her eyes opening reluctantly against the stabbing light. The hand was cool and gentle at her forehead, a tender stroking that brought with it vague dreams and shadowy memories, and then was gone as she struggled up out of the dark void of dreamless sleep.

She cast her thoughts about, trying to sense what awaited, but there was only silence. She attempted to turn within, seeking the power that was like a voice that always guided her, but there was no answer.

There was only a faint hissing sound, occasionally interrupted by a sharp crackle, that she recognized as the sound of fire in a brazier, the soft musical sound of water, and that gentle hand as a cool cloth was laid against her forehead.

Overhead, on the ceiling, were beautiful flowers, hundreds of them, on lush, green vines, trailing down the walls, petals floating so that it seemed she could hold out her hand and catch them. And with the beautiful scene overhead, came the scent of flowers, elusive at first, then washing over her in softly scented waves. Beneath her, it seemed she floated on a soft cloud.

Then vivid memories returned. Of the fierce battle between the Saxon rebels and King William's warriors at Tregaron, the escape through the caverns below Tregaron with King William's knights, her imprisonment, and the discovery that she no longer possessed her extraordinary powers.

Her breath caught as she sat up suddenly, pain jarring through her head, making her wince, a wave of nausea rolling over her.

"Be at ease, child," a voice reached through the pain. "It will soon pass."

"Not soon enough!" Cassandra muttered, pressing fingers against her throbbing temples. Yet, even as she spoke through clenched teeth, the pain quickly subsided, so that she was able to slowly open her eyes.

Always in control of her senses, it frustrated her that her vision focused slowly, but when it did she frowned as she stared at the creature who stood beside the bed.

She seemed ancient, small and frail, long white hair framing her head in a silvery nimbus. But it was her eyes that immediately drew Cass's attention for they were milky white and void of all color. She was blind.

"A minor inconvenience," the old woman said. She cocked her head toward Cass, a knowing smile curving her mouth.

"But I see far more than most who are sighted."

She moved away from the bed in slow, painful steps, then returned equally slow. She held a cup in her hand. "Drink this." At Cass's suspicious expression, she explained, "It's a restorative. It will take away the last of the discomfort."

Cass took the cup tentatively and sniffed the steaming contents. The fragrance was slightly sweet and soothing. Camomile. The old woman smiled as she sat on a bench beside the bed of furs, while Cass slowly sipped the tisane.

"I know something of the healing arts," the old woman explained with a shrug of her thin shoulder. "If

I wished to poison you, I would have." And then before Cass could ask, she replied, "I am called Meg."

In spite of her blindness, Cass felt the old woman watching her, those vacant, white eyes narrowed with speculation.

Cass set the cup on the bench as she swung her legs over the edge of the raised bed. She tentatively lowered her feet to the cool stone floor. When she was confident the room would not begin spinning about her, she slowly stood.

"What is this place?" she asked.

Thoughtfulness knit the old woman's features. "It is called Camelot."

"The ancient fortress? But it was destroyed long ago. Nothing remains but ruins." Cass took a tentative step. The pain was already gone.

The walls glowed soft pink, the natural color of the stone from which they'd been built. A brazier glowed warmly, sending soft golden light playing across those walls and creating the illusion of the dawn. Overhead the canopy of flowers spread the ceiling, each blossom hand painted on the pale, translucent dome as if someone had tried to recreate the sky filled with spring flowers.

"Not quite all in ruins," Meg replied with a cryptic smile. "Some of it remains. 'Tis said, waiting only for the rightful heir to claim it."

"To hold against the dying of the light, and the waiting Darkness of the night," Cass repeated the words of the ancient legend known among the ancient ones for over five hundred years, and whispered among the simple folk who still believed the ancient king would rule again one day. She angled the old woman a wary look.

"How did I come to be here? Who are you?"

There were so many answers, Meg thought. Where to begin? And which would she accept? She sensed nothing of the girl's true heart, nor if the Darkness had already claimed it.

Her arms ached to hold the child she had once held as only a weeks-old infant, had then wrapped in humble peasant blankets and delivered into the care of the Old One for safekeeping all those years ago.

In a single touch, she had recognized the curve of her cheek. In those first spoken words, she recognized the sound of her voice so like another's. And in her turbulent, uncertain thoughts that struggled with the loss of her powers, she sensed the way Cass weighed everything carefully even as she sensed the girl's keen thoughts already contemplating escape.

But Meg could not know what truly lay in her soul for it was closed to her. She knew only that the power was strong in this one, much stronger than in either Vivian or Brianna. This child of the Light had the power of greatness in her. If she would only accept it . . . if she had not yet been turned to the Darkness.

"You were brought here by King William's men after Lord John betrayed them."

"And the one who leads them?" Cass asked, her fingers smoothing over the ribbon that bound her wrist, trying to find some means of removing it.

Whatever its origin it had a strange effect on her, for as soon as the warrior had tied it about her wrist, it was as if she was bound in chains. But she could have sooner escaped chains, for at least chains possessed a key by which they might be unlocked. The ribbon had no beginning or end. Nor was it easily broken.

"He is a knight of the king," Meg replied. "He is called Stephen of Valois."

"There was another with him," Cassandra continued, slowly walking about the chamber, searching for some means to remove the ribbon for she was certain it held the key to the loss of her power. "A tall warrior with a dark beard and a foolish smile."

"Not so much the fool," Meg replied, following the sound of her voice. "Truan Monroe is from the islands beyond the western sea." She sensed Cassandra's next question.

"He does not owe his allegiance to any king. He joins to fight Malagraine."

Cassandra looked at her with surprise as she realized the old woman possessed the gift of thought. She knew there were many who had the gift, but she had never encountered anyone other than Elora. Then she saw the slender blade that hung from the old woman's belt. She carefully hid her own thoughts as she slowly moved toward Meg.

"There was a white wolf," she continued. "What has become of him?"

"He accompanied us from Tregaron, but will approach no one, nor allow anyone to approach him."

"And the other woman who was captured?"

Meg snorted. "She has a vile temper. They should not have brought her here. But they think to bargain with Tregaron for her freedom. Methinks they already have the worst of the bargain."

"And what is to be my fate?" Cassandra asked. "What is my value to King William's warriors?" It was but idle conversation, yet the woman's answer startled her.

"Far more than you know, my child—the entire future of a kingdom."

For a moment, Cassandra hesitated. Robbed of her powers, even the simplest ability, she could discern nothing beyond the woman's words. Yet, there was something in the way she said it, a prophetic sadness wrapped with some small fragment of hope that reached deep inside her, like a half-remembered voice that whispered though she could not clearly hear it.

Yet, she sensed, in that one brief moment, that she knew the old woman. Had known her before in some other place and time.

She shrugged off the feeling. Seizing the only opportunity she might have, she lunged toward the old woman and seized the knife from her belt.

Clever girl, Meg thought. Brave girl. Robbed of her powers by the spellcast that virtually held her prisoner in the mortal world, she was forced to rely on her mortal senses to free herself.

She would need all her mortal qualities as well as her immortal powers for what lay ahead, Meg thought. Then she sensed Cassandra's frustration and anger, her thoughts open and driven by pure emotion. The knife would not cut the ribbon.

"It cannot be cut," Meg told her, wishing she could remove it and calm Cassandra's fears. But she could not, for she did not have the power.

"There is only one who may remove it. The one who placed it there."

The blade hit the wall and clattered to the floor in an explosion of pure human emotion. She sensed Cassandra's growing distress and the fear she fiercely fought to hide.

"It is a spellcast."

Cassandra needed no answer, nor special powers to know that much. "For what purpose?" she demanded.

It was not Meg who answered, but someone who had entered the chamber behind her.

"For the purpose of preventing your escape."

Cassandra whirled around. Stephen Valois stood framed in the doorway of the chamber. He was tall and powerfully built, his warrior's strength no illusion of chain mail armor or thickly padded garments for he wore no protective clothing.

He was dressed in black leggings and boots. A black

tunic molded wide shoulders, belted at his flat belly and narrow hips. Light from the brazier played across lean features and glinted in amber eyes remembered from that long ago day when she had encountered him by chance and he had refused to let her go, traveling through the portal of light though he could easily have died from it. Just as he now held her imprisoned.

"Leave us," he gently told the old woman.

Meg hesitated, a worried look creasing her shriveled face. Then she nodded, seeking the doorway. She paused as she passed the warrior. Her frail hand closed over his arm with amazing strength.

"Everything she knows has been taken from her. She is vulnerable and frightened, much like the child who must learn everything for the first time."

Stephen frowned. "I will not harm her. You have my word on that."

"It was not for her that I was concerned, milord."

No sooner was the chamber door shut and barred behind her than there was an explosion of breaking pottery from inside the chamber.

Meg leaned against the stout door that had only recently been replaced. She shook her head. Anxious thoughts connected with her in the silence of the hall.

"Tell me about her. Tell me everything."

She sensed all Ninian's hopes and fears in the thoughts that joined with hers, as she desperately sought to know something of the daughter she had not seen in many years.

"She has your logic and sensibility," Meg answered, speaking aloud as though there was someone there to hear. "She is slender and beautiful." She remembered the feel of her features, the delicate curve of her cheek, the slight tilt of her nose, the strong angle of her chin.

"She is also stubborn and willful." As another piece

of pottery hit the door, she added, "and, she has her father's temper."

"But what of her heart? Is it true?" And in the unspoken question that did not follow, Meg sensed Ninian's worst fear—that her stubborn, willful daughter might already be lost to the Darkness.

Sadly, there was only one answer she could give. "I do not know, mistress. Only time will tell if her heart is true. If we survive it."

"Put that down!" Stephen ordered, confronting his angry, willful prisoner. "If you break that, I will have you beaten."

In the space of less time than it took for the old woman to leave the chamber, he was already at the point of losing his temper. At the moment, a good beating seemed like an excellent idea.

He ducked as another pottery vessel, one of the few found still intact in the ruins of the ancient fortress, flew past his head with amazing accuracy and hit the wall.

"You will stop this now!"

He had precious little time to duck as another missile was launched at his head.

"That is enough!" Muttering an oath, he went after her.

She was nimble and quick, darting away from him, another piece of pottery in her fast dwindling arsenal held before her ready to launch. When he lunged at her, she threw it and several more pieces in a rapid barrage of flying pottery, metal flagons, and wooden utensils. He grabbed her by the arm as she seized a pottery bowl.

"Do not!" he ordered, his temper all but gone. She looked up at him with those drowned violet eyes and an innocent expression that could have melted the coldest heart.

"Very well, milord," she said with such sweetness of acquiescence and sincerity that he made the mistake of believing her. She held out her other arm and opened her fingers. The bowl exploded as it hit the stone floor.

Stephen was furious. The chamber, one of the few in the fortress that remained intact all these years, was now in shambles. In the space of a few moments she had accomplished what five hundred years of decay and resident rats had not achieved.

"Will you now remove the ribbon?" she demanded, unflinching as his fingers bruised at her upper arms.

"I would sooner cut off my arm," Stephen replied furiously.

"That may be arranged, milord. In fact, you may find yourself without both arms if I get my hands on that blade."

Anger and threats. Meg was right. She was like a child, robbed of the powers she'd known her entire life by the spellcast that bound her wrist, fighting back the only way she knew how, with the only thing left to her—mortal instinct.

But the creature he held in his arms was no child. She was a woman, an extraordinarily beautiful one with violet eyes that shimmered between anger and tears, cheeks that blazed with furious color, skin like pale satin, and soft breasts felt through the layers of clothing with each defiant breath she took.

Her back arched, her body rigid as she strained away from him, the expression on her face one of surprise at the suddenly intimate contact. Her delicate brows, dark as raven's wings against the pale satin of her skin, drew together in confusion.

"Let me go," she demanded, her voice low and filled

with uncertainty, reminding him of their first encounter which might have ended far differently.

Her powers were great, her immortal strength far greater than his own. She could have abandoned him as they traveled through the portal of light, leaving him to an uncertain fate perhaps even death with none the wiser to his fate. But she had not.

When she had touched him, she touched some deeper part of him. As if she had reached inside his soul, a creature of light, not of this world, a creature who haunted his memory and had brought him to an unknown land on a dangerous quest.

Now, *she* needed him.

He slowly relaxed his fingers and released her. He suppressed a smile at the startled expression that immediately leapt into her eyes at a reaction she had not anticipated.

Mindful of her threats he retrieved Meg's knife from the floor. Firmness and patience, he recalled had worked wonders on him as a boy. Along with a great deal of hard work, after being given time to consider his options—that of remaining in his father's empty house with an endless procession of humorless tutors who secretly hated him and beat him mercilessly, or by taking up the sword of knighthood and discovering the man he might be.

First she needed time to consider her options. He slipped the knife into his belt. He looked around thoughtfully.

"You will clean this chamber," he told her, looking about at the destruction she'd caused. Not a choice that he gave her, but an order. A little hard work would give her time to think.

"You will scrub the floors and the walls. When it is clean, you will be given food and fresh clothing but not before. If it is not cleaned, you will go hungry."

Her violet eyes shimmered. Feet firmly planted, hands propped on slender hips, she asked, "You think to starve me into submission?"

She presented such a delightful picture of childish defiance and feminine indignation. He clenched his jaw, suppressing the urge to grin at her. Or kiss her. That way lay danger and he was not of a mind to travel that road for he had seen the perils that lay there for his two friends who had succumbed to the charms of Merlin's daughters as though caught in a spell.

"You need not starve," he said with mock sternness, remembering his own encounters with authority as a child. "You need only cooperate The choice is yours."

"You are a pig," she informed him, wishing she had the power to go along with the words. He didn't even flinch at the insult. In fact, she could have sworn that he almost smiled. Which only goaded her temper further.

"You are worse than a pig! If you do not release me I swear I will—"

He cut her off. "What will you do, Cassandra?" he asked, a smile playing at the corners of his mouth.

She had not known a simple smile could hold such fascination. It transformed his face, easing the lines of severity, reaching those amber eyes that also seemed to laugh at her.

He took hold of her wrist, the ribbon gleaming in the light of the torches as he recalled a spell her sister had once threatened her own husband with on more than one occasion but to his knowledge had never carried out.

"Perchance turn me into a hedgehog?"

His skin was warm against hers, his thumb resting against the pulse at the curve just below the heel of her hand, long fingers braceleting her wrist with a gentle restraint of power.

She had felt that power before at that first encounter

when he had grabbed her as she tried to escape through the portal, and again when she was abducted from Tregaron. She knew the deadly power he was capable of, hands accustomed to wielding the cumbersome broadsword with quick and deadly skill. Yet the hand that closed around her wrist was surprisingly gentle, his touch almost a caress that she could have easily broken.

She finally pulled her wrist from his grasp and instinctively rubbed the place where his fingers had gently closed round her.

"A hedgehog would be an improvement," she informed him, trying to dispel the disconcerting feel of his fingers which lingered on her skin.

"Perhaps you will have that opportunity."

He turned to leave. At the door of the chamber, he paused. "You will be given food, but only when the chamber has been thoroughly cleaned. The choice is yours."

"What you mean is that I will be allowed to live, if I submit to *your* demands."

With maddening calmness as if the outcome did not matter to him, he shrugged and repeated, "The choice is yours, demoiselle."

"It is no choice at all!" she shouted at his back, as he closed and bolted the door behind him.

"Your terms or none at all? I do not accept your terms!" The last piece of pottery hit the door and shattered.

There must be an easier way, Stephen thought, wondering at the notion that all things in life eventually come full circle, the deeds of the child are revisited upon the man, and wishing that he had been a less stubborn and willful child.

Eventually, Cassandra slumped against the wall exhausted. The fire burned low in the brazier. There was no food or water, or any container to hold any for she had broken them all. Those that could not be broken lay scattered across the stone floor. As anger subsided and she was left alone with her thoughts, overwhelming doubt returned.

Her thoughts reached out. *"Where are you, Elora? I need you. You taught me how to use my powers, but you taught me nothing of how to live without them. What am I to do?*

But there was only silence in answer to her anguished thoughts.

She sat against the wall, dozing then waking with a start, disoriented without her senses to guide her. Then eventually her mortal senses adjusted once more, she remembered, and recognized her prison walls.

She heard occasional sounds beyond the door of the chamber as someone ventured near, then passed by. She tried the latch even though she knew it was bolted from the outside. She tried to summon her powers to release the bolt, even though she already knew it was hopeless. Next she tried the windows.

They were wood-frame, arched, and made of a resinous material that had been tinted a soft shade of pink. Late afternoon light shown through the windows, bathing the chamber walls with golden pink light. A royal prison once occupied by a queen.

She finally opened one of the windows, prying loose the swollen window frame with a piece of broken pottery and discovered that she was in a high tower chamber. There was a small ledge outside the window, but no means of escape so far from the ground unless she sprouted wings. And that, at least for the present, she clearly could not do.

She paced the chamber, kicking aside pieces of pottery, her fingers worrying at the ribbon, wondering at its origin—a spellcast capable of robbing her of her powers.

Where had he gotten it? What was the source of its power? Who was Stephen of Valois? Was he a servant of the Darkness? If so, why as Elora had warned, had he not simply destroyed her?

She grew hungry, but ignored the gnawing ache, angrily kicking aside more pottery. Eventually the light faded at the window. It grew dark and cold in the chamber. She sought the warmth of the bed with its thick furs.

There, she curled into a tight ball, arms wrapped about bent knees, and stared up at the ceiling that earlier had glowed like the dawn with those flowers that looked as if they fell on her from above.

The flowers were no longer visible as night fell, but were replaced by a canopy of twinkling light that spread the ceiling and glittered down on her like stars in the heavens.

She dreamed strange dreams. Of warriors and knights from long ago, of the powerful king who once ruled Camelot with strength, courage, and honor, whose words whispered through her dreams with tenderness and longing for a queen he had loved beyond even death.

"Remember . . ."

Seven

Cassandra rose early. She plaited her hair into a long neat braid and tried to bring as much orderliness to her appearance as possible. She left the chamber as it was and waited for her captors to make their appearance.

She hoped the old woman might return, for she had sensed a sympathy in her that might be turned to her advantage. Surely a knight of King William hadn't the time to be concerned with prisoners. She convinced herself, over the loud complaining of her stomach, that she was prepared to defy his demands unless he was prepared to meet hers.

Midmorning she finally heard metal grate against metal as a key was turned in the iron lock. She sprang to her feet and smoothed the fabric of her gown. The expression on her face as the door was pushed open was one of cool defiance that quickly turned to surprise as a young woman entered the chamber.

She was slender as a reed and small, her body that of a young girl beneath the simple wool gown she wore. She was hesitant, dark liquid eyes surveying the damage in the chamber and no doubt wondering if she might be in danger if she entered.

Her hair was unbound in the way worn by young girls, flowing loose to her hips in a thick tumble of rich amber waves. She was pretty with a heart-shaped face, small up-turned nose, and delicate mouth that promised the beauty she would become as a woman. Over her arm she carried a woman's gown, chemise, and soft leather boots. And with her, through the doorway, drifted the smell of food.

The girl said nothing but entered the chamber hesitantly as a warrior appeared behind her, carrying a tray of food. He was the same warrior who had led King William's men into the hall at Tregaron.

Truan Monroe's eyes were as blue as she remembered and his smile, wreathed by close-cropped dark beard, was just as irritating. The platter and metal urn he carried were both covered by a square of cloth. Wonderful smells escaped the cloth, tormenting her as they were no doubt meant to.

He carried the tray to the table beside the brazier, and removed the cloth. The metal urn contained fresh milk. Just the sight of it made her thirsty for she had foolishly shattered the flagon of water against the wall the night before. The food on the platter was simple— fresh baked bread, cold, sliced fowl, and sliced apples. It seemed like a feast.

Her mouth watered, her stomach complaining noisily. She could not seem to take her eyes off that platter.

The girl crossed the room, laying the clothes across the pallet of furs. They were simply made, but clean compared to her own garments stained with the mud and muck of the caverns below Tregaron.

In fact, she had noticed a particularly unpleasant smell upon rising and donning her soiled gown that morning and wondered about some of the stains. They looked and smelled distinctly of horse. Her slippers were covered with the same stains.

She had used her chemise and a small puddle of water at the floor where the flagon had shattered to clean away some of the stains. But now her chemise was ruined and she had nothing to wear under her gown.

"I see you have already made improvements," Truan remarked, eyes sparkling with humor as he surveyed the disheveled chamber. "Milord would be greatly pleased to see the effort you've made."

First a pig, and now a pompous, braying ass! Cass thought murderously, her gaze once more drawn to that tray of food. It took no unusual powers to see the game her captor played with her. He thought to force her into submission by teasing her with food and clean clothes!

"You lead his men. Now he has you doing the work of servants. Perchance he will next have you emptying the relief pot!"

Truan grinned. He liked her spirit. "I think not," he replied, blue eyes laughing. "Since you have broken it, there is nothing to empty. But I am certain you have already discovered that loss." She had, very early that morning. It added to her growing list of discomforts.

"And I do not lead his men. It was necessary so that he and the rest of his men could hide among the Saxon rebels inside Tregaron Hall. If we had all marched into Tregaron," he pointed out, watching for her reaction, "we would have all been slaughtered."

For a moment the humor in his eyes wavered and she saw beneath the jovial facade to the deadly serious demeanor beneath, as though someone else was hiding behind the smile.

"Yet you act the part of the lackey now."

He winced and slapped his hand over his heart as though mortally wounded. "Your tongue, mistress, is as sharp as your aim," he commented. "Has no one ever told you that you will draw more flies with honey than vinegar?"

She tried to ignore his antics. At times, the man truly

seemed the fool. And at others. . . . He slowly poured the milk into a cup.

"I have no use for flies," she replied, determined to ignore his game. "I would sooner kill them—therefore I have no use for honey."

Next he took a slice of bread and spread it with honey, the thick, golden liquid dripping onto his fingers which he slowly licked clean. A juicy apple peeked from beneath the other cloth.

Winking at her, he said, "I will remember that."

Inwardly, Cass groaned as she imagined the thick sweetness slipping down her throat. Then he washed the bread down with milk. Her own mouth watered, her stomach rumbling loudly.

"What was that I heard?" he said with mock seriousness, cupping his hand behind his ear. "Did you say something, mistress Cassandra?"

"You are an idiot!" she said, turning abruptly toward the window so that she was not forced to watch his little performance.

"And you may take that away for I will have none of it. Not until he has removed this wretched ribbon."

He shrugged as he stuffed another piece of bread into his mouth. "If you have no need of food, then perhaps you would care for clean clothes," he suggested. "This chamber is beginning to smell like the stables."

She slowly turned back around. Her gaze instinctively went to the tray now void of all food except one teasing slice of bread that seemed to wait only for her.

"And the price of the clothes?" she asked, wondering what new demands would now be made.

"You must first clean the chamber."

She frowned. "And the price of food?"

He smiled and she knew the answer. It was the same.

"And if I wish to leave this chamber?" She held her hand up, already knowing the response. "Do not say it!"

" 'Tis a simple thing, Cassandra," he said, as the girl carefully picked up the garments and crossed the chamber. She extended her arms, holding the clothes out to Cassandra.

Though simple in design, they were finely made, the wool finely spun into a soft fabric that was clean and without stains or offensive odors.

"Take them away," Cass answered defiantly, for she would not do as Stephen of Valois asked. "Take it all away!"

The girl flinched as though she'd been struck and hastily backed away. In her haste she dropped the leather boots. She glanced hesitantly from Cassandra to the warrior as though expecting a rebuke.

"What is the matter? Can the girl not speak?"

"I am told she has not spoken since her village was burned and her family murdered in front of her by Saxon rebels who fled into the western lands," Truan explained, all traces of humor now gone.

With her unusual powers, Cass had always known the feelings and thoughts of others. But now she did not. It was as if a cover had been placed over her other senses, leaving her only with what other mortals relied upon. And poorly at that for she had blundered and caused the girl pain.

She bent down and picked up the boots. When she started toward the girl, Truan Monroe stopped her with a hand at her arm. The unspoken warning was there in the strength of his fingers closed around her upper arm that could have easily snapped the slender bones, along with some strange undercurrent of energy felt in her blood. She frowned.

"I give you my promise, I will not hurt her."

"Her name is Amber." Slowly, he released her. Cass handed the garments back to her and explained, "Please try to understand, Amber. I cannot accept these."

The girl watched her with wary eyes. Eventually, she nodded and took the garments.

"Please take it all away," Cass told them, turning so that they could not see the doubt and uncertainty in her face. Then she heard them leave.

"Well?" Stephen demanded when they emerged from the chamber. "Were you successful?"

"We were not," Truan informed him, skewering the apple with the tip of his blade and taking a bite out of it.

"You, my friend, have your work cut out for you."

"It has been six days," Stephen said with growing frustration. "Has she eaten anything?"

"She has taken only water," Meg said.

"What of the clothes?"

"She refuses everything."

"And the chamber?"

"Unchanged," Meg replied.

Stephen sat before the fire in the brazier in the star chamber. In the days since they had ridden into the ancient ruins, it had been cleaned of debris. The bodies of the ancient warriors who had fallen where they had fought had been carefully removed. They were buried on the hill overlooking the fortress. But there were still signs of the battle that had been fought here over five hundred years ago.

Though the walls had been scrubbed, the scars remained. The chairs that had once sat around the large round table were gone. They had been replaced by simple benches for he had taken this place to meet with his knights, just as the king had once counseled with his.

The table once more sat upright, its charred pedestal had been replaced. It was the first thing he had ordered when he returned to this large chamber with the damaged, domed ceiling that was decorated with thousands of stars. Thatch now covered the damaged portion, but eventually he would have it repaired.

He slowly circled the table, gazing down thoughtfully at each of the twelve panels with their ancient Latin inscriptions. From the moment he had first seen this ancient place, its ghostly warriors still holding their positions with battle swords drawn, he had felt a oneness he could not explain. A oneness that had compelled him to return, in defiance of his own king, and felt again when he returned after the battle at the Brodmir forest.

Since then, almost daily, people had been arriving at the ruined fortress. At first it was only one or two—a farmer bringing foodstuffs, a mason with skill in building. But their numbers grew each day as word spread until more than a hundred people now inhabited the walls of the ruined castle, with more arriving all the time.

Workmen climbed the walls and caulked ancient stones. Thatchers replaced roofs. Carpenters tore down crumbling buildings that lined the fortress walls and built new ones. Overnight, a city had sprung to life. And also among those who poured out of the surrounding hills, were men who could wield a sword or broadax, and many more who were greatly skilled with an unusual longbow.

From Tregaron to the west, there was only silence. A dangerous, menacing silence that would not last. Of that he was certain.

Stephen vaulted out the chair, pacing the chamber restlessly.

"Is there nothing that can be done?"

"I warned you she would not easily be persuaded in this," Meg reminded him. "You play a game for which she has no understanding."

"This is no game, old woman, but deadly serious. For I do not know if she can be trusted. How do I know that if I yield and remove the spellcast, that she has not already been turned by the powers of Darkness? I would be risking all who have placed their trust and their lives in my hands. And if she has not, can she be persuaded to do what must be done?"

"It is an interesting dilemma, warrior. For the spellcast protects at the same time it prevents you from knowing the truth."

"Is there nothing you can tell me that I may know what truth lies in her heart?"

"I know only the truth of her anger. She has carried it with her many years. Long ago she refused to return to the mist and learn of the ancient ways and the legacy that awaited her. She turned away from those who loved her. I cannot say what lies within her heart."

"If she is as a child," he asked, "then what am I to do? How do I make her understand?"

"You are the teacher," Meg reminded him. "She is the student."

"A stubborn one."

"Then, perhaps first you must get her attention."

Stephen's eyes narrowed thoughtfully. Then he slowly smiled.

The past six days since she'd been abducted from Tregaron had settled into a monotonous routine that at times made Cassandra think she was going mad.

Each morning at precisely the same time, the door to her chamber was opened and a tray of food was delivered. And each morning she refused the ultimatum she'd been given. The routine was repeated each midday and again in the evening. And each time she refused to accept the terms she'd been given. Although, with each successive day, it was becoming more and more difficult to resist. If not for water and the silverberry plant the old woman had brought her, she did not think she could have survived until now.

The third day the old woman had returned carrying the small plant. A restorative she had called it, against any aftereffects of her abduction from Tregaron.

Under the watchful eye of the guards who watched constantly, the old woman had instructed her in the brewing of a special tisane from the leaves of the plant. But Cassandra knew those same leaves provided nourishment as well. For the past three days, she'd subsisted on water and the silverberry leaves.

It was a poor substitute for food. And each time a tray of succulent meats and fragrant bread was brought to her chamber, she found it more and more difficult to resist. Yet, still she mustered the strength to refuse, kicking aside a piece of broken pottery.

During the long hours of her confinement, she searched the chamber from top to bottom for some means of escape, and could find none. Repairs had been made. The door was stout. And the shimmering blue ribbon bound her as surely as chains. She was trapped, until she found a way to persuade Stephen of Valois to release her.

Cass turned as she heard the key grate in the lock. She carefully smoothed her rumpled gown that she was now forced to sleep in. But beneath the gown she had managed a modicum of cleanliness with the water that was brought her each day. What she didn't drink, she washed with.

She squared her shoulders and prepared to meet her guard with a cordial expression for she had befriended the two who usually took turns watching over her. And she was always pleased to see both Meg and the girl, Amber, although conversations were somewhat more limited with the girl.

Her eyes therefore widened with surprise as the door opened, and neither Meg nor Amber delivered the usual meal tray. Instead, her captor filled the doorway, feet planted in a wide stance, arms folded across his chest.

He bore no tray, nor did any servant follow him into the chamber carrying one. Cassandra glanced warily past him, for she saw neither of her guards.

"Good morn, mistress," Stephen greeted her. "I trust you slept well."

He had never cared a wit how she slept. "Well enough," she answered hesitantly.

"The chamber is not clean."

She frowned at the obvious, wondering if he expected an answer.

"Do you refuse to clean it?"

Her frown deepened. What game was he playing now? He waited for her answer.

"Yes, milord. I refuse."

"Are you prepared to accept your punishment?"

Punishment? Her attention focused slowly. Had he decided to have her beaten after all?

"You may do what you will, milord," she said defiantly. "I will not clean this chamber."

His expression was unreadable. Worse, she had no notion of his thoughts. The fear returned in a heartbeat as he said, "I regret that it has come to this."

He crossed the room in long strides, reaching her before she could react. When he raised his hand, she brought her arms up to protect herself. But instead of striking her, he grabbed her and threw her over his shoulder.

The air left her startled lungs in a loud whoosh as his shoulder drove up under her ribs. Inky dark spots swam in her vision and she suddenly felt faint as she fought for the smallest breath.

He adjusted her over his shoulder as if she was no more than a sack of grain, and cool air filled her lungs. When she tried to lever herself up off his shoulder with hands flattened against his back, he smacked her hard across the bottom. She cried out in equal amounts of anger and indignation.

"I demand that you release me!"

He swung around, forcing Cassandra to duck as he left through the chamber doorway.

"Put me down!" she demanded, ending with a shriek as he loosened his hold on her legs and very nearly dropped her off the back of his shoulder.

Her hair swept over her shoulders and face as she was carried upside down over his heavily muscled shoulder, and it rapidly became a struggle just to keep from being dropped on her head.

Her face was buried in the middle of his back. Somewhere along the way as he carried her out of the main fortress and into the open yard, he heard a mixture of muffled curses and threats, and something that vaguely sounded like a promise of what she would do to him when she was able to remove the ribbon.

"Put me down!" she shrieked. "You have no idea what you are dealing with."

"You're wrong, Cassandra. I know exactly what I am dealing with." His reply only infuriated her more. She beat at his back and kicked her legs, determined to free herself.

"I demand that you release me!"

"Very well, demoiselle. As you wish."

The change in his tone should have warned her. But she paid no attention. When she realized that he fully intended to release her, it was too late to wonder why he had so readily agreed.

He shifted her up off his shoulder. One arm cradled her at the shoulders, the other beneath her knees. Then, she was suddenly released. Her startled scream ended on a gasp as she was plunged into the horse trough.

Sputtering and choking, she thrashed in the water,

her soggy hair smothering over her nose and mouth, soggy clothes dragging at her and making it impossible to get her footing.

"I loathe you!" she screamed.

"No doubt. At the moment you are somewhat offensive yourself," Stephen remarked with amazing calm as he stood at the edge of the huge round wooden trough near the east wall.

"You are a toad, a vile, filthy pig—"

The last ended on a shriek as Stephen seized her by the neck of her gown. Her eyes widened as he drew his knife, then widened even further as he sliced her gown from neck to hem.

She wore no chemise under the gown, her skin pale, almost translucent in the early dawn. Though she tried to hold the gown together, it gaped away from her slender body, exposing the gentle curve of hips, a slender waist his hands could have spanned, and firm high breasts. His gaze fastened there as her rose colored nipples puckered and thrust through her splayed fingers as she tried to cover herself.

He was caught off-guard by her sudden nakedness and the equally sudden heat that burned through him and had nothing to do with anger.

Grabbing the twin halves of her gown, trying desperately to hold them together over her nakedness, Cassandra sought the only protective covering available. She submerged below the surface of the water up to her neck.

"I hate you! You whoreson! You spawn of the devil. I hope you grow warts. I hope your manhood shrivels and rots off. I hope—"

Stephen placed his hand firmly on top of her head and shoved her beneath the surface of the water.

"Such foul language for a young lady," he reprimanded her, as a crowd slowly began to gather, including Truan Monroe who had followed him across the yard.

Stephen allowed her to briefly bob to the surface. "Do you apologize?"

"Never! I curse the day you were born. Your spine will become twisted and bent. You will grow a hump in the middle of your back—"

He pushed her beneath the surface again.

"The water is cold," Truan commented as streamers of mist rose from the water in the chill morning air.

"Aye, that it is." Stephen replied, holding her under.

"You would not wish her to be taken ill."

"At this moment, I could wish her simply to be taken from here." He allowed her to bob to the surface and then promptly dunked her again.

With a thoughtful frown, Truan suggested, "I think you should stop."

"When she has had enough." Amid more sputtered curses, Stephen pushed her under again.

"She has had enough."

"This does not concern you."

"It does concern me!" Truan said, a dangerous edge in his voice. Then, as Stephen finally looked up, he smiled.

"You are enjoying it too much. You don't want to drown her."

"The thought had occurred to me." Stephen finally released her. She bobbed to the surface, choking and sputtering colorful curses. Most of it lost in the translation. But there was no mistaking her meaning.

She scooped the curtain of wet hair back from her face and glared at Stephen of Valois. He threw her a horse brush and a cake of strong lye soap.

"Scrub," he ordered. "Everywhere, until you are clean. If you do not do as I say," he leaned over the trough, hands braced at the edge. "I will scrub you myself!"

The brush floated before her like a ship bobbing

about on an uncertain sea. She felt his men watching, waiting to see what she would do.

Her teeth had begun to chatter and her skin was covered with goosebumps. But she dare not leave that water without doing as he said, for she feared he would carry out his threat. She angrily dragged her skirt up and began scrubbing her foot with the brush and soap. She sent lye soap flying as she plunged her foot below the surface and found the other. Much of it splattered across his face and hair.

"Be careful, mistress," he warned. "If you continue in this manner, I will be forced to join you to see the matter properly done."

She glared at him from the middle of the horse trough. "You would not dare!"

"I would," he promised, then repeated, "For I will not abide anyone who smells worse than my horse! And when you are clean and do not smell like a dung heap, then we will talk again. Until then," he leaned closer. She went absolutely still in the water, her lips turning a light shade of blue, caught between freezing and cold terror.

"I suggest you keep scrubbing." His voice was deadly quiet and far more unnerving than when he shouted. "Every part."

Among those who had gathered, he passed Sir Kay as he turned and stalked away from the water trough.

"You may give her something to cover herself with. If she complains, if she utters one disagreeable word, leave her where she is."

Then he turned on his heel and walked back across the yard. Now, he had her attention.

Eight

Cassandra jerked awake, her head coming up from arms folded across her knees.

Metal scraped against metal. The bolt to the chamber door thrown back. The door to the chamber slowly opened. Light from torches in the hallway slanted across the stone floor. She leapt to her feet, weary muscles protesting every movement, every nerve drawn taut with exhaustion.

She had spent the entire day scrubbing the chamber—walls, floors, window openings—until every stone once more gleamed the color of pale sand. Until her knuckles were raw and bleeding; beyond the point where muscles cramped and spasmed. Past exhaustion, lest her captor return and find even the smallest speck of dirt and mete out more punishment; past the anger and humiliation; past tears she had never cried before. Until, exhausted, alone, and afraid, there were no more tears left.

Hours earlier a servant had brought hot water, a bowl of soap, and the clean gown she now wore. Cassandra considered throwing all three out the window. Except for fear of the retaliation it would bring.

Her cheeks were dry now, eyes only slightly swollen as she stood in the shadows near the raised hearth, fists balled at her sides, with no other weapon but her pride as the door opened.

"Tell me!" Lady Ninian's insistent thoughts connected with old Meg's as she stood in the doorway of the chamber.

"What do you sense?"

"I sense fear, anger . . . so much anger, and courage."

"Is she well?"

"Aye, mistress, as well as can be expected."

"What of her thoughts?"

Meg did not answer right away, her own thoughts searching in the ancient way, trying to connect with those of the young woman whose presence she felt and sensed as surely as the warrior who stood beside her. But unlike the warrior who stood beside her, wary and cautious, she sensed nothing.

"Her thoughts are closed to me. I sense only her human emotions. There is much anger, and pain. I do not know where her heart lies."

"You must reach her, dearest friend," Ninian implored her through the connection of their thoughts.

"You must help him to reach her for his fate is entwined with hers. She must be persuaded to accept her legacy."

"I will try, mistress," Meg replied. *"But I cannot make her see what she refuses to see. I cannot make her accept what she has closed her heart to."*

At first there was only silence. Then, the changeling sensed her mistress's despair.

"Then she is already lost, and there is no hope."

Beside the old woman at the doorway, the warrior Gavin de Marte lit another torch. Flames sputtered, then caught the tar-soaked cloth. Acrid smoke spiraled upward as light spread through the chamber, falling across the young woman who stood in the shadows at the hearth like a warrior ready to do battle.

Her back was rigid, feet firmly planted, and shoulders

squared, a defiant, wary expression on her face. Color blazed across cheeks and glittered at her vivid eyes. But the hollows beneath her cheeks and the dark circles beneath those vivid eyes revealed far more.

She may come willing, or dragged kicking and screaming. But she will come. Those were Gavin de Marte's orders.

He prayed for the first with the desperate hope that it would not be necessary to drag her to the main hall. He had seen the confrontation in the courtyard. He sensed how that ultimatum might be received, and decided to lie.

"With sincere apologies," he began tentatively, making it up as he went along. "Milord humbly extends an invitation for you to join him for the evening meal."

Beside him, Meg's head came up in surprise, for she had heard Stephen of Valois's orders and feared the worst. Cassandra also looked at him with surprise.

"These were his words?"

"Aye mistress, his exact words."

"He apologizes?" she asked incredulously.

Sir Gavin swallowed tightly. What difference did it matter whether it was one lie or a dozen? Surely the outcome could be no worse than delivering the ultimatum he'd been given.

"He apologizes most humbly and regrets his earlier treatment toward you. It is his hope that you will forgive him."

Beside him, Meg snorted. "You had best hope for more than that when he discovers the lies you've told and she discovers the deception," she muttered under her breath.

The tension eased out of Cass's shoulders, almost immediately replaced by overwhelming exhaustion and hunger. She swallowed convulsively, hunger gnawing at her until it became a dull ache that pressed against her

backbone. Nearly as painful as her throbbing muscles
and aching back.

"I accept."

"You are doomed," Meg told the warrior softly, a
smile playing at the edges of her mouth. "I shall enjoy
watching this."

"Do you have a better idea, old crone?" he whispered.

"None that shall prove nearly as entertaining."

Cass was stunned by the transformation of the ruined
castle as she accompanied Sir Gavin. It was far different
from the crumbling ruins she had discovered a long time
ago.

As a child, she had heard all the legends about the
ancient castle and the king who had once ruled over five
hundred years ago. Myth and legend entwined in stories
of brave warriors who had pledged their swords to the
king who ruled from a castle made of rare, pale sandstone with gleaming spires, clear domed ceilings that
looked out on the night sky filled with stars, and the wise
and powerful high counselor to the king. Merlin.

It was called Camelot, the legendary kingdom where
warriors served their king with great courage. Warriors
who were as well known as the king, with names like
Lancelot, Sir Gawain, Melador, Sir Hector, and Sir Bors.
Twelve knights who joined around a legendary round
table where decisions were made about the future of
the kingdom.

But war spread across the land. A vast army swept out
of the north and invaded the kingdom, led by warriors
whose helms, swords, and breastplates were as black as
the darkness that filled their heartless souls.

The powers of Darkness invaded Camelot. The king
was betrayed by one of his knights whom he loved and

trusted above all others. Shadows filled the sunlit halls and courtyards of Camelot.

The king was mortally wounded in battle. Merlin was captured and banished to the world between the worlds. The king's warriors made their last stand against the enemy in the great starchamber of the round table. There, with swords drawn they defended the kingdom. And there, they fell, one-by-one, dying with their swords in their hands.

Afterward, with the king and his warriors dead and Merlin banished to the nether world, the great Darkness swept over the land. There were many years of war, sickness, death, and the growing power of greedy and ruthless men like Prince Malagraine.

It was remembered now only in stories whispered to children around the fire at night. But there were those who still believed that the powers of the Light and the powers of Darkness continued to battle for the kingdom of mankind and that one day the Light would rise up against the Darkness to reclaim the kingdom.

Cassandra heard all the stories as a child. But she did not believe them. Until that first time she awakened from a troubling dream and found herself in the starchamber within the ruined castle walls. It was the first time she traveled through the portal of light. When she emerged on the other side, she stepped into the chamber. As she grew older she was drawn again and again to these ancient ruins.

She explored the halls and courtyards, the open-air chambers that looked out on balconies and terraces. Within the starchamber were the ruins of a round table and the crumbling remains of the warriors who died defending the kingdom, just as the legend had said. But the castle ruins she discovered long ago as a child were far different from the hallways and chambers through which she now passed.

Debris had been cleared away. Walls had been scrubbed and floors swept. Seams of new mortar were visible on walls where stones had been replaced. Lights blazed from torches and oil lamps. As she passed another hallway that opened onto a balcony she saw more torches as guards walked the parapet walls. The yard below was dotted with the glow of campfires of a small city that now filled the walls.

Buildings lined the bottom of the walls. The air was redolent with the smells of a small city—cookfires with food simmering, tallow for candles, dust churned beneath the hooves of horses that passed by, the barking of a dog, laughter, and the voices of children.

After five hundred years, Camelot was alive once more.

The main hall was at one end of the courtyard, enclosed by tall doors that had only recently been replaced. Cass held back hesitantly as they reached the main hall, remembering the last time she had seen it steeped in shadows, layers of filth and dust covering the floors, furnishings crumbled to ash, and the fire-blackened walls.

It had seemed like a haunted place, filled with ancient spirits and old dreams. As a child, she had fled, certain the shadows of Darkness chased her. But the great hall was transformed.

The walls had been scrubbed and whitewashed. Fresh mortar patched the walls like a spider's web. A fire blazed on the hearth. Before the hearth were several long tables with chairs along both sides.

Venison roasted over the fire. The tables seemed to bow under the weight of large platters of roasted guinea fowl. Overall, aromas of food mingled with that of new timber, mortar, thick pine logs at the hearth, and sweet, pungent pine oil in the wall lamps.

Conversation suddenly ceased. Someone laughed, a startled sound that ended in a cough as Cassandra entered the hall and wished she had remained in her chamber no matter what the humiliation or cost.

She entered the hall hesitantly, aware of those who stared, aware, too, that Margeaux sat among them like a welcomed guest rather than a prisoner.

She also wore a clean gown. Her hair was pulled back and plaited in a simple braid, decorated with a circlet and sheer length of fine silk that matched the color of her gown. She sat near the end of the table before the hearth, her gaze narrowed and sharp, in stark contrast to the smile she turned on the warrior beside her.

Cass was escorted to the table before the hearth. Stephen of Valois stood to greet her.

"Good eventide, mistress. I am pleased you have joined us."

"Your apology was most persuasive," she replied. "But I was most intrigued by your humility. I had thought you incapable of it."

He looked at his knight, his gaze speculative. "I am intrigued by it as well."

Gavin quickly excused himself and fled. Meg, also left, taking up a perch at the corner of the hearth where she might observe everything that went on, but out of harm's way.

"It seems we have both been deceived, milord," she told Stephen as she turned to leave, determined to escape from the hall as quickly as possible. His hand closed over her wrist.

"Please stay." It was hardly a request, but a command. She felt it in those long fingers that encircled her wrist, trapping her as surely as that unusual ribbon.

"And if I refuse?"

"You already know the consequences."

Her breasts rose and fell sharply beneath the gray wool kirtle he'd sent to replace the one he'd ruined. It was belted at her slender waist with a length of braided silver cord. Long sleeves flared wide at her fingertips and exposed the snug sleeves of the pale muslin chemise she wore underneath.

Her hair was unbound and fell down her back in a torrent of gleaming midnight satin, framing delicate features that bore a strong resemblance to her sisters in the curve of her cheek and the stubborn angle of her chin. But her eyes were the sorcerer's eyes, dark as obsidian that glowed with violet flames beneath the delicate arch of slender brows black as a raven's wing. Vivid color spread across her cheeks.

He imagined what she would like to have called him, but dared not. He saw the anger and humiliation in her eyes, in the sudden color that blazed across her cheeks, and the slender taut muscle at her jaw as she fought to remain calm. She said nothing but finally sat down as food was brought to the tables.

The amount of food was overwhelming. There was roast fowl, venison, fish, baked breads, pickled eggs, and spicy poached apples. The roast fowl swam in a plum sauce. The venison was well turned so that it all but fell from the bone.

"It would be a shame to waste this fine food," he suggested as a servant set a trencher before her.

"What difference does it make to you whether I eat it or not."

"It makes a great deal of difference, and you will eat."

It was on the tip of her tongue to refuse, but she already knew what he would say. She knew the consequences.

"I assure you it is not poisoned."

To prove it, he sliced a piece of meat from the haunch of venison. Thick, succulent juices ran over the venison. Her mouth watered and she swallowed convulsively as he carved off a tender morsel with the knife and popped it into his mouth.

"If I wished to poison you, I could have done it days ago in the water you drank."

Next, he sliced a plump drumstick from the guinea hen swimming in a sweet plum sauce. Then, he relaxed back into the chair, long legs stretched before him, booted feet crossed at the ankles, and began nibbling on the drumstick. Inwardly, Cass groaned.

The table at Tregaron had never boasted anything so abundant or pleasing as the food laid out before her. The cook at Tregaron was a disagreeable woman whose husband and son provided the meager meat for the tables.

The evening meals usually consisted of fowl or wild boar, seared on the outside, uncooked on the inside. She rarely ate in the main hall, preferring instead the simple food she prepared herself and ate in her chamber.

It was agony watching him clean off the drumstick and reach for another. She was so hungry she almost felt physically ill. He hesitated, the drumstick with succulent golden skin glistening with plum sauce. He looked over at her.

"Perhaps you would prefer roast fowl to venison," he suggested, offering her the drumstick.

Stubborn pride battled hunger and common sense, while she couldn't seem to take her eyes off the drumstick. He saw the conflict in her eyes, at the stubborn angle of her chin, her convulsive swallow as her mouth watered, and the moment when hunger and common sense finally won out. Eventually, she reached out and took the drumstick.

She held it in slender fingers, her tongue darting out to tentatively taste the plum sauce. Her small, perfect teeth flashed, gently nibbling as she bit into succulent golden flesh and tasted where he had tasted. Her lips glistened with the sweet juices, her tongue darting out to catch a drop of juice at her lower lip. An innocent gesture that made his mouth suddenly go dry as desire spiraled through his veins.

There was something almost intimate in the way she carefully took a bite in exactly the same place he had, plum sauce glistening on her lush, curved lips, as if she tasted what he had tasted. As if . . . she tasted him. He suddenly felt as if she were the captor and he the captive.

The drumstick was neatly stripped clean, the gleaming bone quickly returned to the platter, the muslin cloth that had covered it used to wipe her hands. He pushed another platter toward her with slices of venison, a portion of bread, and spiced apples. Her watchful gaze met his, still cautious, still wary.

Stephen said nothing but bent over his own plate, slicing a portion of venison and skewering it into his mouth, giving her the choice, food or hunger, in the silence that lay between them.

She ate sparingly. Eventually, she pushed the platter away unable to eat anything more for the fear and uncertainty that coiled a knot at her stomach while all about them there was an almost festive atmosphere. Even Margeaux seemed to feel at ease among them, conversing with the warrior beside her.

The old woman was never far away. The girl, Amber, served food and filled goblets. She moved silently along the tables. Unlike the other serving girls she was not fondled by the knights and warriors, but remained close to Truan Monroe.

As appetites were satisfied, the sounds of eating gave way to animated conversations, the retelling of old stories and colorful tales spoken in a mixture of languages. But laughter was the universal language as Truan Monroe entertained them with slight of hand tricks and simple conjurements that brought delighted squeals from a serving girl as he magically plucked a flower from behind her ear, and then produced an egg seemingly out of thin air from behind the ear of a kitchen servant.

"You must be careful not to break it," he warned, mischief gleaming in his blue eyes.

When the woman's oversized, gangly son, Gryffyd, asked to be shown the trick, tables were pushed back and encouragement shouted from all corners.

Truan bowed to his audience and stepped to the center of the hall. The boy followed like an oversized puppy, lapping at his heels.

With an amiable grin on his handsome face, Truan showed the boy and his captive audience several different slights of hand and tricks of illusion—gold coins that disappeared one-by-one in front of everyone, then magically reappeared in the boy's pocket; a dove perched one moment in the palm of Truan's hand and disappearing the next.

At first Gryffyd was disappointed when the bird did not immediately reappear. Then, suddenly he jumped with surprise at a sudden movement in the front of his breeks.

All about him were guffaws of laughter, lewd comments, and shouts of encouragement as one of the serving girls eyed the front of his pants enthusiastically.

His cheeks spread with color. Eventually, he carefully dug a hand into his pants to find the cause and discovered the dove, struggling to free itself. Once freed, the dove escaped high into the rafters amid hoots of laughter about the lad's manhood that had just flown away.

Cassandra could stand it no more.

"Why have you brought me here?" she demanded. "What do you want of me?"

His amber gaze was contemplative, measuring as he sat back in his chair, a goblet of wine loosely clasped in long fingers. His hair spilled loosely about his shoulders, framed by the light from the fire at the hearth behind him, a russet mane that gave him a leonine appearance as he studied her with thoughtful eyes.

The relaxed angle of his warrior's body in the chair was deceptive. His fingers drummed the arm of the chair while he continuously swirled wine in the goblet held in the other.

They were large, powerful hands capable of wielding a broadsword, or crushing slender bones. She remembered the warmth of those fingers about her wrist when she encountered him on that fateful journey.

That encounter was burned into her memory in such a way that she had only to think of it again and she experienced that disturbing heat at her skin once more.

"I am of no value to you. Nor am I a threat to you or your men. If you think to ransom me or make terms for my return . . ."

He did not answer, in fact he seemed to pay her no attention as Truan Monroe performed his next trick with a bucket of water, slowly and precariously balanced upon the tip of one finger, his hand extended high overhead.

She slanted a look at her captor, but he watched the performance intently as Truan slowly removed his finger from beneath the bucket which amazingly remained suspended in mid air. The boy, Gryffyd, was delighted and begged to perform the same trick.

With encouragement from everyone who watched, Truan carefully instructed him on how the trick was done. All were silent as Gryffyd hoisted the bucket of water high overhead, slowly removed one hand, while repeating certain words over and over like an incantation.

Cass frowned at the foolish, nonsensical words that meant nothing, but only encouraged the boy. Then, just as Truan had instructed him, Gryffyd slowly removed his finger from under the bucket.

To the amazement of all who watched, the bucket remained suspended above him. Gryffyd grinned and took his bows. Stephen's men shouted and applauded enthusiastically.

Watching the performance, Stephen finally replied, "There will be no ransom. Nor will there be terms."

Her head came around, her startled gaze met his. All of a sudden there were cries of surprise followed by an explosion of laughter as the bucket suddenly wobbled, tipped, and the entire contents spilled over Gryffyd's head and shoulders.

"But surely you cannot think to keep me here," she replied aghast as all about them the hoots of laughter slowly subsided, amid growing speculation as Truan Monroe approached their table. But by the expression on his face, she knew it was exactly what he intended.

"A bit of entertainment perhaps to bring a smile to the lady's face?" Truan suggested. "A simple trick. I will read your thoughts."

Cass was stunned. She hardly heard what he was saying. When he reached across the table and seized her hand, she instinctively tried to pull away.

"No, please . . ." She had to get away, leave this place.

He smiled, differently than before. Not the fool's smile, but a hidden smile that appeared briefly out from under the fool's mask.

"It will be your chance to prove the fool is a fool." He would not take no for an answer, but instead instructed her on how the trick was to be done.

She was to draw a picture on parchment with a piece of coal, showing it to no one. The parchment was then to be folded and given into the care of the girl, Amber, for safekeeping. He would then attempt to *see* what she had drawn.

Realizing he would not go away until it was done, Cassandra took the piece of coal and drew the picture from one of the ancient rune stones, the sign of the bird in flight—symbolic of freedom. When it was done, she folded the parchment and handed it to the girl.

"Now, you must think only of what you have drawn on that piece of paper."

He closed his eyes, pressing his fingers against his temples as though he might find the answer there.

Come back, Cassandra. Unspoken, the words whispered through her thoughts.

You must come back. Remember . . .

"I have it now," Truan announced, turning about. His head slowly came up and he looked directly at her.

"The image you put on the parchment was a creature." His brow furrowed as though trying to discern it more clearly. Then he stared at her intently.

"It is a bird." He slowly smiled, the fool's grin firmly back in place once more. He skewered a piece of roast bird from the platter.

" 'Tis a guinea fowl!" he announced, grinning widely, holding the skewered carcass aloft to much laughter.

Across the hall, calls went out for Amber to show what she had drawn on the parchment. She unfolded the paper and displayed the drawing for all to see. There were bursts of laughter and demands for Truan to be skewered for his poor tricks.

But Cassandra heard none of it. She stared down at the length of ribbon that bound her wrist, the trick already forgotten.

"I demand that you release me," she said softly for it was all that was left to her.

Stephen heard the change in her voice, the quiver of anger wrapped in fear.

"I regret, demoiselle, that I cannot release you."

"Cannot or *will* not?"

"Very well, Cassandra," he replied. "I *will* not release you."

Too late he saw the knife in her hand.

Nine

The blade flashed, laying open the skin from his cheek to jaw. A narrow ribbon of blood glistened along the seam of flesh.

Stephen grabbed her wrists and pinned them behind her back. When she struggled he pulled her against him, hitching her wrists up high against her back until she cried out in pain and ceased struggling.

The hall was suddenly silent. There was only the hiss of the fire at the hearth, and the ragged sound of each breath dragged into her lungs as conversations and laughter ceased all about them.

Holding her imprisoned with one hand clamped over her wrists, Stephen tenderly probed the cut at his cheek.

"It would seem, mistress, that your aim *is* as sharp as your tongue."

Her eyes were wide, dark, and filled with shadows. In those haunted eyes, the same color as the sorcerer's, he saw fear, anger, and surprise.

"Nay, milord," she replied through thinned lips as she struggled to free herself. A slender dark brow arched as she informed him, "I missed."

She gasped as he angled her wrists up more sharply against her back. Eventually, he felt the fight go out of her. The knife fell from her fingers and clattered down onto the table.

Stephen twisted his hand in her hair and pulled her head back. Defeated, surrounded by his men, completely helpless without the hope or possibility of escape, her eyes glistened with angry, defiant tears.

Meg hovered close by, hands twisting, powerless to help her. In the center of the hall, Truan watched with sharp eyes, hands clenched into fists, every muscle taut, ready to spring.

All about him, Stephen's men waited expectantly. The very least she deserved was to be beaten. But that would only harden her defiance and deepen the anger. He could have her stripped naked and chained in the yard as he'd promised, but that would only humiliate her. His hand tightened in her hair.

He twisted it about his hand, coiling it like a thick, satin rope, his fist at the nape of her neck angling her head back farther so that she was forced to look at him.

"I do not intend to miss," he told her, the moment before he kissed her.

His mouth angled down over hers. He tasted her startled breath, the pliant curve of her full lips, then the sudden, yielding softness of her mouth.

He tasted the surprise, then the anger. She tried to escape. He tightened his hand in her hair, holding her imprisoned as he deepened the kiss, forcing her to open to him, forcing her to yield as he plunged his tongue inside. Then he tasted heat.

It moved through her with the power of a thousand suns, burning through her blood and across each nerve ending. It was a kiss that was part anger, part punishment, and all desire.

Feelings and emotions she'd rarely experienced before with her unusual powers that protected her from human frailties, suddenly exploded within her. Anger, pain, and fear. Then confusion and humiliation. And finally, something completely new—desire.

It moved through her senses like mist, slowly curling around the anger and fear, like the warmth of the sun after a long cold winter on her face, like the slow heat of a fire that steadily glows like a resting ember and then suddenly bursts to life.

Her mouth moved against his, first in angry protest as she fought him, her body arched as far away from his as she could with her arms pinned behind her. Then on a startled breath as she trembled violently. And finally in breathless confusion when she no longer fought him.

Anger glittered in his golden eyes as he abruptly ended the kiss, his face a mask of harsh planes and angles, the ribbon of blood glistening at his cheek.

Her eyes were large, dark pools, glistening with unshed tears of anger and humiliation. Her skin was pale and translucent as candlelight. Her lips were slightly parted and faintly bruised, her breath coming in startled gasps.

The pulse at her throat beat like the fluttering of a bird suddenly caught and frantically trying to free itself. He stroked his fingers across that frantic pulse, her blood pumping hot and wild beneath his fingers as he closed his hand around her throat with terrifying tenderness.

"The next time you draw a blade, mistress, you had best kill me." He backed her up against the chair, the edge catching her at the back of her knees.

"Or the price will be far more than a kiss."

"Release me, and you will have no need to fear a blade in your back as you sleep!"

He backed her up farther, forcing her down into the chair. He leaned over her, hands braced at either side at the arms of the chair, his face so close that the ribbon of blood blurred in her vision. So close that all she saw were his eyes, golden and dangerous.

"I see no reason to fear it at all, mistress," a dark brow arched, "unless you choose to join me in my bed."

Her eyes widened. Humiliation burned across her cheeks. She started up out of the chair.

"Not even if you were the last man in the kingdom!"

He pushed her back down, fingers lightly bruising as he cupped her chin. His lips brushed hers with each word.

"Then neither of us has anything to fear."

Silence filled the hall. She felt the stares of his men. She was the enemy. In their own minds, they had perhaps already condemned her to death.

Her skin felt bloodless, drawn taut across her bones, frozen one moment then blazing with angry defiance the next. Defiance and anger were all she had left. That and the strange, stirring emotion that still pulsed beneath her skin as if something alive awakened deep inside her, clawing to get out.

Outside the main hall, a commotion was heard. It grew increasingly louder until it was just outside the main doors. Then the doors were suddenly thrown open.

His knights, seated at the tables around him, seized their swords and quickly formed a protective perimeter between the tables and the doors. Stephen seized his own sword and rounded the end of the table. There he was joined by Sir Gavin and Truan Monroe.

There were shouts of surprise and much confusion throughout the hall. Several of his men could be seen quickly moving out of the way to let someone pass among them. Others leapt out of the way amid the sounds of snarling and growling.

Stephen's hand relaxed about the handle of his sword as four of his own men slowly made their way through the hall, dragging something behind them with much effort. As his men nearby parted to let them approach he saw what they dragged behind them, and the cause for all the commotion. It was a large white wolf.

They restrained the beast with nooses suspended from

stout poles, one to either side, and slipped over the beast's head. When the creature tried to lunge in either direction, it was pulled up short by the opposite noose, thereby restraining it the safe distance of the poles.

He immediately recognized the creature. It was the white wolf he'd encountered in the forest. His men had seen it again from the walls of the fortress, but it refused to come near. Until now. Somehow the beast had been caught. Now, it fought wildly against the restraint.

It was a magnificent creature, long-legged and rangy, completely white in color, and easily standing the height of a man's hip. Its eyes were not the keen yellow of wolves he'd seen in the far eastern mountains of Europe, but silver gray, the color of the mist. It fought with the strength of ten hounds, battling the four men who struggled to restrain it.

"The creature has been raiding the peasants' farms. They've lost many cattle and sheep. It dragged down a man full astride his horse and killed him. We snared it outside the gates."

All about them, his men called for the creature to be killed. Exhausted from fighting, the wolf hung between the twin nooses, tongue hanging limply from the side of its mouth, sides heaving as it struggled to draw air. Those silver eyes had not the look of wildness about them, but the look of wisdom as the creature stared at Stephen.

"Nay! Do not!" Cassandra cried out as she came out of the chair, and rounded the end of the table.

Several of his men moved to stop her, raising their weapons to block her path. Exhausted as it was, the creature exploded with sudden energy.

It lunged first to one side then the other, the nooses tightening with each frantic movement as Stephen's men fought to restrain the powerful creature. Blood appeared at its mouth. Still it fought on, as though fighting to reach her. Or protect her.

"Do not fight them," Cassandra cried out in her thoughts, but it could not hear her. She pushed past one warrior, then challenged another as she struggled to reach the wolf, risking her own life against those drawn swords. Her head came around, the midnight fall of satin hair framing her pale drawn features and pleading violet eyes.

What did he see in those eyes? Capitulation? Never. Heart-rending sadness for the creature? Possibly. In the creature's fate he saw an advantage that might be turned to his favor.

"Hold!" he commanded. "Let her pass."

He saw the surprise that leapt into those vivid dark eyes, then she turned and pushed another of his men aside. When they did not move quickly enough, she fought her way through them, pushing and shoving until she reached the open space that had cleared around the wildly thrashing wolf.

Robbed of her gift, Cassandra was forced to rely on her mortal abilities. She prayed Fallon would hear her. Then she prayed he could be calmed for she had never seen him this way.

She whistled softly, a sound familiar between them. Still, the wolf struggled, snarling and snapping, choking itself as it continued to fight. She whistled again, but Fallon could not hear her so great was the animal's distress.

"Let him go!" she pleaded. "You're choking him. As long as you restrain him, he will continue to fight." She turned to Stephen, her heart in her eyes.

"Please!"

In that single word and the torment he saw in her eyes, it seemed as if she was the creature, begging for her life, those nooses bound around her neck as surely as the spellcast that bound her wrist.

"He will not harm anyone! Please, they're killing him!"

With a look at his men, Stephen nodded. Everyone except the two men holding the thrashing wolf cleared a safe distance away, their swords drawn. Finally, one moved away, lowering the pole to the floor. Then the other moved away, laying his aside as well. Everyone backed away from the wolf as it swung first in one direction, then the other, shaking its head repeatedly, trying to rid itself of the dragging weight of those heavy poles.

Cass whistled softly. There was no response. Fallon simply stood there, sides heaving, lips pulled back over his teeth, bloodied foam staining the corners of his mouth. She whistled again as she slowly began to circle round so that he could see her.

He saw her movement, whirling around sharply, head down, a glazed look in his silver eyes. He snarled a warning, lips curling back.

"He will tear you to pieces," Stephen warned.

"He will not!" she whispered fiercely. "He knows me. He will not harm me." But even she had her doubts as she slowly continued to circle around the wolf so that she was facing him straight on.

For the first time in his life, he'd been abused and badly treated. Extraordinary creature though he was, who had watched over her and protected her with uncanny abilities, he still was ruled by the form of the wolf. Wild at heart, wary of mortal man, and justifiably so.

Now the special bond that had always linked them had been removed. She could not reach him as she always had, communicating with him in the way of a changeling with that instinctive understanding of all creatures. She was now fully mortal, left only with her mortal abilities. She could not even be certain that Fallon would know her in this mortal form. But she was willing to risk her life to save his.

She whistled softly a third time, then spoke the words that had always connected them.

"Be at ease, old friend. I will not harm you." She slowly approached closer, going down on hands and knees, lowering herself in that way of creatures showing subservience to those more powerful and stronger than they. Then, she slowly began to crawl toward him. From the corner of her eye, she saw the gleam of a sword and wondered if it was for her or the wolf.

Still she crawled forward, slowly gathering the hem of her gown and inching forward.

"It is me, old friend. You know me," she spoke softly. "We have walked the forest trails and meadows. We have hunted. You know me, Fallon."

She was now within only a few feet of the wolf. She crouched lower still, leaning low on her side, imitating the way of dogs when together, lowering herself before the wolf as she moved closer still, slowly extending her hand so that he could gain her scent. If she was wrong, if the bond no longer existed between them on any plane, then she was dead. He would be on her in less than a heartbeat, tearing her apart.

She had seen other creatures when they attacked. It would be swift, but brutal. Without her powers she would be unable to stop him, or the pain as she was torn limb from limb.

"Come, Fallon," she said softly, whistling again, extending her hand farther. He jerked back uncertainly, lips curling on a snarl of flashing teeth and bloodied foam. She whistled again, moving lower, closer, reaching out.

She saw the moment when he accepted her. That sudden break in his gaze, the exhausted confusion, and then the soft whistle at his own throat in response. His stance changed, rigid muscles easing, the tentative brush of his tail, the ears that eased forward.

"Come, Fallon. You know me."

Then he caught her scent, nose extended. He took a hesitant step forward, then another. Ears lowered. He whistled softly in his throat and slowly walked toward her. At a single touch upon his head, her slender fingers going back through the long silver white fur, the wolf collapsed, its great head laying across her lap.

"Bring me water." It was said with such quiet authority that several of his men moved at once. A bowl of water quickly appeared, slowly pushed toward her.

She scooped water in her hand, dripping it into Fallon's gaping mouth. The water mixed with foam and blood to stain her gown. She gave him more water, searching those half-closed slits at his eyes for some sign of response.

His breathing was labored, each breath dragged into that massive chest, then wuffing out to brush against her cheek as she bent low over his large head.

"You must not go, my friend," she whispered, bringing him more water. "I need you. Please, Fallon."

For the longest time, they simply stood there, those armed warriors surrounding a slender girl bent over a large white wolf. Eventually the creature's breathing eased. The tongue lapped at the water from her fingertips. Those wise, silver eyes opened, staring back at her with recognition. The silver tail thumped slowly. The wolf struggled to its feet, sending warriors leaping back several paces.

"He will not harm you," Cassandra told them. But they were not persuaded. Finally, it was Truan Monroe who came forward from beyond the circle of warriors. Unafraid, he strode toward the wolf. He slowly knelt down, until like she had, he was on a level equal but not subservient to the wolf.

"Ho, Fallon," he said gently. "You are a fine beast,

but I will not kneel to you. You must accept me as I am, and I shall do the same."

The wolf cocked his head, silver eyes gleaming. Slowly, he reached out with his muzzle, gaining the man's scent. He did not immediately retreat as he usually did with mortals, but instead those large ears angled forward in acceptance.

"Do you think he believed me?" he asked, turning that laughing gaze on Cassandra.

"Perhaps he is more fool than you are, to approach a creature in such a way."

"Why not?" Truan asked. "You did."

"But he knows me. I raised him since a pup. He has no reason to fear me."

"Nor me," he answered solemnly, startling her with the sudden intensity in those dark blue eyes. Then he smiled and the fool returned. He shrugged.

"Animals have always liked me. Rabbits, birds, and such." Behind him, Amber tentatively came forward. She did not reach out to Fallon, but let him catch her scent.

"The wolf is still wild," one of Stephen's men reminded him. "It has killed many animals and now a man."

"Not true!" Cassandra defended the wolf vehemently. "He hunts only from the forest, or what I provide him. He has never taken from any farm or village. And he would never attack unless he was threatened." She looked around at their unconvinced expressions.

"You see how he has accepted me. He is tame. There is nothing to fear!" If she had her powers she could convince them with but a single thought. But she had nothing but the words she spoke and the sincerity that came from her heart. She could not bear it if anything happened to Fallon.

"Please!" she asked again, turning to Stephen, realizing he had no reason to grant her anything after what she'd done. In his eyes, she was no better than what they accused Fallon of. Still she begged.

"Stay your weapons," he told his men after much consideration. "We will see about this wolf of yours, mistress," he told her.

"But until we know his true nature, he must be confined."

The thought repulsed her. Fallon had never been confined, but allowed the run of the countryside, and even the halls at Tregaron though little to John's knowledge. For with her powers, she had been able to make certain the wolf was not seen. Only once had he startled one of the servants who entered unannounced and came upon the wolf laying across the foot of her bed.

But when the hysterical woman looked again, all she saw was a sleek white fur pelt where moments before she thought she saw a white wolf with gleaming silver eyes.

Cassandra reluctantly accepted his terms, knowing that it was equally dangerous now for Fallon to return to the wild. He would be hunted down and surely killed.

"Very well, I agree."

"I did not seek your agreement, mistress. Those are my only terms, for you are equally as imprisoned as the wolf."

"I ask only one more thing," she added.

"What is that?"

"That I be allowed to care for him, for he will take food from no other."

Old Meg eased to his side, laying a thin, bony hand on his arm.

She had appeared out of nowhere, without even a sound. It was always a little disconcerting how she did that. That and the sightless color of her eyes. Even though the Lady Vivian assured him the old woman was blind, he was not so certain.

"This might be turned to our advantage," Meg whispered as she sensed she had his full attention. She sensed too his uneasiness whenever she approached him—that instinctive wariness that came after an encounter with the other world.

This mortal, whose life threads were interwoven with those of the daughter of the Light, had survived what few other mortals had—a battle with a creature of the Darkness that unleased such terror and power that most men never dreamed of.

He had survived but not escaped unscathed, for his body bore the scars of that encounter, the horrible slash marks that had torn his flesh as he was stripped of his weapons one by one, then left with all that he possessed to face the Darkness. His courage.

It was for that reason that he'd been chosen, just as the others were chosen by the guardians, though he little understood it. He believed he had only to find the daughter of the Light and convince her of the legacy she must fulfill.

"Explain yourself, old woman."

She smiled, for beneath the warrior's battle shield, within the warrior's heart, she sensed a fierce passion. A passion only recently glimpsed in that single kiss. And she knew that already another thread was woven.

"She will not be broken by force. You have already seen this," Meg pointed out. "How much better to have her cooperation than her enmity." She sensed when she had his full attention and smiled shrewdly.

"You hold the fate of something she values highly in your hands. You need her cooperation. Use one to gain the other. And remember, once she has made a promise, it must be kept."

Stephen saw the direction of the old woman's

thoughts. Cassandra was grateful that he had spared the wolf. How much more grateful might she be for the wolf's continued welfare?

Stephen nodded as he told Cassandra, "I agree to what you ask, provided I have your word you will not attempt to escape."

He watched the play of emotions across her face, the inner struggle revealed in each expression. And the moment when she capitulated.

"Very well," she said stiffly, her gaze fastened on the wolf who now stood quietly at her side. "I will not attempt to escape."

"I have your word on it?"

"Yes."

"Say it."

Her violet eyes flashed angrily as she looked up at him. "You have my word that I will not attempt to escape."

He nodded, then gave instructions to Gavin to see a proper place prepared for the wolf. Until he was assured of the creature's true nature, it must be confined. But the moment Gavin tentatively approached, the wolf snarled at him.

"It will be necessary for me to go with him," Cassandra pointed out. "Unless your man wishes to lose an arm." She saw the refusal in his eyes, then turned his own words against him.

"After all, milord," she said in open challenge, "you have my word that I will not attempt to escape."

Ten

"He keeps you well guarded," Margeaux commented as Cassandra returned to her chamber and glanced up to find her stepsister waiting for her.

She quickly closed the chamber door behind her. It was the first direct contact with her stepsister in more than two weeks that they'd been there.

"And you are not guarded at all, it would seem," she said in a low voice as she came away from the door.

"I am as well guarded as you, but I have learned to show more humility toward my guards. I pleaded a female complaint," she explained, her eyes taking on a shrewd expression.

"I complained so pitifully of it, that they were only too glad to allow me to seek out your chamber." She snorted. "With no other women except that old crone and the mute girl, Amber, they were only too happy to do anything to ease my suffering. You would be best advised to use similar methods to our advantage."

Margeaux crossed the chamber, listened at the door to make certain no one listened, and then turned sharply.

"You endanger us with your defiance," she told Cassandra bluntly. "If you continue, Lord Stephen will have us both put in crow's cages and left for the birds to pick our bones. But if you cooperate, then perhaps he will think it worth his while to bargain for our release."

Cassandra shook her head. "John will not bargain for our release."

"He will!" Margeaux replied adamantly.

"And part with some of his precious gold? He would sooner let his own blood."

"Malagraine will see to it," Margeaux said confidently. "And John dares not defy Prince Malagraine. He will align all the nobles and the Saxon rebels against the army of the English king and this fortress will crumble to dust."

"How do you know this?" Cass asked, suspicious of Margeaux' certainty. "What have you done?"

"I have guaranteed our release because I have something Malagraine wants more than anything else." Her eyes gleamed.

"His son."

"Son?" Cassandra replied incredulously. "What are you talking about?"

Everyone knew that throughout the years of his marriage with the Welsh princess, no child had been conceived. And there were rumors as well that none of his mistresses had conceived, for Malagraine would not hesitate to set aside one wife to take another if she got herself with child. But such had not happened. Malagraine had no heir to succeed him.

Margeaux smiled slyly as she smoothed the soft wool of her gown over her flat stomach. Comprehension slowly dawned with images of Margeaux naked beneath Malagraine's thrusting body.

"And the woman's complaint that persuaded the guards to bring you here?"

Cassandra found it impossible to believe that Margeaux was with child. There was certainly nothing in her appearance to suggest it.

She favored all the Tregaron predecessors in her angular height, wide shoulders, narrow hips, and flat chest, features that leant themselves more to that of a young boy. With a shudder, Cassandra remembered the sight of her, the shallow breasts more like that of an underdeveloped girl, the dark nipples tightly puckered instead of engorged in anticipation of a child. And the narrow span of stomach between sharp hip bones, equally flat, that gave no hint that a child grew there.

Margeaux shrugged. "The guard did not care to hear the details of the complaint. He is like any man and more than willing to deliver me here to prevent hearing of it."

"Does Lord Stephen know of this?"

"He will know of it when it suits me."

"But how can you be certain that Malagraine will learn of it?"

"There is always a way," Margeaux answered slyly. "No one is completely loyal. Everything has its price. But you must cooperate. It will do no good if he throws us in the dungeons or in chains because you cannot keep a civil tongue in your head."

"I have given my word that I will not try to escape," Cass reminded her.

"Your word?" Margeaux laughed. "A convenient lie given at a particular moment in exchange for something you wanted. You are a prisoner. No one would expect you to remain bound to such a promise."

"I expect it and I am bound to it. I cannot break my promise."

"All for the life of a worthless cur? A wolf and one that will be killed when it suits these warriors. Who is the fool, my dear?"

"He gave his word the creature would be spared. I must trust in that."

"Do as you will," Margeaux said in disdain. "But do

nothing to jeopardize my own escape." She shook her head. "You have always been a strange one, always keeping to yourself. It would be a wonder if any man looked favorably upon you."

Her stepsister had always been sharp-tongued. Those who fell victim to her tongue-lashings found ways to avoid repetitions. When she got into those moods, Cass usually escaped to the forest.

Only with Malagraine did Margeaux carefully watch every word, curbing her sharpness lest he take some offense when he was in residence at Tregaron. But now, there was no escape and for some reason her words had the power more than ever to wound deeply.

"When will you leave?" Cass asked.

"Soon I hope. I cannot abide these warriors with their foreign ways and strange habits."

Cass smiled inwardly wondering if her stepsister spoke of their unusual discipline, loyalty, and steadfastness to young Lord Stephen, for it was certain her stepbrother had never commanded such loyalty. His own army was comprised mostly of mercenaries and Saxons who had fled across the western borders from England after King Harold's death.

They were unkempt and undisciplined, preferring to eat his food and drink his ale until they fell into a drunken stupor. Hardly better were the Welsh nobles, too easily swayed by the likes of Malagraine into fighting a war they had no skill for fighting or hope of winning.

She had heard it rumored that when no cause could be found for fighting newly crowned King William of England, then one was invented—the brutal deaths of several of King William's knights, their heads sent back to London in baskets as a warning.

But why pursue a war that could not be won? As always these past few weeks there was no reply that whispered in her thoughts.

There was a sound at the door. No longer was it kept bolted from the outside. In that at least she was no longer treated like a prisoner. But this was the sound of the latch being lifted. Margeaux looked at her sharply. Even though her own guard had been persuaded to deliver her to the chamber, there was no certainty that another would feel the same. Margeaux stepped back into the shadows behind the door.

Old Meg shuffled into the chamber, immediately aware of the girl's presence so attuned had she become to her these past few weeks. The first hesitance the girl had shown her had been replaceed by a grudging acceptance after the wolf was spared. But now as she stood in the chamber her meager senses told her another was there as well. Someone who hid in the shadows. She frowned as she turned toward Cassandra, guided to her as she always was, like a golden sun in a great vast darkness.

If only she knew and would accept, Meg thought with that growing sense of urgency. Time was running out. But soon, soon she would know all and must be persuaded to accept her destiny.

"Milord wishes to see you," she told Cassandra, her senses still aware of that lingering presence like a shadow that blocks the sun.

Since that night when Fallon was dragged into the hall, Cassandra had hoped to meet again with him. For there were questions that still went unanswered. Who was he? What did he want of her? What was it that was in the power of the spellcast that she now had no powers at all?

But he had no time to speak with her these past weeks as additional repairs were made to the fortress walls against attack. Almost daily more people arrived, an equal number of young men willing to take up sword or battle-ax against her stepbrother and Prince Malagraine.

Their numbers swelled the population of Camelot. Lord Stephen had no intention of retreat or surrender. He made plans for war, certain, she heard it rumored, that it could come any day once Malagraine united his forces.

"I will gladly meet with him," she told the old woman, stepping outside the chamber and quickly closing the door behind her so that the old woman was not tempted to go inside.

"Do you accompany me?" Cass asked.

"I am an old woman," Meg replied. "My bones ache with every step I take. He has asked that you meet him in the starchamber. He said you would know it."

Cass glanced back hesitantly at the door of the chamber. If she protested the old woman remaining behind it might raise her suspicions. She nodded.

"I know it well." She turned, praying Margeaux had enough sense to remain hidden for a while longer, at least until the old woman was gone.

Long after Cassandra had gone, Meg still sensed that lingering presence. She frowned, heartened that it was not Cassandra whose dark presence she sensed, at the same time worried about the presence she did sense. She laid a hand at the latch, thinking to search the chamber, then hesitated, when she sensed that disturbance no longer.

Inside the chamber, Margeaux waited until she no longer heard voices. Then waited a few moments longer. As she was about to leave the chamber, she was suddenly overcome by a wave of pain so violent that it drove her to her knees.

It centered low at her belly, tearing through her as if some creature were clawing at her insides, trying to get out. Moisture beaded across her forehead at the same time she felt cold and clammy. Nausea swelled into her throat and she fought it back. She loathed sickness.

Her mother had been sickly, never strong. She had seen her mother's sickness as a child. Indelibly etched in her memory were the sights, sounds, and smells of the sickroom. Interlaced were all the times her mother had conceived yet another child in the hope of giving her father yet another heir to Tregaron—a son as strong as the daughter she had borne, not like the only son who had survived. But she had grown weaker with each dead child she had borne, until it seemed she wasted away to nothing.

Those were the memories that haunted Margeaux, the memories she fought back as the illness swept over her and then slowly receded. Her hand trembled violently as she smoothed it over her belly, no longer flat but now slightly rounded as though just in the speaking of it, the child had grown.

After all the times she had gone to Malagraine, she had begun to lose hope of conceiving. She had not even been truly certain of it until now, having last laid with him only those few weeks ago. She knew little of bearing children but what little she knew it seemed strange that she should show only a few weeks gone.

She knew of some women at Tregaron, including those loathsome creatures her brother took to his bed, who hardly showed through their entire confinement. Others of course grew to enormous proportions. She shuddered at the thought of her body being so distorted, experienced a deep loathing and ambivalence for something she had vowed she would never allow to happen.

But this child promised far more than she had ever hoped for. Her eyes gleamed at the thought of the power she would have within her grasp. Soon Malagraine would know of it, perhaps even at this moment word was being carried to him. And when he learned of it, he would come for her.

Cassandra had not been to the starchamber since that last time when Fallon led he and his men here with its ghostly dead gathered about the crumbling round table. As with the rest of Camelot, she discovered the starchamber greatly changed.

The debris and ruin of centuries had been cleared away. The walls once more gleamed pale and golden, the floor made of gleaming, polished malachite. Candle holders the height of a man were set all along the perimeter of the chamber, their golden flames fluttering in the sudden gust of air as she opened the door, then resting quietly and burning steadily once more as she closed the door behind her.

She went no farther into the large room where legend had it an ancient king had once met with his war counselors and knights ruling a vast kingdom, but stood just inside the doorway, remembering another encounter all those weeks ago. The memory of it drew her gaze to the clear domed ceiling overhead. It had been repaired as well, dark solid patches of thatching covering the holes.

She felt a wave of disappointment, recalling that first time when she had encountered Stephen of Valois after he made the return journey through the portal. Since then, it seemed their lives were inextricably intertwined. Now she was his prisoner.

She rubbed her fingers over the blue ribbon that bound her wrist, wondering again at the source of its power. Was it a power of the Darkness as Elora had often warned her as a child? Or had someone else sent him? And to what purpose?

She slowly walked down the steps into the oval cham-

ber that had drawn her as a child as surely as travelers
followed the lodestar. Circling the chamber, she ran her
fingers lightly along the smooth walls, the perfectly cut
pale stones glittering with thousands of tiny facets that
reflected the light of the candles and with the stars shin-
ing down from above made it seem as if this place was
all the known universe.

The Voice had first brought her here as a small child,
as though drawing her to something that waited for her.
Here she had first discovered those ancient warriors,
long dead, who had laid down their lives for that ancient
king. A legendary castle, legendary warriors, and legendary king. All real. All waiting in this ancient place.

She had felt their presence, other voices that whispered to her, telling her that she must remember. They
were like the shadowy images that came to her in dreams,
faces of those she should know but could not remember.

Father and mother, were what others called them.
But she had no emotional essence of them, no connective bond that assuaged the loneliness she felt in those
last moments before sleep each night when Elora sat
rocking in her chair and Fallon lay at the foot of her
bed. And not even their loving presence could ease the
ache that filled her mortal heart and brought tears to
her eyes.

The wolf and the old woman were her only companions then. This place was her haven, a secret place of
legend and myth where she and Fallon roamed. In her
imagination, fed by Elora's stories, she saw it as it had
once been. Alive with brave knights and warriors, and
a golden queen who was loved by a powerful king. And
in her imagination there was no betrayal. They did not
die, but lived on.

Then came the day when she was suppose to journey
through the mist to that other secret place. The place,
Elora had also spoken of. The place where she was

born. But she stubbornly refused, insisting that she had no parents. For how could they abandon her? How could they not hear her thoughts that she wished to be with them? How could they not know of the tears of loneliness she cried every night?

She had wanted nothing of such heartless creatures and stubbornly closed her thoughts to all Elora's entreaties as well as those gentle voices that spoke of love. Now she was truly alone, Fallon imprisoned in a cage, and without even her powers to protect her. She saw the sudden fluttering of candles and turned as Stephen of Valois slowly walked down the steps.

He watched her from the doorway of the chamber, trying to assess her mood as he had each day the past two weeks since granting her the life of the wolf.

He had gradually given her more freedom as long as one of his men accompanied her. And the old woman had also taken to accompanying her, attempting to persuade her through thought and the sharing of memories of her family, of the destiny that awaited her.

Time grew short, the old woman reminded him. With each passing day the powers of Darkness grew. She had warned him just that morning that the days no longer carried the fullness of light. He explained it away to the change of seasons. Winter was almost upon them, but even he could not deny that a strange darkness seemed to settle over the land just beyond the walls of the castle as though held at bay by some invisible hand. And all the while came rumors of the army Malagraine assembled.

Soon the passes in the mountains that surrounded the valley would be closed by winter snows. But with the spring came the certainty of war.

She turned, the flame of a nearby candle reflecting in the depths of those violet eyes, her expression watchful yet without the usual mistrust of their last confrontation.

"You sent for me, milord?"

"A request, Cassandra. Not an order," he reminded her, hoping this time might be different, that they might find some level ground between them, rather than the uneven ground they constantly fought over— her request that he remove the spellcast and his refusal.

A delicate brow angled slightly. "A request in exchange for whose life now, milord?"

He fought back the usual response that came from frustration and no small amount of anger at her stubbornness.

"A simple request not in exchange for a life, but the gift of a life to do with as you wish," he explained as he approached her, one arm cradled across the front of his tunic, his other hand tucked inside so that for a brief moment she feared he might have been injured.

He slowly drew his hand from the front of his tunic, a small ball of fur, cradled in the palm of his hand. It was tightly curled, wrapped tail to nose so that it was impossible to tell which end was which.

The body was dark, bands of lighter colored fur striping one portion that might have been a tail. The ball of fur nestled in the palm of his hand, shivering. For the moment all animosity between them was forgotten. Unafraid, Cassandra reached out a finger to lightly stroke the trembling fur.

There was a feeble stirring. A tiny masked face peered from the knot of fur. Two dark eyes looked back at her with not enough strength even to be afraid. The tiny creature was dying.

"One of the peasants found the nest in a hayrick," he explained, watching her intently as she stroked the soft, dark fur. "Two others from the litter were dead.

The mother did not return. This was the only one left alive."

"And not by much," she said softly, letting the baby raccoon get use to her scent, instinctively knowing that fear might just as easily kill it as weakness from lack of food and whatever other ailment plagued the wee creature.

She frowned. "It will only die. Why have you brought it here?"

"You seem to have a way with creatures. A gift," he explained, recalling another—her sister—who also possessed such a gift.

"They trust you."

"Because they have no reason to mistrust me," she retorted on a harsh whisper. "I do not beat them, starve them, or string them up in nooses. Nor use them to get something I want."

Her gaze met his briefly over the small ball of fur cupped in his hand and still cradled against the warmth of his chest. Not for the first time, he wondered just how much of her powers of perception she still possessed.

"If you do not wish to care for the creature, I will see that it is returned to the hayrick. Perhaps the mother shall yet return for it."

"She will not!" she answered vehemently, an expression of pain filling her eyes. "Once she has abandoned her offspring she will not return." Her voice softened as she disguised the pain once more.

"It is the scent of man within the walls. Once the hayrick was brought inside, she no doubt fled in fear. They are already forgotten. 'Tis the way of things. I will take the poor thing, though I doubt it will live long. It is small and weak."

"But with a fierce heart," Stephen commented, showing her the bite mark at his finger. 'It took a good chunk out of me for my efforts."

"No doubt you deserved it," she muttered. She curled her fingers over the creature, lightly brushing his. "It must get use to my scent so that it will accept me," she explained, her head angling low beside his. Then she gently blew out her breath, warmly caressing the creature so that the air it breathed was what she breathed.

The touch of her fingers, the gleaming satin of her hair spilling over her shoulder to brush his sleeve, the sweet warmth of her breath between softly parted lips, were reminders of that last encounter and the taste of her on his lips. The anger, the stubbornness and defiance, and then the capitulation when he wondered who had surrendered, were gone.

Light from the candles played across her features, settling in the deep violet of her eyes as she gazed down at the creature. For just this moment there was no anger between them, only the bond of the trembling creature, her hand wrapped around his, the sweet fragrance of her hair, the shared warmth.

His head lowered beside hers, the silk of her hair brushing his cheek, her lips so close that he had only to turn his head to taste her again.

"Aye, no doubt I deserved it," he replied, thinking of all the ways he'd wounded and humiliated her. Her gaze came up, her eyes wide drowned pools of violet fire and for a moment longer there was that connection first experienced all those weeks ago outside the royal hall, when he had encountered a beautiful young woman and followed her through that portal to this place, her hand clasped about his.

Her lips parted, her breath warm against his. Her tongue flicked between the deep, lush curves to wet her lips.

"Milord, I . . ."

He heard the confusion in her voice, heard the warning in his own head that it would be unwise to take advantage, and ignored it as he slipped his hand beneath the curtain of her hair, fingers lightly stroking across the back of her neck.

Her breath came out in short, startled sounds. Her other hand came up in protest as he gently kneaded the muscles at the back of her neck. Her dark gaze fastened on his mouth, her lips parting on some last, desperate sound they both knew he would not heed.

"Please . . . ?"

Whatever else she might have said, he kissed from her lips as his mouth closed over hers. His lips gently stroked hers apart and on a startled sound of pleasure, he slipped inside, caressing past her lips, dipping into the silken warmth of her mouth, sinking into her. Just as he longed to stroke those other soft lips apart and on a startled sound of pleasure slip inside, caressing, dipping into her silken heat until all that he felt was her, all that he tasted was her sweetness.

Her hand fluttered against his chest, like the feeble movements of the creature he'd given her. She ended the kiss, suddenly pulling away. But the look in her eyes was dark, glowing with heat, her breasts rising and falling beneath the wool of her gown, her skin ablaze with color that was neither embarrassment nor humiliation.

"If I can save the creature, may I keep it?" she asked, wetting her dry, faintly bruised lips, tasting him all over again as he still tasted her.

She had never asked him for anything, and he had denied her everything. He nodded and answered gruffly, struggling with desire and duty.

"You may, in exchange for a small request." He saw the wariness then anger that immediately leapt into her eyes, and knew what she thought. That he had tried to seduce her to gain something. He had.

"There is always a price is there not, milord?" she asked furiously.

"I ask only that you take this and look upon it." From the table he retrieved a thickly rolled length of fabric. The tapestry the Lady Vivian had woven, which he had carried from London.

She frowned. "A gift, milord?" The sarcasm had returned along with the anger. "I had not thought you so generous."

"There is very little time, Cassandra. Perhaps only a few weeks. This was sent—"

"I have no need of such things," she replied angrily. "After all, I am only a prisoner. What need has a prisoner of such finery?"

She scooped the tiny raccoon from his palm, nestling it beneath the curve of her breast.

"I thank you for the gift of the creature, milord." Then she turned and fled the starchamber.

"Damn!" Stephen muttered. He felt the shift of air in the chamber, then saw the wraithlike form that moved slowly at the top of the stairs.

"She refused to look upon the tapestry," old Meg said with great weariness, already knowing without the need of seeing the tapestry still rolled and upon the table.

"You must find a way, warrior. Or all is lost." For she saw far more than she revealed. She saw a child, yet unborn, that brought with it either hope for the future or an end—the end of all mankind.

Eleven

"Has anyone told her she is not the first woman to bear a child?" Old Meg said as she placed more wood on the brazier.

"It would not matter," Cassandra replied. "Margeaux has no tolerance for discomfort. And in truth this confinement of hers seems particularly difficult." She wiped her stepsister's mouth of the sickness that seemed to plague her almost from the beginning.

It had been only weeks since Margeaux announced the news that she carried Malagraine's child, but it seemed more like months. She had been abed almost constantly since, with one complaint after another while her body rapidly expanded so that now her belly was quite rounded, her condition visible beneath the slender gowns that had always hung on her.

To make matters worse, it had snowed heavily several days earlier, confining everyone within the castle walls. Even within those walls, moving from one building to the other was difficult except where paths were cleared.

"This herbal remedy is of no use," Cassandra said with growing frustration. "She simply grows weaker and more irritable."

Meg harrumphed. "A natural condition from what I see."

Cassandra smiled in spite of the fatigue that pulled

at her from attending Margeaux all night. If not for the old woman and the girl, Amber, she might have gone mad these past weeks, confined with Margeaux.

The old woman knew many stories and was wise beyond her years. In many ways, she reminded Cassandra of Elora. In old Meg's easy companionship she found something of what she'd lost when Elora died. Amber was tirelessly patient, caring for Margeaux when Cassandra needed a respite. They often joked that it might be well to be deaf with a patient who complained constantly. In many ways, Amber was the sister she'd never had, for it could hardly be said that Margeaux had been as a sister to her. More like a shrewish maiden aunt.

Even the raccoon, Pippen, who had miraculously survived and now romped about the chamber with all the enthusiasm and mischief typical of raccoons, was given to hide in the woodpile or under the furs at her pallet when Margeaux's complaints grew wearisome.

Cassandra set aside the cloth and pail of water. When Pippen scuttled across the floor from his latest hiding place and tried to follow, she deposited him onto Amber's shoulder for he favored the girl almost as much as Cassandra.

"I'll be back," she told them. "With a remedy that will ease her discomfort, or I swear she won't survive the night." Amber giggled shyly, her eyes dancing with merriment, reminding Cassandra that she was a very beautiful girl when she wasn't so sad.

"If you do not," Meg added for measure, "I may murder her myself."

"You all hate me," Margeaux wailed weakly, then she began to cry. "Do you think I feel this way because I wish it? Would that I could get this child out of me now."

"I think," Meg added smartly, "that you have just what you deserve for spreading yourself beneath a man.

And a loathsome one at that." For Margeaux had spared no one in her tales of how Malagraine would come for her once he learned that she carried his child. That had been weeks ago. There had been no word from Malagraine or her brother. And now it was winter.

"Hurry," Meg urged her. "Do not delay!"

She closed the door behind her, amazed as she always was when there was not the usual cold blast of frigid air that was always present in the halls at Tregaron. Camelot had been laid out to take advantage of the warmth of the sun in winter, and cooling breezes in the summer.

Though winter light was meager and short-lived, there were still several hours of the day when it was not storming, when sunlight slanted through those amber-colored windows to the west, throwing warm light across floors and walls.

That shimmering gold light always caught her by surprise, unexpected after the dreary darkness of Tregaron, pale walls washed with warmth.

It took her some time to find him. One of his men eventually informed her that Lord Stephen was in the starchamber. It was late morning. Many of his men were either riding out about the countryside, watching for any sign of Malagraine's men coming through the mountain passes, while others supervised the fortifications of the castle.

She entered the starchamber unannounced and suddenly stopped when she saw he and his men gathered about the round table.

"My apologies, milord. I was not told that you met with your men."

Stephen rose from his chair, one of twelve that surrounded the table. One other was empty. Sir Gavin had ridden out with his men to check the passes. He was due back soon. She turned to leave. It was rare that they encountered each other, rarer still for her to search him out.

"Do not leave, mistress. We have finished our business." His knights, and Truan Monroe, rose from their chairs, gathering together maps, charts, and weapons. Every man at Camelot kept a weapon constantly at his side.

"It is a trivial matter," she said hesitantly as his men moved past her. Their expressions as they acknowledged her were by turns, respectful, curious, and amused.

"What do you smile at, sir?" she demanded of Truan Monroe, uncertain why the man irritated her so. Perhaps it was because he seemed to take nothing seriously, but was always conjuring up some stupid slight-of-hand trick which amused Amber highly, but then she was a child.

"I'm smiling at you, mistress," he replied, trying very hard not to burst out laughing, then leaned close to whisper.

"You have soot smudged across your nose and the look of a charwoman."

"And you have the look of a braying ass!"

He did burst out laughing then. "And the temperament of a charwoman as well." Then he was gone, his laughter reaching her from the hallway.

"You wished to speak with me, Cassandra?"

She scrubbed her nose with the sleeve of her gown, then turned around. He stood at the far side of the table. Late morning light streamed down through the clear, domed ceiling, gleaming in the deep russet shadows of hair that fell to his shoulders.

As he had that first time she saw him, he wore black— black tunic, breeches, and boots that encased the length of leg to his thighs. The tunic was belted at his waist, emphasizing the narrow span of waist, lean hips, and contrasting with wide shoulders.

The last time she had been to the starchamber it had been night, the room bathed in shadows with only the light of those candles. But now, in the light of day, she saw the embossed walls, newly exposed with a rich tapestry of carvings that told a story in themselves. The story of a king as a young boy and the kingdom he had grown to rule. Camelot.

She saw this magnificent room as it had been then, when Arthur was king, standing perhaps just where he stood now, recently seated among his knights, brave and fearless men who would die for him. And had.

She slowly crossed the room, feeling some strange energy within the room. An energy of light and sound and memories that all seemed to whirl around her at the edge of her vision, illusive as a dream. But when she looked this way or that, the vision was gone.

"It is about Lady Margeaux."

"What about her?"

"She is not well. 'Tis the child. Some women have great difficulty. There are remedies which would ease her discomfort."

"And no doubt her complaining as well?" Stephen speculated, for old Meg made no secret of her dislike for the woman.

"That would be an additional benefit," she admitted.

"For us all."

She looked up at the teasing laughter in his voice, and found herself trapped by his smile—understanding and filled with no small amount of sympathy.

"You may have whatever you need."

"What I need cannot be found within the castle walls. It is a tuberous root that grows in the forest. It has a purplish leaf, but the tuber that grows beneath the soil holds the healing remedy to ease her discomforts."

"Is there any danger with this medicine?"

"None to her or the child. More's the danger without it."

"Meg threatened her, did she?"

"With violent harm, if I do not quickly return."

"Not a man in Camelot would blame her for it."

"Not a man in Camelot has ever borne a child," Cassandra spoke out in defense of womanhood if not her stepsister. " 'Tis a great burden to carry and then see safely brought into this world."

"Most men are not afraid of pain."

His reply surprised her. "You would trade places with a woman and bear the child?"

He thought of the knight, Rorke FitzWarren, who was like a much-loved older brother or uncle, and the agony he had suffered during Lady Vivian's confinement.

"Can you truly say that a man does not suffer perhaps the more for his helplessness in watching the woman he loves go through such agony to bear his child."

"I cannot imagine such love," she answered truthfully, for it could not be said that Margeaux's child was created of love, but of cold-hearted ambition. She thought then of her own parents, of whom she knew little, and wondered fleetingly if her father had loved her mother in that way.

"Nor can I," Stephen replied truthfully. "But I have seen it. I have seen it humble a warrior to his knees, begging God to take his own life in exchange."

"Then I may have the medicine?"

"With my blessing. I will see that it is provided for you."

"Thank you." She turned, eager to end the conversation about things for which she had no understanding.

"In exchange I ask one thing."

It was always that. Everything was always a bargain. Something given for something received in return. She slowly turned back around, wondering what price he would demand. She waited expectantly as he slowly rounded the table. As he approached closer, she remembered the last time she had been in this room.

He saw the subtle change in her breathing, the rapid rise and fall of her breasts beneath her gown, the way she kept her gaze carefully averted, the sudden dryness at her lips and the way she nervously wet them. He reached for her hand and felt her instinctively pull back. He held her hand firmly in his, cupping it with palm turned up.

"Our bargain," he said, placing a rolled cloth lengthwise across her palm, "you shall have the medicines you need. In exchange you will agree to look at the tapestry."

It was on the tip of her tongue to refuse, to throw it back in his face. Then she thought of Margeaux and all who would suffer if she refused. It seemed a small price to pay for relief to many.

"Very well," she agreed. "I accept it."

"You will look at it," he insisted.

She chose her words carefully. "I will look at it." She gave him no opportunity to alter the agreement by adding other stipulations, but turned and quickly fled up those stairs and out of the chamber.

She returned to her own chamber briefly and set aside the rolled tapestry. As she was about to return to Margeaux's chamber, the light from the fire burning low in the brazier, caught the light of threads dangling loose from the end of the rolled tapestry.

They were rich colors that immediately drew the eye and the hand. As she reached out the threads shimmered and glowed, taking on several different hues, as if they were alive. As if they reached out to her. She was about to untie it when Amber appeared at her door. At the girl's pleading, desperate expression the tapestry was forgotten.

True to his word, Stephen sent a huntsman, familiar with the forest surrounding Camelot to Margeaux's chamber. Cassandra described the plant she sought with great detail, stressing that the tuberous root must be intact, for it was the tuber that contained the healing medicine Margeaux needed to ease her malady.

He returned just before late in the afternoon with the plant she'd asked for. Cassandra quickly brewed up a tisane from a cutting of the tuber, wrapping the remainder in a wet cloth for safekeeping. Then she gave Margeaux the tisane.

It was a bitter brew, the sort that one questions which is worse—the disease or the cure. But Margeaux was not given a choice nor was she in any condition to protest. The tisane quickly took hold and soon Margeaux slept soundly to the relief of everyone.

Cassandra stood, easing the ache in her back from bending over Margeaux's bed most of the day. She seized a heavy woolen mantle Meg had brought her one day. It was a fine wool, in a shade of deep blue and woven through the wool were faint silver threads. It was a mantle fit for a queen. But when questioned where she had obtained such a fine mantle, Meg merely shrugged.

I found it lying about. No one wanted it and it is much too long for me.

As Cassandra settled the mantle over her shoulders and tied the cords against the cold, Pippen scurried across the room and disappeared in the swirl of her skirts. She felt him brush against her ankle.

"Very well, you may come." As if the small ball of fur understood, Pippen shot through the door as she opened it, both of them eager for the sharp sting of winter air.

Snow crunched under her slippered feet as she crossed the inner courtyard. She passed through the gate, unhindered as the guard recognized her. As always, she sensed the shadow that fell into step a few paces distant. Her guard dutifully followed behind her.

It had snowed almost constantly the last week, the first break in the storm was just that morning. Now, she turned her face to the winter sun, feeling its warmth steal into her bones as though the winter had been months long instead of only the first storm of the season. She felt exhilarated, every nerve tingling expectantly, heat like the warmth of summer sun burning through her veins.

Pippen seemed to catch her mood. He had almost doubled in size on a diet of goat's milk and honey, and recently began foraging for scraps when no one was looking. His legs had doubled in length as well but still not long enough to make his way through the snow which reached almost to her knees.

Instead, he was forced to jump from one of her footprints to the next, disappearing completely into each new hole. Soon he had fallen far behind, and set up a loud chattering. Cassandra retraced her steps, scooping him from a deep impression several paces back and settling him in his favorite spot snuggled atop her shoulder within the folds of her hood, his pointy nose poking out to catch each new scent, his eyes sharp as a hawk's.

With the recent snows, it had become even more important that she visit the shelter where Fallon was caged twice each day. He was by nature a wild creature and grew restless at the confinement. Unable to hunt for himself, his very survival now completely depended upon her. It was an arrangement neither of them cared for.

Though they were natural enemies in the wild, Fallon accepted Pippen, without question, so that now the raccoon kit romped through the slats in the enclosure, chattering away at the wolf, tangling his long legs and doing what a raccoon did best which was to make a cheerful pest of himself. For his part, Pippen, simply had no understanding that it should have been any different.

"How are you my old friend?" Cassandra greeted the wolf as she opened the gate and released him. He immediately came to her and she buried her face in the thick ruff of his neck, each communicating in the ancient way that bound them—by touch, scent, and sound. Growls low at his throat, her gentle words in answer. His muzzle thrusting at her shoulder, her hand stroking back through thick fur the color of freshly fallen snow. The way he buried his nose in the curve of her neck, the way she laid her cheek fearlessly against his shoulder with arms wrapped about his powerful body. Then, the playful nip at her hair.

"You want to play!" Cassandra laughed, then laughed all the harder as Pippen suddenly popped up through the snow as if adding his voice to their play.

"Gentle! Fallon," she commanded the wolf as he nuzzled the fur ball. "You are bigger than he and should know better." He turned wise, silver eyes on her, but his lips pulled back in what seemed like a grin. Then he lunged at Pippen, scooping him with his nose, and rolling him through the snow.

Pippen rolled end over end, snow coating thick fur, so that when he finally rolled to a stop and popped his head up in anticipation of more, all that looked back at her were two sharp beady eyes from a snow creature face.

Cassandra called to them both, unaware that they had become the center of attention as peasant and warrior alike stopped their work to watch the strange, beautiful girl who was a prisoner of Camelot frolicking in the snow with a wolf and a raccoon.

She threw clumps of snow at Fallon. He caught them in his mouth, shaking his head at the cold, while Pippen ran round and round them, until he collapsed in an exhausted fur ball. Then Fallon launched himself at her, narrowly missing each time he made a pass, leaping through the snow. She laughed all the harder, her cheeks bright with color, the hood of her mantle fallen back to her shoulders, her midnight dark hair pelted with snow.

Stephen watched their play. She was like a child, innocent and pure, with none of the darkness about her that he'd been warned of. Was it possible for a deceptive heart to live with such laughter? Such innocence of joy? Such passion?

Like his men, he felt spellbound, captured by her joy and sheer happiness in the day, and like them found himself drawn to her, crossing the inner courtyard, stopping a peasant who pushed a cart along a cleared path and then slowly approaching the clear space in the outer courtyard where his men usually trained.

He laughed as Fallon gently clipped her at the back of the legs, and sent her sprawling flat on her back in the snow. Pippen was immediately on her, burrowing at her neck, while the wolf nipped playfully at the toe of her slipper.

"It is difficult to tell which is the creature and which the fair maid," he remarked as he approached the playful threesome. She sat up in the snow at the sound of his voice, her hair and lashes tipped with crystals. Her lips glistened and her eyes sparkled.

Fallon immediately caught the scent of meat purchased from the peasant's cart and to Cassandra's amazement approached him without hesitation.

"But not difficult to tell which is the traitor," she

pushed to her knees and immediately fell back again, hopelessly tangled in her skirts and the dragging weight of the mantle. Not to be left out, Pippen the more cautious, slowly approached and nipped an apple from his outstretched fingers.

"You as well?" she remarked, giving up on any hope of extricating herself from the soft, deep snow. "I am surrounded by traitors whose affections can be bought for a mere piece of food."

"More than a mere piece of food," Stephen confessed as he extended another strip of venison to the wolf. "Between the food you have given him and what I have brought him, it is a wonder that wolf has not grown fat as a monk."

At her look of stunned surprise, he shrugged. "I said he must be confined, not that he must be starved. Besides," he gestured to Fallon who stood a few feet away with a satisfied look on his face, tongue lolling out the side of his mouth, ears pricked forward in anticipation of more food. "You did not keep your part of the bargain either. He is not caged."

"And what of Pippen?" she asked. "Have you turned him traitor as well?"

Stephen snorted. "He is a thief of gigantic proportions. In the past week alone I am missing several medallions and the stone with the unusual carving."

"He is most fond of shiny objects," she admitted. "I am teaching him to be more selective. Gold coins only. Preferably those of King William."

"The thief and her apprentice," he said with a laugh. "If you perchance find my belt would you be good enough to return it. I find it necessary to keep my breeches from about my ankles."

"That would be a sight to see. The lord of Camelot brought low by a raccoon."

"Lord of Camelot?"

"Aye, is that not what you are with your knights of the round table?"

He stood and extended a hand to her. "I thought only to find a place that was defensible against Malagraine. If these walls stood for five hundred years, then perhaps they can stand for five hundred more."

She stared at his offered hand, considered the alternative with the snow soaking through her mantle, and finally accepted it. She quickly found herself extricated from the clinging snow, standing so close to him that she felt his warmth in spite of the afternoon chill that had set it with the sun below the western wall.

"You speak of a kingdom, milord." Her breath plumed softly on the cold air. He did not immediately release her hand.

"I am no king," he said softly, his voice edged with pain and bitterness. "I am the disinherited. A man with no land."

"Desdicado," she whispered, recognizing the Latin word carried upon his shield. Her brows drew together upon a memory of a legend once told to a small girl.

"A kingdom is found in the heart, not in earthly possessions." Her gaze met his, her expression thoughtful as though trying to see more than what was before her.

"Did you not know Arthur was a warrior king with no land to claim, until Camelot."

" 'Tis a legend," he replied. "Nothing more."

"Aye," she said with a faint curve of a smile. "Just as Camelot is no more than a dream and the round table merely the fabric of stories told to children about the evening fire." She hitched up her skirts and the sodden hem of the mantle, then called to Fallon.

But the wolf would not immediately come to her. He stood muscles braced, ears pricked forward, that silver gaze staring in the direction of the main gates just as the cry went out from the watch towers. Riders approached.

Warriors and knights filled the yard. The residents of Camelot came out of their huts and cottages, cook fires were stirred in the main hall. The signal was given from the gate tower. Sir Gavin and his men returned.

Slowly the gates were opened, lowered on massive ropes across the icy span of river that surrounded the castle on three sides, the only access in winter with the lake frozen but ice too thin to support even a single man afoot. But the men who rode through those gates were hardly recognizable.

Sir Gavin rode before them, his crest barely visible for the blood on his tunic. Beside him rode John de Lacey, his face haggard and drawn. Behind them less than half the men they had left with. Orders were given for the gates to be immediately closed when it was determined that no more followed afoot.

John de Lacey reined in his horse and quickly dismounted, but not quickly enough as Sir Gavin slumped forward and toppled from his saddle. Stephen caught him, easing him to the snow covered ground.

"What happened?"

"We were attacked in the northern pass between here and Tregaron. Three score men. They wore no crests and carried no banners, but wore this." He pulled a black plumed helm from his saddle.

"Mercenaries," Truan said as he joined them, all traces of humor gone from his face. "They've thrown in their lot with Malagraine. Ruthless bastards who would sell the souls of their mothers for a meal. This is the banner they carry. The color of death."

Cassandra knelt beside Sir Gavin in the snow and laid her hand against his forehead. He burned with fever, but at the touch of her cool hand his eyes opened.

"I can fight, milord," he gazed past her to Stephen. "My sword."

Stephen knelt at his other side. "You'll fight no more this day, my friend. Be at ease, you are home." His gaze met hers across his stricken friend's body.

She lifted the edge of his tunic. Even in the waning light she could see the blood that soaked through thick layers of undergarments, the cleaved edges of flesh opened to the bone at his shoulder. She did not understand how the man had ridden as far as he had. Only the extreme cold had saved him, slowing the flow of blood and the spread of infection.

"We must get him inside."

Stephen did not hesitate or question, but slipped his arms beneath his friend and picked him up though Gavin was much heavier and weighted down with battle armor. He turned and carried him through the snow through the inner courtyard and into the main hall.

The others followed, many with wounds. Those who were not wounded were quickly rid of their battle armor and fed. The west wall of the main hall was still not fully secure against the weather. It had suffered much damage in the siege all those years ago and there had not been sufficient time to close in the wood roof. Patches of thatch covered large areas, sodden with the weight of the snow. The fire struggled to keep those within warm.

"Not here," Cassandra said. "He must be kept warm."

Stephen turned and headed for the steps to the chamber he had taken for his own. It was on the second level, the private chambers that had suffered less damage. It was very near her own chamber and that occupied by Margeaux. John de Lacey went ahead of him, throwing open the heavy door. Stephen followed him, gently laying his friend on the pallet of thick furs before the brazier.

Cassandra had not seen this chamber before and hesitated as she realized that it was the king's chamber, the pale sandstone walls embossed with the ancient crest of the king and beside it the more delicate crest of his queen.

Then it was all forgotten as she quickly gave instructions to the servants for the things she would need as Stephen and John de Lacey efficiently and gently removed layers of tunic, battle armor, chausses, and protective underpadding until Sir Gavin lay clad only in soft woolen shirt and trews.

The blood had soaked through all, the flesh gaping open across his shoulder and chest. She could clearly see the bone beneath, shattered fragments in the cleaved flesh, and the glossy sheath of muscle that was all that protected his heart.

"Father in heaven," John de Lacey whispered. But Stephen wasted no words as he turned to Cassandra. His face was a mask of tormented emotions that he didn't bother to hide.

"Will he live?

She shook her head with uncertainty. "Even if the flesh could be mended, there is the bone beneath. It has been shattered. Pieces of it lie in the wound. The muscle is all that protects his heart."

"You have the ability to heal."

She nodded. "With herbs and powders. But this is beyond that."

"I do not speak of herbs and powders." His intense gaze burned into hers. "Bones that can be melded until they are whole and strong once more, flesh can be healed with barely a mark." He tore open his own tunic, revealing the long scar from a wound not unlike Sir Gavin's—the mark of a seax—that should have taken his life but had not.

She swallowed convulsively that he still carried such a mark and wondered at the wound that had left it.

"I have felt the healer's touch."

"Then you were most fortunate. If you can find such a healer bring her here."

"She is here," he said, seizing her by the wrist. "The power is strong in your family. You can save him."

"I have no family. None that will claim me, nor that I wish to claim."

"Then you have what lies in your heart," Stephen told her. "Gavin has been a friend to you. Do not let him die."

She felt as if her heart was breaking. He above all need not remind her of Sir Gavin's friendship when not even he had a kind word for her.

"He is very nearly dead now. I cannot give life back to the dead."

"You can save him. As long as he still breathes air. I have seen it."

"You ask for much."

"I ask for the life of my friend." He nodded. "Aye I ask for much."

"And what are you willing to do in return?"

The anguished expression on his face turned angry.

"I will not bargain for his life!"

She extended her other wrist before him, the blue of the spellcast ribbon gleaming in the light from the brazier.

"You have nothing to bargain with," she said. "Release me. It is the only way I may save him."

Twelve

Stephen stared down at the spellcast that encircled her wrist. He had been warned that it was the only means by which he might protect himself against her if she had been turned to the powers of Darkness.

Below her slender wrist, lay the shattered body of his friend who had risked his own life many times protecting an inexperienced young knight who was more reckless and headstrong than wise.

That same recklessness had brought him to the west country against the orders of his king, and now guided the only decision he could make no matter the outcome. He owed Gavin his life. The least he could do was give him back his life in return.

"Be certain of what you do, warrior," Meg whispered beside him for she had heard everything, quickly rumored among the servants.

Stephen seized Cassandra's wrist. In her stunned gaze he saw disbelief, then incredulity as he seized the knife from his belt and prepared to cut the blue ribbon. It was not necessary. At the first touch of his fingers it separated and fell from her wrist.

"I ask only this, that you honor the vow you have made to heal the wound," he reminded her. "Once a promise is given, it must be kept."

"You know much of our ways."

He nodded. "Learned at the killing end of a sword wielded by the warriors of Darkness. It was a lesson I learned well."

She realized then what he thought, what even the old woman had thought. That hers were the powers of Darkness, and the spellcast had been used to protect against those powers.

"Will you honor your promise?"

"Sir Gavin is my friend," she reminded him. "You needed no promise, you needed trust."

His hand closed over her wrist, stopping her with a warning. In his eyes she saw doubt, in his thoughts she understood the reason as she searched deep in the old way and relived what he had lived through his memories.

"If you harm him, I will kill you."

She did not remind him that with her powers, he would be unable to harm her.

"You have seen this done?"

He nodded, the memory of it vivid and painful even now. For the healing he had seen had been his own father, the king.

"All others must leave," she said softly.

As John de Lacey and the others left, Meg announced, "I will stay. Though I may be blind, the old ways are known to me. I am not afraid."

"Then stay, but do not interfere."

"Interfere?" Meg snorted. " 'Tis old I am. Far older than you can guess. More I have seen than you know with all your powers. I can ease the warrior's pain, and you can begin what must be done." The old woman moved unerringly to the other end of the pallet.

Kneeling down on ancient knees, she placed her thin, bony hands one at either side of Gavin's head. Those blind old eyes closed as she gently eased the pain from his unconscious thoughts. Her breath caught. She winced as though his pain became her pain.

"You may begin child, but do not take overlong. The life force is weak within him."

"What can I do?" Stephen asked.

"What must be done, only I can do," Cassandra said softly, her anger at his doubt of her ebbing away his anguish for his friend. She laid a hand over his.

"Stay beside him as you would on a field of battle, for if I should fail I would have those about him who have loved and fought with him."

She was deeply moved as Stephen took Sir Gavin's hand in his. There was nothing unmanly in the gesture, but a tenderness of comaraderie, of lives shared, and now possibly death.

"I am with you, my friend," Stephen told him even though Gavin could not hear.

"As you have been the shield at my back and the sword at my side, I will be your sword and shield now." Then he nodded to Cassandra. "Do what must be done."

It had been many weeks since she had summoned the power within. But it was like a wellspring, first discovered so long ago as a small child. It was like that now, feeling the power that moved within, guided by her thoughts, summoned by images she created, moving through her blood, expanding to the tips of her fingers.

All her thoughts became one thought, the concentration of the healing touch, a memory glimpsed of herself as a child discovering a deer with a broken leg in the forest. Her heartbreak as the creature thrashed about trying to stand, her innocent need to help as she reached out; her confusion as the creature eased to the ground at her touch and lay perfectly still; and then the mysterious almost frightening thing that happened next as bones straightened and mended once more whole again beneath her fingertips, and torn flesh healed barely leaving a scar.

The wounded doe had laid there as though in a deep

sleep. Her breathing had eased, the fear leaving her.
Eventually those large, brown eyes opened and in them
Cassandra glimpsed herself. A part of her became the
soul of the creature, and the creature part of her. Afterward, rested, her strength regained, the doe had
slowly gotten to her feet.

She had moved off through the woods, and Cassandra had followed, glimpsed by the Old One, Elora, who
saw two does where there had previously been only one
and the child who playfully followed.

Cassandra had been five at the time, the powers growing stronger within her each day. First the power of
thought, then the knowledge of the ages as she sat at
the Old One's knee. Then the healing way that eased
the discomfort of others long after Elora was gone. The
power was strong in her, Elora had said, stronger than
any of the others—sisters she had never known; strong
enough to open the portal of time itself.

Softly she spoke the ancient words, all but forgotten
except by those who passed the knowledge on from
mother to daughter, father to son. The flames of the
oil lamps and the brazier lowered, coals glowed as if
resting. Then through those ancient words she summoned the fire, felt it as it burned through her, searing
through her blood, until it seemed that she was on fire
as she gently pressed her fingers against the shattered
bone and severed flesh.

Stephen had seen his father healed in such a way. He
had experienced it himself, certain he was dying. He
knew the great and terrible pain that moved through
Gavin even as Meg tried to protect him from it.

It was a pain worse than the pain of the wound, for
it was the mending back of shattered bone, the seaming
of severed tendons, muscles, flesh, and each nerve ending. Gavin's body spasmed as the fire moved through
him from the bond of her touch. In her thoughts she

became one with him, she felt every fragment of bone as she sealed it back into place, experienced each fiber of muscle being bonded back to severed muscle, tendons eased back into their natural place and reattached where they had been torn away from the bone.

It was a slow process, this mending of flesh and bone. The mortal body so strong, yet so fragile. He had lost so much blood. That she could not mend. Twice she sensed his heart weakening, and infused him with her strength until his heart once more beat in unison with her own.

She slowly opened her eyes, releasing the bond that connected her to Sir Gavin. Weakness poured through her. It had taken all her strength to hold onto the life force within him as she sealed the wounds and mended shattered bones. Her hands were bloodstained as she looked across at Stephen.

The look in her eyes was not human, nor was it the look of Darkness. For he had seen it and knew it well. Hers was a look seen on a battlefield. It was the look of someone who has seen death and lived to tell of it.

"It is done," she whispered, then collapsed in his arms.

"Take her from here," Meg commanded like a field general. "She has proven herself this day. Now she must rest."

When he hesitated, torn between loyalty to his friend and the needs of the young woman cradled in his arms, she assured him, "You have seen her power for yourself. It is stronger than her sister's. Your friend will live, warrior. Now she must regain her strength for what lies ahead."

Stephen eased her against his chest. He had seen the power within her. He had seen that inhuman look in her eyes as she looked upon him with that power. But the creature he now cradled in his arms seemed very human, and suddenly very small and fragile.

* * *

She awakened slowly, like emerging from a dream. Images moved through her thoughts, an awareness of things around her, beyond the walls of the chamber, the thoughts and dreams of others. And the memory of the hours past.

It was night. Soft golden light played across the pale sandstone walls, created by flames that burned low on the brazier. She recognized the arched mullioned window with that unusual amber glass, the raised hearth, and the bed of thick furs with the heavy bed-hangings closed round her, like a protective cocoon.

She knew this place. It was her room, but not her room at Tregaron. Then, gradually, it all came back to her. Images replaying themselves with painstaking slowness as if she had been ill for a very long time and only now remembered everything—the afternoon before, the sudden ease between her and her captor, and then the return of his knights bloodied and wounded with Sir Gavin near death.

She shivered faintly, drawing the thick furs more tightly about her at the sudden weakness that moved through her. It was always that way after the joining of her power with a mortal life force. But as her hand smoothed over the soft fur, she felt a warmth of air brushing against her hand, a breath expelled, and beneath her hand the length of warm body that lay the length of hers.

Fallon. In that familiar way, her thoughts communicated themselves to the wolf. As if she'd said his name aloud, he raised his head, silver eyes gleaming through the cloaked darkness as he stared back at her and whistled softly in his throat.

She had no idea how he had come to be in the chamber, only that she was grateful that he was no longer confined to the cage, for the night had held the promise of another snow and she had feared for him without the protection of a true shelter to keep him warm.

"I am well, old friend," she assured him in the way she'd grown accustomed to the past few weeks with her powers restricted by the spellcast. He responded with a thumping of his tail on the pallet of furs. Somewhere near her head, she heard the soft guttural sound of Pippen, a round, tightly curled lump of fur at her pillow.

Her eyes drifted closed as she cast her thoughts afar and reassured herself that Gavin de Marte was indeed alive and rested soundly. Then she too slept, her fingers curled in the thick ruff at Fallon's neck.

She had no idea how much later she awakened, but the lethargy that had gripped her earlier was almost completely gone. Fallon had abandoned the bed to lay on the floor. When she sat up, Pippen curled into the warmth where she had lain, sighed without opening his eyes, and went back to sleep. She swung her legs over the low platform of the bed, her feet brushing cold stones at the floor.

Fallon raised his head and looked at her as she pushed aside the bed hangings, then rested his head once more on his paws as she left the bed.

Her legs were unsteady beneath her. She had forgotten just how exhausting the healing way was. She steadied herself with a hand at the wall and noticed for the first time that she wore nothing at all under the covering of furs on the bed.

Her gown and chemise lay in a pile on the floor, lacings cut through as though with great impatience, and then both hastily tossed aside. They were cold and still wet to the touch, a reminder of her play in the snow the previous afternoon with Fallon and Pippen. There had been no time to change after Sir Gavin and his men returned.

As her thoughts cleared, she looked about the room,

trying to remember but could not. Then she turned her thoughts inward searching for the memory within her subconscious.

She remembered being carried to this room, the solid strength of arms that held her, the fierce beating of a heart where her head rested against a heavily muscled chest.

She had made no protest as powerful hands, capable of wielding a deadly sword, gently touched where no man had ever touched as her clothes were removed.

It had seemed the natural way of things, a familiarity in his touch that soothed and gentled, and brought sudden heat to her cold skin after she had ventured so near death herself to save Sir Gavin's life.

When he laid her on the pallet of furs she had instinctively waited for him to join her there, longed for his warmth beside her with an intensity that seemed to come from her immortal soul, of something predestined.

When he had not, she experienced a sudden aching of emptiness and loss that came back to her now in waves of physical memory so intense she shivered and gathered the thick fur more tightly about her shoulders. But except for Fallon and Pippen, she was alone.

She stood and walked to the raised hearth and the warmth of the brazier, trying to understand these feelings, drawn out of memory of the last hours for which she had no understanding. Surely, she thought, they would ease as mortal emotions and feelings always had, a duality that was part of her, but that always seemed a shadow part of her, dominated since childhood by the greater forces of her immortal powers.

It did not lessen, even as she built up the fire in the brazier and its heat radiated into the chamber warming her skin, but the coldness of emptiness remained inside—an emptiness of unknown longings.

Stephen had sat here after he had undressed her and

placed her on that pallet of furs. She felt his essence as if he had only just left the chair and his warmth still lingered.

She closed her eyes, summoning the power within as she focused on that essence—the rich deepness of his voice, the penetrating gaze of his amber eyes as if he saw inside her, the intensity with which he moved like a caged animal, the scent of him, heated with essence of sandalwood, his touch, powerful and urgent one moment, surprisingly tender the next, and the taste of him. . . .

For a moment, the memories of him were so strong, so vivid and powerful in her senses that it was as if she had only to open her eyes and she would find that amber gaze looking back at her, only to part her lips to again experience the sinking, possessive heat of his kiss. On a soft gasp of remembered pleasure, she opened her eyes. But there were only night shadows and the rolled tapestry that lay on the table before her.

Light from the fire gleamed on threads visible at the edges, colors that shimmered as if with a life of their own, recalling the promise she had made to look at it. She looked at it now, and bound by her exact words, it was all that was required.

She had thought to appease him at the time and so carefully spoke so that nothing more was required of her than to take the tapestry. But now she felt regret for the slight deception. These days past the tapestry had lain in her room, *looked at,* but untouched.

As she tentatively extended her hand toward the tapestry, the fabric seemed to glow as if surrounded by light. When she withdrew her hand the light wavered and faded.

"What once was, can be again . . ."

The words whispered from the walls and sighed through the still cool air as if in answer.

She rose from the chair, retreating across the room,

refusing to look at the tapestry. But as she did, she experienced a loss so intense that it drew the air from her lungs and caused intense pain as if her soul was dying.

She no longer felt Stephen's presence, the warm essence of him on her skin. It was as if by refusing the tapestry, she had lost him, lost the memory of him, and so, lost herself.

She returned to the chair, recapturing that essence, drawing it within her even as she extended her hand once more to the tapestry.

At a single touch, the ribbon that bound it fell away. It slowly uncurled. As if guided by some unseen power it unfolded before her, revealing vivid, shimmering images woven among the threads.

From left to right a story unfolded in brilliant detail—of a great battle led by a fierce warrior and the beautiful flame-haired healer with unusual powers who was taken captive; the life of a king saved; lovers entwined in graphic display; then a growing darkness that began at the edges of the tapestry and slowly wove through, like evil snaking through the brilliant threads of life; a confrontation and the evil destroyed with a mighty sword.

"Excalibur," Cassandra whispered, her mortal soul disbelieving, even as her immortal soul knew that it was true.

Like the chapters of a book, the next panels of the tapestry revealed the image of a beautiful golden haired maid with the powers of a changeling, a creature transformed who saved the life of a warrior who journeyed to the far north country; a golden chalice lost for centuries until it was thought that it existed only in legend, guarded by a horrible creature of Darkness; the journey to an island shrouded in mist and the battle between the creature of Darkness and the powers of the Light to reclaim the lost golden cup known to mortal men as the Grail.

In the next set of panels she saw a dark-haired girl, the threads of her gown woven through with an unusual shade of thread that shimmered blue one moment then dark violet the next and matched the color of her eyes.

Cassandra jerked her hand back from the tapestry. The ends immediately curled in on themselves. The images no longer glowed with the light of life but grew dull and faded, then disappeared altogether from sight as the tapestry once more lay rolled before her.

She stared down at the tapestry. For a moment she tried to convince herself that she had not seen those images. That it was all her imagination or a trick of the light at the fire. But in her soul she knew that what she had seen were images of the recent past, the threads woven by a hand with powers almost as great as her own.

She felt it even now, the sense of it lingering at her fingertips where she had traced the images woven in thread, as if there was a connective bond between the weaver and herself, felt in the almost human touch that reached out through those images.

Sister. On a single thought the truth came to her, along with emotions and feelings too long denied. Childhood anger wavered and gave way to need—the need that had always lain just beneath the anger. The need of her mortal self for that connection to those of her blood.

Sister.

She slowly reached once more for the tapestry, willing herself to see all of it, no matter what the images revealed. As before, the tapestry unfolded beneath her touch, those vivid panels spread before her and in the shimmering images of one she was certain she saw tears upon the cheeks of the flame-haired young woman, her expression slowly turning from sadness to a smile.

It might only have been a shift of the light across the threads, but as she had already discovered, the images seemed alive, like a living memory woven in thread. Then she passed her hand over the rolled right side of the tapestry. It opened beneath her hand, revealing the dark-haired young woman—herself—a warrior whose fate was connected to her own, his outstretched hand clasped about hers; then the uncertain, partly woven images of a golden orb set atop a staff—the Oracle of the Light.

These images overlay many others, a relief of scenes upon scenes, created in painstaking detail, a tapestry of life, the past in the images of a kingdom lost; a beautiful half-mortal woman who carried the fabled sword through the world of the mist to the one imprisoned there. And two more words slipped through the anger and whispered in a broken sound from her lips. Words she had denied herself.

"Mother. Father."

It was all surrounded by waves of growing darkness that engulfed the last panels of the tapestry in shadowy images of death, destruction, and the end of mankind.

She sat there long after the fire burned to embers in the brazier and gray light appeared at the edges of the window openings. Eventually she stood. Gathering the fur tightly about her, she left the chamber. Fallon padded silently beside her as she sought the one place that had always drawn her. The place of lost hopes and dreams, the place where she had first encountered her own destiny.

The starchamber was dark and silent, steeped in shadows. She was alone. But as she turned her thoughts inward, drawing on the powers that were strong within her family, she saw images of the final struggle here all those centuries ago, when brave knights whose king already lay dead, made one last stand in a fight against the Darkness, and one-by-one laid down their lives for what they believed in.

She felt their fierce loyalty, their anguish and pain as they were cut to pieces by an enemy they could not vanquish, yet continued to fight, until the last man fell, his blood staining the wood of the round table. She placed her hand over that exact spot, long ago washed away by time and the elements that had claimed Camelot in the ensuing centuries. It was as if she touched his blood now, rich, warm, the last dying essence of bravery, faith, and hope in a world of growing darkness.

She was no longer alone. She sensed the presence of another at the door of the chamber.

"He has gone to find those who attacked Sir Gavin," she said with a certainty in her heart, for nowhere else through the halls or even in this place where he had come so often did she sense any presence of Stephen. Only in her chamber where he had sat and watched over her, then made his decision, and left.

"Aye," came the answer through the stillness of the starchamber, a voice at the same time familiar but with a much older memory that was gone as easily as it had come to her.

"Before dawn," Truan said as he slowly descended the steps into the chamber.

"And left you to defend Camelot?" she turned, her gaze meeting his, for a moment connecting on some other level, causing her to frown as she struggled to understand. She frowned as it fled beyond even her abilities and she felt a tingling of fear.

"A fool to guard the kingdom?"

The fool's grin was once more in place, his intense blue eyes filled with self-deprecating laughter as he bowed slightly, waving his hands gracefully through the air before him and when he opened his fingers, produced a flower.

It was no small trick to produce a flower in the midst of winter, but still a trick none-the-less, a minor accomplishment, she thought impatiently wondering at the contradictions in the man—a warrior who fought with slights of hand and childish illusions. She did not understand why Stephen's men tolerated him.

"A fool," he replied, smiling at her, "and near a hundredfold warriors and knights."

Her startled gaze met his. "Has he taken so few with him?" For with the loss of Sir Gavin's warriors and so many remaining behind, it meant that less than a handful rode with him against far greater, deadlier numbers.

"In his mind the greater need lay here," Truan replied.

"And I suppose you were more than willing to remain behind, to practice your poor conjuror's tricks!"

He looked at her with bemused expression. "I remain where I am needed most."

"I find great comfort in that thought," she made no attempt to disguise her sarcasm. "If we have need of flowers or shiny trinkets plucked from our ears then we have nothing to worry about."

As if to irritate her, he reached out, his fingers gliding beneath the fall of her hair at her shoulder to pluck an object seemingly from the air. When he uncurled his fingers he produced a medallion, much like the smooth, flat rune stones in the necklace Elora had given her. She snapped it from his fingers.

"Have I interrupted something?"

They both looked up to find Margeaux standing in the doorway at the top of the stairs. It was the first time she had ventured from her bed since her confinement. It seemed the tisane had greatly revived her. Though there were still circles of fatigue beneath her eyes, she seemed completely relieved of her earlier complaints.

Instead of pinched with pain, those cunning eyes looked upon the two before her with amusement.

"Is it possible to find something to eat in this place?" she asked. "I find that I am quite famished. I feel as if I could eat a roast boar. But please," she implored, with a knowing look in her eyes, "dress yourself first, my dear. These halls are drafty and cold. You would not want to come down with a malady."

It was only then that Cassandra realized she wore only the thick fur wrapped about her. She realized how it must have looked standing there with Truan, her shoulders bare above the fur.

"She seems greatly recovered," Truan commented, his blue eyes narrowed on the place where Margeaux had stood only moments before.

"I think perhaps her illness was preferable."

For the first time, Cassandra laughed at something he said. She was in complete agreement with him.

"Did Lord Stephen say when they would return?"

Truan's blue gaze turned to her. He saw something more than mere concern for her own safety and the safety of those who remained behind.

"When it is done."

She did not ask his meaning, for she understood without the need for explanations. He had gone to hunt down those who had attacked Sir Gavin and his men. He had gone after Malagraine.

It snowed the next five days and each storm brought new concerns. Many times she returned to the star-chamber with the thought of using her powers to go to him and each time she stopped, bound by the promise she had given Stephen—that she would not let Gavin die.

His progress was slow. The first two days he lay in a

deep sleep unaware of everything about him. Twice he hovered so near death that she feared even she could not bring him back. She fought for his life, for in fighting for it and fulfilling her promise, she felt nearer to Stephen. Then, the third day he seemed to drift near waking, his eyes moving as though he dreamed, responding in a brief twitch or flicker to sounds around him.

Bones, muscle, and flesh healed. But the spirit healed less quickly. In his subconscious thoughts relived in dreams and through the stories told by his men who had survived, she learned of the attack they had barely survived. Through his thoughts, she saw what he had not seen, the darkness of evil in the midst of the warriors who attacked.

Days turned to one week, then edged nearer to two. Gavin became strong enough to spend several hours each day in the main hall with his men. There, he assumed the command and protection of the castle, consulting with Truan and the other knights and warriors who remained behind.

Margeaux too had rejoined them, glorying in the glow of impending childbirth that was still months away. As she was seen more and more about the common rooms of Camelot, returning to her previous sharp-tongued nature, everyone tried to stay out of her way.

Meg threatened to put a sleeping draught regularly in her morning tea so that they would be spared her shrewishness. Amber, usually sweet-natured and patient, more and more became a shadow.

She came upon them suddenly in the passage just outside the great room one evening after many had already retired to their pallets for the night.

Through that long evening, Truan and Gavin had formed a foursome with Amber and another knight and played at a board game. Amber had won several times, giving Cassandra cause to wonder at the honesty of her opponents for the girl was greatly liked by all at Camelot. And in the time she had been there, it seemed that she had lost much of the haunted look in her eyes. In that it seemed that Truan's friendship had served a purpose.

But as she suddenly rounded the corner, steeped in soft shadows, she heard Truan's gentle laughter and saw the movement of pale yellow wool at the gown Amber wore that night. Then they passed by one of the oil lamps at the wall, light playing across Truan's laughing features as he conjured another trick. But the expression in Amber's eyes was far more than amusement.

It was heartfelt, open, completely unguarded, the pain of the past fading before some intense longing that darkened at her eyes. In a movement so sudden that the soft yellow of her gown seemed to blend with the light of the lamp that spilled the walls, she reached out slender arms, and encircled his neck. Her mouth opened beneath his as she drew him down for a sudden, deep, impassioned kiss.

Caught off guard, he was for a moment, visibly stunned. Then, a side she would not have thought existed in the laughing fool exposed, Cassandra watched as he returned the kiss.

His hands plunged back through Amber's hair, molding her small head until it seemed he might crush her. He lifted her against him so that her slender body molded the length of his as his mouth angled across hers.

From Amber's silence came a soft, yearning sound of need deep at her throat. Instead of stopping him, it was as if that sound, the first the girl had ever made, was some long lost endearment spoken only for him. He molded her against him, hands stroking the length of her slender back as if he might pull her inside him.

He deepened the kiss, as intimate as anything Cassandra had ever experienced or longed for. He was a man transformed, the fool no longer but a man filled with a man's hunger and longing to be joined with a woman.

She saw it in the veins that stood out at his hands as he clung to the girl, in the way he arched his body against hers as if he would tear the clothes from her and take her there; in the scent of passion that came to her even there in the shadows—his strong and potent with the human need to be physically joined; hers sweet, hot, and innocent with the first arousal of sex; and then in the fierce gleam of his blue eyes as they slowly opened.

For a moment, Cassandra feared that he would take the girl there in the hall. Then, as suddenly as it had happened, Truan's fingers closed around Amber's arms. He made a sound, deep, harsh, and wounded as if a part of him were being torn from him someplace deep inside as he set her away from him.

The expression on Amber's face was stunned, filled with confusion. His expression, head thrown back, eyes closed, was filled with agony. His words where harsh, felt along the stones of the walls and in the very air, though spoken low. Still, Cassandra felt them.

"No, Amber. This cannot be."

The girl's questioning gaze searched his. The haunted, wounded look had returned.

"You are only a child," he whispered. "What you feel is friendship, nothing more. In time, you will have other feelings."

Amber shook her head adamantly, refusing what he was saying, her expression now a mixture of wounded anger and tormented sadness.

"You will!" he told her adamantly, hands at her shoulders, shaking her as if he could forcibly make her understand. "You must. I am not for you. You must find a young man more your own age and in time these feelings will grow as they should."

Even as Cassandra heard the words and knew the right-
ness of them, she knew Amber did not believe them. She
was only a child, no more than fourteen or fifteen. Truan
was a man, far older in years and experience.

She could listen no more, for Amber's silence had
turned to soft weeping. In Truan's tormented answer
she knew he spoke the truth. He would put distance
between himself and Amber. Even now, he turned away
from the girl, fists clenched at his sides.

"It is late, Amber. Return to your own chamber. Meg
will be waiting for you." Then he left, the sound of his
footsteps rapidly receding in the hallway. For a long
time, Amber stood there, tears glistening at her cheeks.
Then she too turned and left, weeping softly. Cassandra
was left with her own uncertain emotions, stirred by
what she had seen and felt, and the emptiness that grew
sharper within her each day.

With the deepening snows, it became more and more
difficult for the men to ride out on patrols beyond the
walls of Camelot. With increasing frequency they were
forced to seek the warmth of the fire rather than ven-
turing out in storms that would have endangered both
men and horses. And still there was no word of Stephen's
return.

They had been gone nearly three weeks. The mood
inside Camelot became more and more subdued with
each passing day. Even Truan has ceased his tricks and
games, becoming silent and withdrawn. He no longer
shared company with Amber but sought the company
of Gavin and his men. Amber became hollow-eyed and
more silent, if that was possible. She was rarely seen in
the main hall.

Margeaux seemed oblivious to it all. She enjoyed her
role as pampered prisoner. No longer confined to her
bed with illness, she gained health each day, her figure

expanding as Malagraine's child grew within her along with the certainty that her rescue was imminent.

Cassandra spent as much time beyond the confining walls of the great hall as possible. At each fleeting break in the weather she wrapped herself in the woolen mantle and set out with Fallon and Pippen, tramping through the snow from cottage to hut that housed the residents of Camelot seeing to their illness and complaints, returning only when it was absolutely necessary.

More than once she was caught outside the main hall as a new storm set in. It would have been foolhardy to attempt to return even by way of the network of ropes strung to guide the warriors and knights from the stables to the inner courtyard and then from the courtyard to the front doors of the hall. When that happened, she was more than happy to accept the hospitality of those she had gone to help, sitting with them before a comforting fire, sharing their simple but abundant food, not haunted by the emptiness of the king's hall and the nagging fears that Stephen and his men might not return.

Well into the fourth week the storms finally broke. The dull silence of snow drifting layer upon layer at the doors and windows momentarily ceased. She turned Fallon out into the courtyard. He was no longer restricted but was seen constantly at her side wherever she went about Camelot. Pippen sniffed the sharp air, determined that it was not yet spring, and scuttled off in the direction of the larder to see what he could raid from the cook.

At the sound of Margeaux's sharp voice as she encountered the raccoon in the hallway, Cassandra made her escape, following Fallon's path through the snow. She took advantage of the break in the weather and spent the entire morning in the cavernous storerooms that had once contained food for an entire city, taking inventory, calculating the supplies of food brought by the farmers and peasants who had returned to Camelot, bringing their earthly belongings with them.

A man by the name of Goodoe assisted her, taking down the marks she tallied, clearing a path through crates, hogsheads, sacks of grain, and bundles of carded wool. Stephen had made him the keeper of the records and the man took his position very seriously.

He was a miller by trade and before the first snows had put the finishing touch to repairs made to the ancient granary that in the coming season would hopefully provide grain for the larders at Camelot.

Permanence. The future. She realized more and more with each passing day that these simple people had quietly returned, family by family, centuries after their ancestors had once dwelled here, with new hope for a future once promised only in legend.

How fleeting might their hopes be? she wondered, with thoughts of the uncertain images of the tapestry, the past, present, and the shadowy portent of what lay ahead for them all.

They ate at midday and continued to work, taking advantage of the respite from the weather, with no notion how long it might last. It was midafternoon when she finally emerged from the huge storage barn.

The sky was gray with the portent of another storm, the air sharp and crisp, bringing with it the smell of cook fires, the sound of voices from the cottages that lined the walls of the city. She returned to the hall reluctantly, just as the first new snow began to fall.

She glanced at Gavin as she entered the hall. A slow shake of his head told her there was still no word from Stephen or his men.

She did not take her meal in the hall that night but retreated to her chamber with Fallon and Pippen. The wolf sensed her mood and lay on the floor beside the fire, his sad silver eyes watching her intently. A night creature by habit, Pippen sought escape, scuttling through the door as she opened it on his way to raid the kitchens. Somewhere along the way he again encountered Margeaux.

Cass heard her shriek, then several curses. Not long after Margeaux passed her chamber door still muttering about wild creatures allowed to roam the halls. Some time later there was a scratching at the door and she opened it, the raccoon waddling through, his sides bulging with some treasure he'd discovered in the larder. Probably the apples he'd grown fond of. He found a favorite place at the corner of the raised hearth where the stones radiated heat from the brazier and set about cleaning his face and paws.

She paced the chamber restlessly, returning again and again to the tapestry, trying to see some emerging pattern in the dark unwoven threads, finally pushing it away from her in frustration. The fire grew low. She threw several more pieces of wood on it and then sought the warmth of the bed.

How many hours later she awakened, she did not know. Only that she sensed a change in the air. She rose from the bed, taking the largest fur with her. When Fallon raised his head in question, she commanded him with a single thought. Stay.

The hallway was cold and empty. She heard no sound. But still she sensed something. She crossed the hall, her hand at the heavy iron latch. She pushed the door to the king's chamber open.

Fire burned in the brazier, casting pools of light across pale walls, the thick fur at the pale sandstone floor, the gleam of new wood at a chair, and the man who stood before the brazier, hands extended toward the flames as if he would take hold of the fire.

At first glance, he was the same. But as she looked more closely she sensed a weariness that pulled at him and seemed to drain the strength from him. She saw it in the slight sag of those shoulders and in the way his head hung forward as though he possessed so little strength that he might fall over at any moment.

As she slowly walked into the chamber, her senses and thoughts frantically searching his, desperate to assure herself that he was indeed unharmed, he finally seemed aware of her.

His head slowly lifted, and in the haggard, drawn expression on his face and in the haunted look in his eyes she saw the deepest pain of all. She saw what Stephen had seen; what he and his men had encountered; she saw the unfolding threads of the tapestry in a canvas of horror, death, and destruction.

Her gaze searched his, fear welling inside her at what he had seen and experienced, as she looked for some ember in those golden depths, some small flame that still existed. Then she saw it as his gaze met hers, a flame of life struggling up out of the misery of darkness as he saw only her.

She slowly walked toward him, terrified that the light would die, terrified of what he had seen and endured yet forcing herself to see those same images, to take them within herself so that she might understand, so that she might lessen his anguish.

The gaze that clung to hers was haunted, burning almost feverishly as he fought his way out of the darkness. She felt the pain that tore through him, the horror at the death he had seen, the lives lost, the blame that he carried.

Wordlessly, she let the fur drop to the floor at her feet.

Thirteen

"My men." Stephen's voice was low and harsh at his throat, an agony of pain mixed with impotent rage at what he had found.

"I know," she whispered. But even before the words were out, he was reaching for her, dragging her against him, his powerful warrior's hands bruising as he pulled her to him, his lips hungry, consuming as his mouth crushed down over hers.

There was no tenderness in him, only desperation. A desperation that came from what he had seen and carried back with him in every fiber of his memory. A memory that haunted and would continue to haunt as long as he lived, even as he tried to burn it out with the fire that leapt between them as they came together.

His hands drove back through her hair, tangling it, twisting it as he angled her head back, exposing her throat to his lips, lifting her as if she was no more than air, a wild sound at the back of his throat as his mouth closed over her breast.

Cassandra gasped at the wildness in him, the barely controlled power that bordered on frenzy, as if with her touch, the taste of her, he could wipe out the horrible memories. And at the wildness in herself as she arched her back offering all of herself to him, holding him clasped against her, the longing inside her becoming a far different ache as she watched him suckle her as if he drew life itself from her breast.

She caressed his cheeks, his eyes, the hard curve of his jaw, touching each part that she had memorized the past weeks, then kissed him with all the longing he'd left her with and the aching uncertainty that he would never return.

"Make me forget," he whispered against her throat, clasping her against him. "You have the power. Take away the pain."

As his hand stroked down her back, Cass circled her legs around his waist, angling his head back for her kiss.

"Give me your pain," she whispered against his lips, her thoughts moving through his, her body burning as she discovered far more beyond the painful memories and then discovered the desire that had lain there from the moment they had first met.

She closed her eyes, allowing his thoughts to become hers, in all the vivid images he had imagined the past months—all the ways he longed to make love to her, sensual, erotic, stunning images—touching her, caressing her, the moment when he had undressed her, the longing that had raged through him to take her then, images of emotions and feelings when he had kissed her, his tongue plunging inside hers as he imagined his body joining with hers.

Emotions and longings so intense that they became her longings. Physical hunger so deep and painful that it became her hunger. The need to be joined so strong and vivid that it pulsed deep within her like a waiting heartbeat.

"Give me all of yourself," she whispered, dragging the tunic back from his heavily muscled shoulders. Her tongue caressed the hard ridge of scars that webbed his flesh and made him only more beautiful in her eyes.

She grazed her teeth across a flat, male nipple, lingered, then suckled as he had suckled her, bringing a fierce choked sound from deep in his throat.

"Give me your heart."

Her eyes closed again as she tasted the skin at his throat, caressing the scar that angled low across his chest and might have taken his life, taking the essence of him deep inside of her with each stroke of her tongue.

"Give me your soul."

As if he could bear it no more, he dragged her head back, with a fist knotted in her hair. His amber eyes were ablaze with desire and an almost desperate anger. In the anger she sensed his thoughts, the doubt, and the unasked question. Was she a creature of the Darkness?

In the desire that burned there, like a fire beyond control, a fire that reached out to her, she saw his own answer as he carried her to the pallet in powerful strides. There was no gentleness either as he laid her back across the thick furs. Only urgency.

Urgency as he peeled off his tunic, tore open the front of his breeches and kicked them aside, thickly veined flesh—exquisitely beautiful flesh—springing taut against his belly. He was long and proud, fully engorged, the tip flared and deep red, the skin sleek and stretched to bursting the full length of him, thrusting from that thatch of dark hair that swirled about twin pouches of heavy flesh.

Urgency as his weight dipped the edge of the pallet, his fingers lightly bruising at her knees as he drew them apart. Her own growing urgency in the sudden quivering of her body in anticipation, reaching for him, slender nails digging into powerful muscles that sheathed his shoulders; in the instinctive arching of her hips, as if with her thoughts joining his, she already felt that fierce sweet physical joining.

Then, that moment when his flesh first touched hers, the wet heat of her body easing him past pale flesh wreathed in dark satin, the quiver of her body as her body resisted, the veins that stood out along his arms as he held himself above her, then the harsh, fierce cry low in his throat as he thrust deep inside her.

She felt a sudden twinge of pain that quickly gave way to wonder as her thoughts joined with his. She felt sinew, muscles, and flesh molding around his proud warrior's flesh, then saw it in her thoughts. The tender invasion, the length of him pressing deep inside. Her flesh yielding, stroking, molding his until he lay fully sheathed inside her.

Then the sensual, erotic images of his flesh stroking powerfully inside her, withdrawing to thrust even more deeply inside as if he wished to lose himself inside her.

She met each powerful thrust, her legs clasped around his waist, her fingers digging into his shoulders, head thrown back as the images washed over her. And finally, that moment when the first spasms quivered through her body, her startled cry, the harsh sound that came from someplace deep within him, and the moment when she felt his release deep inside her.

His body was racked with spasms, his skin glistened, the mane of dark hair molded his face and shoulders. He clung to her, fingers bruising as he held her hips, as if he poured himself into her slender body.

Eventually, the spasms eased, his eyes slowly opened and in them she saw all of his anguish followed by the dawning awareness of what he'd done.

"Nay," she whispered fiercely, then again tenderly, silencing him as she pressed her fingers against his lips. Reaching for him when he would have withdrawn in disgust and self-loathing for the way he'd taken her. Pulling him down with her on the pallet of soft furs, her body still entwined with his. Holding his flesh deep inside as he curled exhausted about her. Taking away the demons of his memories with her thoughts, leaving him with only the warmth of his body safely nestled in hers as he slept deeply and without dark dreams for the first time in days.

When he first awakened he thought the sightless, soundless cocoon that surrounded him must be what death felt like and for a moment as memories began to crowd back in, he would have welcomed it.

Then he gradually became aware of thick furs beneath him, a current of cool air that invaded between the parted bed hangings, the light from the brazier that pooled across the floor, memories of hours past, and the gliding, silken warmth that eased over his body.

In the soft glow of light from the brazier he saw the dark satin of her hair covering a pale shoulder, spilling to her waist in a torrent of midnight silk, revealing a glimpse of pale breast, then the brush of her fingers along his thigh, tentative, hesitant, a question asked, then answered as her hand stroked upward and found his thickening flesh.

"Cassandra?" he whispered through the darkness, praying it was not a dream.

Her breath whispered in answer where her fingers led, encircling him, stroking him until he thrust proud between her splayed fingers.

Hands at her arms, he tried to stop her. But on a husky, throaty sound her lips brushed his belly.

"Nay, milord," she said fiercely.

Then he felt the softness of her breasts stroking across his belly and chest, her slender legs parting to straddle him, hands gliding up the length of his arms, pinning them overhead when he would have resisted, the sweet wet heat at the center of her caressing him with a slow roll of her hips.

He could have stopped her. And then he could not.

Not when she moved in his blood, burning through him as surely as fire, sweet and hot, her mouth finding his in the dark cocoon that surrounded them and kept the world at bay; not when her slender hands released his and glided back down across his chest, lingering almost tenderly at the patchwork of scars. Not as she came up on her knees, her hand closing around his throbbing flesh as she guided him to her. Impossible as he felt the feather stroke of her fingers like a butterfly wing, then heard her soft sigh of pleasure as she eased him inside her.

"Cassandra, you must not." His hands clamped over her hips, as if even now he might stop her. "What I have seen . . ."

Above all, she knew what he had seen for she had seen it as well. She had felt his agony at the slow, brutal deaths of his men, an agony he poured into her the first time he joined with her. This time would be different. This time there was no outside world.

"It cannot touch us here."

Her fingers laced through his. Her back arched as she slowly stroked the length of him, heat against heat, flesh against flesh, until he was buried deep inside her once more. The waist-length mane of her hair spilled down her back, the ends brushing across his hips and thighs as she slowly began to move, lifting her hips, then easing back down over him in movements as old as time, building the heat, gasping as she took him deeper with each slow stroke, luxuriating in the joining so complete, so perfect as if her body remade itself for him, until she felt his body answer in the slow thrust of his hips, filling her completely until she felt him thrusting at the opening of her womb.

Then, in a movement so swift she caught her breath, he turned, pulling her beneath him, taking away control as he pinned her wrists above her head. In the glow

of light from the brazier she saw the battle he fought
as he pinned her hips with his, felt the agony of the
desire that pulsed through his flesh.

"Cassandra!" he whispered savagely.

As effortlessly as if his hands were made of water, she
escaped, her own hands gliding around his neck, lips
softly parted, her eyes wide and luminous as she lay
beneath him, her answer in the movement of her hips
against his, stroking him, sensing the moment when he
cast aside the demons and sank deep inside her.

The hunger was still there, communicating itself in
the touch of his hand, his soft bruising kiss, the stroking
heat as he teased a nipple into an aching, tormented
knot of desire. In growing agony she drew him down
to her other breast, arching against his mouth and lips,
crying out as he drew the taut flesh between his teeth.
But he did not give her the fulfillment she craved. He
lay still within her, firmly buried, hands stilling her restless hips, forcing her to slow beneath him. A torment
that was only worse as he nipped and stroked at her
breast, until she lay breathless beneath him.

He cursed softly as he thrust deep inside her again,
lost in the sound of her passion, the startled catch at
her throat, the sudden arch of her back, and then the
fierce spasms of her muscles clenching him like a tight
fist. And then he was lost in her, his heat spilling deep
inside, filling her, as if the darkness could not enter.

Afterward, he gathered her against him, her leg riding his hip, their bodies still intimately joined, her hair
spread like midnight satin across the bed. Their scents
were as entwined as their bodies, heat upon heat, that
dusky sweet smell of sex.

He closed his eyes in silent agony as he pulled her
more tightly against him, in agony for the child they
may have already created. A bastard child, like himself,
in an uncertain and dark world. But like the unfolding

images in the tapestry he knew he was powerless to stop it. As powerless as he was to fight the need to feel himself deep inside her.

They slept, the world beyond the gates of Camelot forgotten. When she awakened, Cassandra awakened to a delicious spreading heat that curled low inside her. She opened her eyes to stare into the amber gaze of the man who lay beside her, his hand resting along her thigh straddled over his hip.

Amber eyes blurred in her vision as he bent over her, his hand slipping through her hair as his mouth sought hers with almost aching tenderness.

He caressed her arm, down the curve of her hip, then across her thigh. For now the haunted shadows were gone from his eyes, replaced by a heat that burned at his kiss.

She tasted herself at his lips, the sweetness of lavender suckled from her breasts and other tastes and scents discovered as he'd made love to her. Now they slowly washed back through her senses in building waves of desire.

His hand moved low between them, stroking through damp curls to the place where his flesh joined with hers. She quivered as his fingers began a gentle exploration, parting her tender flesh, stroking with his thumb at the place above where his flesh quickly swelled once more within her.

It was magical. It was wondrous. It was agony, as he slowly made love to her in new ways, with his mouth, his hands, and his body, parting smaller folds of flesh until he found the tiny nub hidden there.

Again and again, he returned, stroking her in that hidden place as he slowly moved his hips against hers. She cried out at the wondrous feelings that poured through her. She ached from his loving of her, and at the same time ached for him to make love to her again.

Her muscles contracted then glided over him as he

drew honey from her once more, sweet golden honey that gleamed the length of his flesh and gleamed at his fingers as he brought them to her lips. Her eyes widened, dark violet, smokey with desire as she drank her sweetness from his fingers then gave it back to him in a kiss.

As he tasted her, she felt his control slip away. He pulled her beneath him, burying himself deep inside her as he tasted her dark honey on her lips. She closed her eyes, losing herself in the fire of passion, no longer caring if dawn ever came.

He had been changed by what he found in the northern passes. In the days following their return, Cassandra sensed it more and more. As if something had died within him.

He did not speak of it, and she did not ask for she understood in that way that only she could in the joining of their thoughts, and at night, in the almost desperate joining of their bodies.

Winter was full upon the land. Camelot settled into an icy cocoon, insulated from the outside world, protected from the darkness that hovered just beyond the walls.

They had wood for their fires and food to last the winter. The men played board games of an evening, or games of skill in the inner courtyard when there was a brief respite from the storms. Truan still performed his foolish tricks and illusions, but his rare smiles disappeared completely whenever Amber appeared.

Contrary to what Cassandra expected after what she had seen between them, Amber did not become weepy and clingy. She seemed to have grown up a great deal in the past months at Camelot. If not happily, she went dutifully about her chores, throwing herself into work until every room in the castle was clean and glowing.

Margeaux did not find such industrious outlets for her wayward moods. One moment she was sharp-witted and chose to join them for evening meals, the next she was sullen and withdrawn. At all times she was peevish. As her belly grew larger, so grew her unhappiness.

She had been insistent in the early days of winter that Malagraine knew of the child she carried. It would have been easy enough in fair weather for one of the peasants to carry word to him.

Yet no word came of ransom offered for her release. And with the attack on Sir Gavin's men in the northern pass, it seemed less likely than ever.

Sir Gavin as well as those others who had been wounded and returned with him, recovered from their wounds. But like Stephen, he had seen things he would not speak of.

Meg was usually found sitting near the fire for the cold of winter had settled into her bones, making it painful to walk. But not too painful to speak of the tapestry.

"It was woven by your sister. The power is strong within your family. But it is unfinished, a portent of an unknown future. A legacy which you must not deny."

"They abandoned me," Cassandra reminded her, for she considered Elora the only one who had truly ever loved her. Elora had died, she had not abandoned her. And even in death, she still sensed the Old One's presence.

"I have no family."

"It is in your blood," Meg had replied softly. *"You cannot deny it."*

Only in the courtyard when weather permitted, or the chamber she shared with Stephen was she able to escape the old woman. But even there, the images in the tapestry constantly reminded her.

The new year came and went. February brought ice storms as brutal as any she had seen, confining them all to the warmth of the fires. And with this added confinement Margeaux's temper grew even darker. She was restless and quarrelsome. Everyone was a target, but especially Cassandra.

She tried to be understanding and sympathetic toward her stepsister who had bargained foolishly.

"I do not know why you tolerate it," Stephen told her as they retreated to their chamber one night in spite of the fact that it was much colder there than in the great hall with the large hearth that burned day and night. Stephen sat in the large highbacked chair before the brazier, long legs spread toward the heat. "Perhaps a few days in the lower regions of the castle would sweeten her temper."

Cassandra burst out laughing. "You do not know Margeaux. She glories in her moods and then finds new ways to make people suffer."

She moved about the room, loosening the ties of her kirtle, slipping out of the soft wool gown until she stood before the fire in the brazier clad only in her chemise. With the glow of the fire behind her, the chemise left little to the imagination.

" 'Tis nothing to the way you make me suffer."

A slender brow arched upward. "You do not seem much tortured, milord."

"An hour when I cannot touch you is torture." He seized a slender wrist and pulled her into his lap. He brushed aside the heavy satin of her hair, his fingers untying the ribbon over her breasts with amazing efficiency, soft pliant flesh spilling into his caressing hands.

He had only to touch her and she grew hot and wet for him, the place he had claimed aching until he claimed it again. Her nipples puckered and grew taut in anticipation of his lips. And the hunger began, a hunger that would not be quenched until she felt him full and hot within her.

Her slender hands released him, her lips caressing his as he eased the chemise up over her hips, her mouth making love to his as he settled her over him, sighing with pleasure as he thrust inside her.

He slowly began to rock her hips against his. With hands braced at his shoulders, she arched her back, taking him as deep as possible and then deeper still.

"My God," he whispered. "How I love the look of you when I'm deep inside you." His mouth caressed her throat. "There is a wildness in you that takes my breath away, as if you're stealing my very soul." His lips skimmed her shoulder and then the slope of her breast.

"How I love the taste of you," his teeth grazed her nipple as he drew her into his mouth. "The sweetness that pours from you, the heat that burns where I touch you." He drew her full within his mouth, his tongue swirling the tender, taut nipple, nibbling it between his teeth until she cried out.

"The strength in you," he whispered, the words aching out of his lungs as his hands skimmed the arch of her back, down over the curve of her bottom to that wet hot place where he glided deep inside her. Then his voice was a harsh, almost painful sound as he felt the liquid fire that slicked her body and his.

"The fire in you."

He stood then, carrying her with him to the pallet of furs. He laid her back across them, sinking down with her, sinking into her.

"The passion in you. The sound you make at that final moment."

As he thrust inside her, she arched, her breath catching as need sharpened, coiling tighter and tighter until she thought she could not endure it.

She tasted the saltiness at his skin, and felt the powerful muscles suddenly clench at his back. Her thoughts turned inward to that place where they joined, the desire that claimed them, the heat that seemed brighter than a thousand suns, and that moment when he held her against him. Heart pressed against heart, soul touching soul.

Fourteen

Everyone grew increasingly short-tempered at their confinement because of the weather. But Cassandra did not consider it so. As long as winter snows blocked the mountain passes, the valley and Camelot were safe. Malagraine could not enter, and Stephen could not ride out with his men. And she could believe for a few weeks more that things might always be this way.

She no longer thought Truan's silly tricks and illusions a fool's game. Many the night he entertained them, constantly adding to the variety of tricks and conjurements that he claimed to have learned in his travels.

Amber was now the one who thought his tricks foolish and a waste of time, refusing to participate, retreating instead to the corner with Meg or to the kitchens where she practiced the blending of herbs and powders the old woman had begun teaching her.

Mornings Margeaux sat before the hearth, her swollen ankles propped upon a stool, a sharp, watchful look on her face, her temperament more disagreeable than ever.

This morning, Stephen and Gavin had left earlier with Goodoe to inspect the supply of food in the storage houses. For his latest trick, Truan conjured an apple, seemingly out of the air, and held it out to Pippen who had been covertly sneaking closer and closer to the basket of yarn at Cassandra's feet. As she wound carded yarn into balls for the weaver's loom, she deposited them into the basket where they rolled invitingly.

Now, distracted by his appetite, Pippen who was very nearly full grown, snatched the apple from Truan's outstretched hand and scurried off to find a corner in which to eat it without being disturbed.

"I do not know why you indulge that foul creature," Margeaux snapped.

"Perhaps, because I find him far more companionable than some people I know," Truan replied pointedly.

She was vain, argumentative, and at times cruel. But she was not stupid. She knew exactly whom he spoke of.

"A clown and a fool," she said with disgust. "Perfect companions."

Truan ignored her as he sat down beside Cassandra, straddling the bench she sat upon, and seized a card of wool from the pile in another basket at the floor.

He skewered the spun wool onto his long fingers, holding it aloft as she rolled the yarn which was to be woven into warm woolen garments.

"She is the perfect companion for herself," Truan commented in lowered voice. "Both equally disagreeable."

Cassandra laughed. "I wonder what would happen if she did not like herself so much?"

"They might come to blows," he quipped.

Their conversation went from silly to ridiculous. "Then at least we might be spared one of them."

"Dare we hope for both?"

Her eyes danced with merriment. "That would be too much to hope for."

" 'Tis good to hear you laugh, Cassandra. You should laugh more often."

"There has been little of late to laugh about."

"Aye," he agreed, his dark blue eyes studying her. "Lord Stephen does not laugh often."

She thought of private moments between them when there had been much laughter. Laughter and passion.

"Perhaps more than you know."

"And more than you will admit, too?"

The expression in his eyes was not mocking, nor was it the expression of the fool, but instead slightly amused.

"Perhaps."

He laughed again, a rich sound that rolled from his chest. The yarn tangled on his fingers and Cassandra was forced to free him or else lose several feet of it hopelessly snagged with knots. It was a complicated process for he was like a playful pup that somehow managed to become more ensnared the more he tried to free himself.

Finally, she did the only thing that made any sense. She did not usually rely on her own powers for it was difficult to explain to some people. But a simple thing such as untangling yarn was innocent enough. On a single concentrated thought the yarn unwove itself as if it had suddenly come to life, fell from his fingers, and drifted down onto the table into a neat coil.

He scooped up her hand and complimented her, "You have a truly magical touch, mistress." Now he seemed more the fool, intent on making her laugh.

"I am merely not so clumsy. You had best stick to conjuring apples for Pippen."

It was her soft, musical laughter that Stephen heard, her hand clasped in Truan Monroe's, as he and Gavin returned to the great hall.

"Or perhaps, *more* perfect companions," Margeaux remarked slyly as she watched their play, her eyes narrowing with new possibilities at Stephen's expression as he saw them together in what appeared to be a very intimate conversation.

"Have you now taken to spinning wool?" Stephen asked as he poured a goblet of wine and sat down across from them at the table.

Truan shook his head. "Cassandra has convinced me that my talents lie elsewhere, lest all of Camelot be forced to go naked because of ruined yarn."

She laughed. "But at least there will be plenty of apples."

Stephen glanced from one to the other as if they had both lost their minds. He set the goblet down with a dull thud that sent wine sloshing over the rim.

"I should think your talents would best be applied to things other than yarn and apples. Perhaps the sword. You will have more need of it than apples when we face Malagraine, unless you chose to beat him to death with fruit."

Suddenly the conversation was no longer humorous. Stephen had been in a dark mood since early morn. It had not improved.

"It was merely a joke we shared," she tried to explain.

"It would appear you shared far more."

Cass threw the yarn ball into the basket. "A bit of laughter, no more. Surely laughter is not against the law, milord."

"No 'tis not," he replied. "But shrewishness should be." He turned to Truan. "What think you, my friend? Should we outlaw shrews?"

"I think there are enough laws already, 'tis the application of them that is most important," Truan answered diplomatically. "But if you feel the need for more, then the counsel of knights might best decide."

"Aye, the counsel," Stephen snapped. "Eleven knights and a fool."

Cassandra suddenly rose from the bench. Anger blazed in her vivid violet eyes.

"Perhaps there should be a law against pig-headedness," she suggested.

"Do you have someone in mind, mistress?"

"I am looking at him!"

Margeaux cackled with laughter.

"Perhaps you would care to discuss this in private," Stephen said between his teeth.

Cassandra picked up the baskets of yarn. "I see no reason to discuss it at all." With a toss of her hair, she left the hall.

Stephen did not follow her and she was glad of it, for she was afraid of what she might say. *He'd* been the fool, and no reason for it. His words had cut deeply, but especially his cruelty to Truan who was a good friend.

Reaching the chamber, she chucked the baskets into the far corner. Just before she slammed the door, Pippen scuttled into the room and found the basket of tightly wound yarn balls—a perfect place to nap and then play.

At the loud thump of the door, Fallon raised his head from paws as though disturbed from his sleep. The expression at his lean, angular face sometimes seemed almost human.

"I do not wish to discuss it!" she told him.

She quickly undressed and slipped beneath the thick furs. It was some time later when she heard the door open, light from the hall slanting across the pale stones. Beside the pallet, Fallon rose and quickly padded across the chamber. The door closed behind him.

The fire had long since burned low at the brazier. The room was steeped in darkness. She listened as Stephen crossed the room, the sounds he made as familiar and dear to her as breathing. Even in anger. Then a loud thump, a muffled curse, and Pippen's disgusted chatter as he was roused out of sleep by a boot that connected with the basket.

It was quiet in the chamber once more, then she felt the sudden intrusion of cold air followed by stirring heat as his long, lean body curled around hers. She felt his fingers stroking up from her waist and the answering desire that swelled her breast into his hand in spite of her efforts to remain passive.

She squeezed her eyes tightly shut, turning her thoughts inward, determined to resist him. But her mortal body betrayed her immortal soul as his hand moved lower, down across her belly at the same time his lips stroked across her shoulder.

"I know you are not asleep," his breath whispered across her skin, desire spiraling through her at that simple contact and the remembered way his breath had warmed other places in the past. Still she refused to answer, refused to respond in any way that was of her own free will.

His hand moved lower, those long fingers stroking between her thighs until they found the hot, wet center of her. She silently groaned even as she heard the harsh sound that came low at his throat. Then, he was dipping inside her, caressing, stroking, until against her free will, a broken sigh shuddered out of her.

He scooped her hair back from her neck so that he could taste her. She was sweet and warm there, soft and giving, as the soft woman's flesh he dipped into. He began a rhythm, gently sinking his teeth into her shoulder at the same moment he thrust his fingers inside her, then stroking with hand and lips, then biting and thrusting, until he felt her back arch against him in that way that connected them beyond anger, beyond harshly spoken words, beyond even another man touching her. And with each tender bite, with each thrust, he reclaimed her.

"You are mine," he whispered as he opened her and stroked deep again.

Her head went back with unleashed pleasure as his teeth grazed her skin. His leg moved between hers and she felt the press of blunt hot flesh low at her back.

Then his fingers stroking her open. In one fluid movement he was inside her.

His hips cupped hers, his hands stroked up to cup her breasts. Instinctively she arched her back, opening herself completely, taking him deeper inside.

"Mine," he whispered again, a harsh thrilling sound that found an answer deep inside her.

The need to touch was almost unbearable. She stroked her hand low at her body, her trembling fingers finding that place where their bodies joined, stroking the length of his engorged flesh, then that gliding moment as his body disappeared inside hers once more.

Possession. It was impossible to know who possessed whom.

She heard the sound low at his throat. Then felt the sudden spasms beneath her hand, and those deeper within at his moment of release.

Though she tried to deny it, she found she could not as her traitorous body answered with deep, racking spasms that spiraled from the deepest center of her, possessing him with every contraction of her own muscles until she was as spent as he.

She did not sleep, but listened to his breathing as it eventually became even with his own sleep. Then she eased from his side, crossing the chamber on icy feet, wrapping herself in a warm fur. She fed pieces of wood to the fire in the brazier. For long hours she sat there, staring down at the unformed images in the tapestry spread at the table. One image now clearly revealed itself. That of a journey into an uncertain land, but she could not tell who it was who made the journey or if they returned.

"How many more weeks of winter?" Truan asked, one day very near the end of February as the ice storms finally ceased. Snow once more fell softly, blanketing the towers so that they looked like gnomes with fat hats hunched along the walls.

Cassandra looked at him in surprise for she had not heard him approach.

"By the seasons, six more weeks until spring." She looked out across the inner courtyard, which had disappeared under a fresh mantle of snow. "But I think no one has told the weather that it has only six more weeks."

"And how much time before the child?"

Her hand hesitated above the journal where she had been making entries, a record of food supplies and livestock. Then with great concentration she made the next entry.

"Three months," she replied. "Though I doubt any of us can stand Margeaux that long."

"I was not speaking of Margeaux."

Her startled gaze met his.

"You have not told him," Truan concluded.

Denial sprang to her lips, words that she had rehearsed over and over the past few weeks since she had become certain that she was with child. In his fool's gaze that was hardly that of a fool, she saw that it was pointless to deny it, especially to him. He was far too quick-witted, those dark blue eyes far too clever so that she wondered again why she had ever thought him a fool. Though he seemed to wish her, and everyone else, to think it.

"How did you know?"

" 'Tis not hard to see," he replied. "If one knows what to look for." At her raised brow, he explained. "There are obvious signs among all creatures. In a woman, it is a certain radiance of beauty." Then, rolling his eyes near the direction of the hearth where Margeaux sat, he corrected himself.

"In some women. In others it appears to breed peevishness."

She didn't know whether to laugh or cry. She hoped no one else had guessed. At least not yet.

"You speak as if you have some experience in these matters."

He shook his head. "Only by observation, not by deed."

"Though not for lack of experience?" she suggested, remembering the encounter she had seen between he and Amber, a passionate encounter that had stripped away yet one more layer of disguise to reveal a far different man beneath the facade he presented to everyone. Since then she had seen many a young peasant girl at Camelot, twitch her skirts invitingly in his direction.

He laughed and shrugged. "Some, perhaps."

She guessed far more than some, for he was a handsome man. No doubt more so beneath the close-cropped beard.

"You cannot keep it a secret for long," he said gently. "There are some who will take notice of it more quickly than others. Those," he added pointedly, "who have nothing better to do with their time than look for such things."

She knew he spoke of Margeaux and assured him, "I will tell him when the time is right. But there are matters which weigh heavily upon him. The winter has been especially long and hard. Food supplies are low. He worries about the people of Camelot. And with the spring, he will take his men into the northern passes to seek out Malagraine. I would not burden him with more."

He bent low over her hand and brushed his lips across the back of her fingers. "If such a lovely lady carried my child, I assure you it would be no burden."

There was no right time to tell Stephen in great part because she could not be certain how he would take the news. She knew of his own bastard birth. He spoke little of it, but she knew that his father's inability to set aside the duties of the king and acknowledge the duties of the father, had left a deep wound that had never fully healed. She understood those feelings all too well, for they were not unlike her own toward the parents who had abandoned her.

Now his child grew within her, a spark of life created in passion, mortal and immortal, with the blood of the ages flowing through its veins.

How might he feel about his own bastard child? And what of the future? An uncertain future shrouded in Darkness and death. A future that she was part of. And because she was part of it, so then too was her unborn child.

In the moments when she was alone, nights when Stephen came late to their bed, she lay alone, tears hot on her cheek, her hand resting over the life that she had sensed the first moment it was conceived.

Her child. A child of unknown powers. If it lived.

That was her greatest fear. Not that Stephen would not accept their child, but that she might not be able to protect the new life that grew within her through what lay ahead.

Briefly, in a moment of mortal weakness and uncertainty, she had thought how different things might be if the child did not grow within her.

There were ways, known to healers. And other ways, known to those of her powers. On a single focused thought, she could have swept that new and fragile life from her womb as if it never existed. But at what price? For her powers drew their soul and substance from the Light, from the source of all life itself in the universe. If she relinquished the child, did she then relinquish her powers to the Darkness, death, and destruction?

What of her mortal self? That part of her that was human? Her heart and soul? Even as she thought of it, briefly plagued by mortal doubts and fears, the answer came from her soul.

She could not. The child within her had been created from love and passion, unlike any she would ever experience again. And she would give her life to protect it.

The platter shattered at the floor.

The expression on the servant's face was one of horror as he stared at the precious food that had taken hours to prepare and was now scattered across the stones at the floor.

"I will not have you looking at me in that way!" Margeaux exclaimed. "I know what you are thinking. But I am the daughter of the Lord of Tregaron. I carry the son of Prince Malagraine. I demand that you show respect!"

The poor man dodged her booted foot as she tried to kick him when he swooped low and tried to gather some of the food.

Cassandra intervened, but her stepsister did not hear her, so intent was she on venting her anger and frustration on the servant.

She had grown increasingly quarrelsome the past few weeks, turning on anyone who ventured near. No one had been spared, until Stephen swore he would ban her to her room.

When she paid no heed, Cassandra gently tried to draw her away. But she misjudged Margeaux. She did not think her capable of actually harming anyone and so therefore did not see the knife she seized from the top of the table.

She sensed the danger too late, the blade of the knife slicing through the soft wool at her shoulder. So surprised was she that it was a moment before she felt the pain, then another moment before she felt the warm stickiness of blood.

Truan was first upon her, seizing Margeaux by the arm in a firm grasp. She hurled several curses at him as the knife fell from her stunned fingers. At the commotion several knights suddenly appeared at the hall, with swords drawn. Stephen was among them.

"What's happened?" he demanded as he crossed the hall, his men flanking him.

Margeaux glared at Truan, then turned her sharp gaze on Cassandra. "A bastard for a bastard," she smirked, making an ugly game of it, taking her revenge with words.

"But which bastard seed has spawned the child? The warriors or the fool's?"

"What is she talking about?"

"A bastard for a bastard," Margeaux repeated. "If you do not know, then you should ask the bastard's mother."

"Enough!" Truan swore as he whirled Margeaux about. His hand slipped over her shoulder. On a startled sound of protest, her eyes rolled back and she slumped unconscious. She would have fallen to the floor if one of Stephen's men hadn't caught her. He quickly handed her over to the nearest servant.

"Get her out of here!" Truan ordered, then turned back to Cassandra. The look in her eyes stopped him before he could make some foolish joke of it all or deny Margeaux's mad ravings.

The expression on her face was stricken, filled with anguish. She looked at Stephen, but saw only anger.

"What was she raving about?" Stephen demanded, looking from one to the other, suspicion growing dark about his heart.

"What you should have known without having to be told!" Truan told him bluntly.

Stephen turned to her. The anger was still there, along with questions in the hard set angles at his face.

"Do you mind explaining this to me?" he demanded.

Then he saw the blood that seeped her shoulder. Anger drained from his face. He reached for her.

Cassandra had never been sick a day in her life. She had never once been ill even after she discovered she was with child. But now pain stung at her shoulder. Nausea backed into her throat at the smell of blood.

She slowly backed away. She wanted only to get away from all of them. Then, suddenly it was as if her feet were weighted with stones. Heaviness dragged at her. She felt herself falling, crumbling as if she was no more than a rag doll, and expected at any moment to feel the cold hard stones of the floor beneath her cheek. Instead, she felt strong arms closing around her.

She protested, pushing against that broad muscular chest. She couldn't bear Stephen's anger.

But it was not Stephen who carried her, nor Stephen who whispered against her ear.

"Eich le, mo chroi." Strange, ancient words, comforting words that spun from some long lost memory and were then gone in the dark miasma that closed round her.

She drifted in a warm, soft cocoon. Occasionally voices entered the cocoon, floating through her subconsciousness, then slipping away.

There was no anger in this warm, safe place. She no longer had to hear Margeaux's vicious lies.

She drifted, slept, then drifted again, preferring to stay in this place for now. Aware of the sweet, warm liquid that slipped between her lips and down her throat. Silverbark tea. She smiled at the sweet lethargy it brought, then drifted again.

"Why was I the last to know?" Stephen demanded angrily.

"Because you chose not to know," Meg whispered. She chuckled softly as she set the cup of tea aside, a simple restorative that allowed Cassandra to sleep and would harm neither her nor the child. She snorted.

"There are none so blind as those who will not see."

"Will she be all right?"

"The wound at her shoulder is slight, even now it heals with the power that is strong within her. As for the rest . . . ?" She did not finish.

"Is the child safe?"

"It is strong within her, and her power protects it. No harm will come to the child as long as she lives." She sensed his uncertainty and again chuckled softly.

"You bedded her with a passion to shake the very walls of Camelot and did not consider the possibility of a child? Who is the fool?"

"It is not that I had not considered it."

"Then perhaps you already have a wife, or children by another woman and wish for no more."

"I have no other children," Stephen answered fiercely. "I have always made certain of it before."

"Yes," she answered. "Always before. Now what will you do, warrior? Your child grows within her. But be assured she will ask nothing of you. She is far too proud to do that. Nor does she need you. She more than any other knows that a child can survive without its parents. The choice is yours."

"Leave us."

When she hesitated and looked at him sharply with those wise, blind eyes, he assured her, "No harm will come to her or the child."

After she had gone, Stephen sat for long hours in the chair before the hearth, staring at the pallet of furs and the slender girl who lay there pale and unmoving, adrift in a deep, healing sleep.

Her hair spread the furs like rich satin. A shoulder gleamed pale above the furs. A slender hand lay curled beneath her cheek. A hand that had once reached out to him and saved his life. A hand with such incredible tenderness and warmth of passion that when he closed his eyes he could feel her touch.

A bastard for a bastard.

The words cut at him. But not because of any pain it caused him. Long ago he reconciled himself to his bastard birth. The anger that remained between him and his father, was one of old arguments and stubbornness. The circumstances of his birth, he realized now, had merely been the excuse he looked for.

The pain he experienced now, to the very depth of his soul, was for the slender girl who had brought him such incredible passion, who now cradled his unborn child in her womb, and had kept the secret to spare him pain.

What if? he questioned.

Her power protected the child, as long as she lived. What if the knife had struck true? Could he bear losing her? Could he bear losing the child they had created together?

He moved out of the chair, removing clothes as he crossed the chamber. He slipped naked beneath the furs, finding her warmth there, joining his warmth with hers as he pulled her to him.

Even in sleep he felt her resistance, so deeply had he hurt her. She stirred, trying to move away from him. He would not allow it but gently pulled her back against him, the silken cap of her head curved at his shoulder, his hand laying protectively over her belly and the small life that grew there.

When she awakened, the stiffness that remained in her shoulder was the only reminder of the injury. The flesh was neatly joined together. All that remained was a narrow ribbon of scar that would soon fade with her healing powers.

Then she felt the familiar warmth at her back and remembered. She stiffened, trying to move away from him. She immediately realized that he did not sleep, but lay awake beside her. She hesitantly turned to him, wondering what to expect.

How long had he lain there watching her? Even now she could feel that warm amber gaze, sensed the turmoil of feelings that he struggled with, and the words that lay unspoken between them.

"There is nothing between me and Truan. He is a friend, nothing more," she began hesitantly, only to feel the warmth of his fingers against her lips, silencing her. Then, she felt the warmth of his hand stroke down low across her belly, lingering over the still flat span between her hips.

She felt his weight shift in the bed beside her, then the tender, stunning warmth of his lips as he bent and kissed her there. His arms encircled her waist. He lay low beside her, his cheek resting against her belly as he tenderly held her.

Humility and tenderness were alien to him, yet he humbly, tenderly held her, cradling her as if she was fragile as rare glass . . . cradling, too, the child that grew within her. It brought tears to her eyes. Tears as warm as those she felt beneath his cheek at her belly.

She stroked her hand through the thick mane of his hair, bound by passion and love in the single touch of a hand, holding onto him against the darkness of the night.

Fifteen

A warm wind blew from the west, a falseness of spring that was still a few weeks away, but brought a brief respite from the harsh winter.

Snow melted in the courtyard, making it possible to reach the dwellings that lined the streets of Camelot for the first time since the new year. The stables were thrown open, advantage taken to exercise restless horses. Carts slogged through the muddied streets, bogging down, drivers helping one another with the simple joy of being able to be outside no matter the gruesome task.

The morning meal was long past. His men had already left to make the most of the break in the weather with predictions from the peasants that it would not last. For a brief, rare moment, they were alone. Even Pippen had ventured outside, no doubt in search of edible treasure different from the apples even he had grown weary of.

It was peaceful here, the pale walls of Camelot glowing around them as the sun poked tentatively through an uncertain sky and Cassandra was loathe to leave, but there were countless chores to see to, and she had promised to teach Amber more about the healing arts. She rose from her chair and felt the warmth of Stephen's hand closing over hers. Wordlessly, he pulled her to him.

The lines had eased about his eyes and mouth the past weeks, as if some great burden had eased. Or as if some decision might have been reached. But he had not spoken of it. In truth, there had been few words between them, and none about the child. He held himself from her, as if the knowledge of the child had changed his feelings for her. Changed them in a way that left her feeling empty and aching with loneliness.

But now, the expression on his face and in his eyes was different, the same as it had been that first time after learning of the child when he had humbly come to their bed and cradled her in his arms through the night.

He gently pulled her down upon his lap, his fingers lacing through hers. He turned her hand in his, gazing down at her slender, pale fingers entwined with his as though seeing something she could not see even with her great powers. Then he lowered his head, his lips caressing the opened palm of her hand as it lay in his, with such incredible tenderness that it took her breath away.

"You are my life," he whispered. "You are my blood, my heart, my soul, the very air I breathe." His eyes were closed, thick dark lashes laying against bronzed cheeks. Then his eyes slowly opened as he looked up at her. The expression in them was tormented. The expression of a man who senses things spinning beyond his ability to control them.

The words tore at her heart. She tried to still them with her fingers against his lips, the words painful as if they were wrenched from his soul and bringing tears to her eyes.

"Milord, please . . ."

But he would not be silenced. "I have heard that for some women the bearing of a child is a difficult thing. I would gladly bear your pain. I would gladly spill my blood in your place. But if anything were to happen to you because of me, I could not bear it."

This then was what had kept him from her these weeks since learning of the child. Suddenly she knew it with a clarity that startled her. She had tried to pluck the reason from his thoughts and had not realized that it was not to be found there, but instead in his heart. He feared for her because of the child.

In all their time together, she had rarely tried to know his thoughts. It seemed somehow important to her that he express his feelings through the touch of a hand, his mouth against hers, his body within hers in the most elemental way between mortal men and women. And the only time she had shared her own thoughts with him were in those impassioned moments when they came together and she gave all of herself to him, allowing him to see, feel, and experience what she saw, felt, and experienced as they came together, in a way that gave deeper meaning to their joining as if in those shared moments they truly became one soul.

Now, the only way to make him understand the enormous strength and power that flowed through her, protecting her from his worst fears, was to give him that part of her again. To open her thoughts, the very essence of her, in a joining that went beyond the physical as her lips tenderly sought his.

Familiar warmth flowed between them, then deepened as she took him with her into that place where her power dwelled, that place where their child grew strong and protected. So that he saw within her, saw the strength of the ages that flowed within her, and in the sweet, tender passion that connected them, saw, too, the son sleeping safe within her.

As the kiss ended, his eyes slowly opened. They glowed with a tenderness of love she had hoped but never believed she might see. His hand spread across her slightly rounded stomach, as if he might touch the son he had just seen. Tears welled in his eyes. Her name whispered from his lips as he laid his forehead against hers filled with awe and wonder, his mouth again seeking hers with a sweet, stirring of passion.

"The morning is young, milord," she whispered. "Everyone is gone. No one will notice if you are gone a while longer."

Stephen laid her across the pallet of furs with the greatest of care, his hands trembling as he removed her clothes—the bliaud, woolen gown, and finally the whisper thin chemise that had tormented him for weeks with glimpses of her slender body—until she lay gloriously naked before him.

There in the light of day that broke feebly through the amber-colored panes, he noticed the subtle changes. The slight roundness of her belly below her still slim waist, the fullness of her breasts, tiny veins visible beneath the pale skin, the dusky nipples, thick and engorged, then taut and puckered in the chill air.

But she seemed not to feel the cold that still gripped the chamber in spite of the sun as she reached for him with fevered hands. When her fingers tangled in leather lacings first at his tunic, then at his pants, she grew frustrated and impatient and willed them away. But relieved of the lacings, she preferred the mortal way as she slowly divested him of his tunic, peeling it back from powerful muscles at his chest and shoulders that leapt beneath each stroke of her mouth that followed her seeking hands.

Next his boots, followed by pants, which she slowly skimmed down over firm buttocks and heavily muscled thighs, her breath whispering across tormented places, his fists clenching at his sides, veins standing out at his neck and arms as he held himself from her and let her have her way with him. Then he felt her slender hand gliding down the shaft of his aching flesh, stroking the length of him from tip to base, fingers stroking through the nest of dark hair to cradle sacks of heavy flesh.

He groaned and swore at the same time, then swore again as her mouth followed where her fingers led, her tongue gliding wetly down the length of him, her breath tickling the hairs, then her tongue gliding lower as she suckled heavy flesh into her mouth.

His hands went back through her hair in silent agony, as if he could not bear it, as if he would push her from him, then gliding back to cup her small head, holding her against him as she slowly made love to him with her mouth, tasting every part of him, slowly returning up the length of that throbbing shaft to take the swollen, engorged tip deep into her mouth.

He tried to slow her, but she would not, or could not. Some deep inner hunger seemed to take hold of her. Glorious color spread across her skin and gleamed in her eyes, as she suckled him deeper and deeper between her lips, until he felt himself deep at her throat. His skin gleamed. Sweat beaded across his chest and shoulders.

"My God, Cassandra," he cried out, feeling what little control he had left surrender to her sweet, suckling lips. Still, she refused to release him.

Her lashes lay like sooty crescents against her cheeks, quivering, then slowly lifting. The eyes he stared into were not mortal eyes, but glowed from that immortal soul within her.

She felt the first spasm at the heavy hot flesh cradled in her hand, that moment when his seed poured forth from the very center of him in violent quakes that shuddered through him; his hands going back through her hair as he held her, and the sudden hot sweetness of him exploding at the back of her throat.

She took all of him, suckling him in rhythm with the

spasms that rocked through him, in unison with the first spasms that began low inside her.

Her eyes glistened. Her lips glistened with his sweetness as he slowly withdrew. Her full breasts rose and fell in torment of the desire that waited within her. One hand slipped about his neck as she pulled him down to her. Her other hand brought his still rigid flesh to the aching opening of her.

"Cassandra?" The question she heard in the sound of her name was wordlessly answered as she pulled him deep inside her in one, long clean thrust.

She arched beneath him, her head going back as her slender hips clung to his. Again and again she met each thrust, with a powerful strength that was stunning, almost frightening in its intensity and need. Then he felt her shudder and the beginning spasms that rocked through her. Her breath caught at the back of her throat in that sound that moved through his soul, then expelled as she cried out his name.

"The walls have begun to talk," Meg remarked at the midday meal. "They even speak names. Particularly names," she said with the curve of a smile as she turned toward Cassandra.

"I think I heard milord's name as I passed by the upstairs chamber this morn. It must be an omen."

Cassandra practically choked on her thick slice of buttered bread. From his chair at the hearth where he took his meal with Truan and Sir Gavin, she felt Stephen's heated gaze upon her and then the laughter that sprung into his eyes as he heard Meg's comment.

Margeaux was conspicuously absent, much to everyone's relief. The mood was greatly lightened because of it.

"Or perhaps," Meg speculated, turning that pale

sightless gaze in the direction of the hearth and the men's voices there. "It was a hungry rat."

"We do not have rats," Cassandra said firmly, hoping to steer the conversation in another direction even as she grew warm once more at the memory of the hours past. Even now her full breasts swelled with desire, straining the front of her gown.

"Perhaps mice then," Meg continued her speculation.

"Aye," Stephen agreed, his amber gaze smoldering at the memory. "Hungry mice."

"I think I am needed elsewhere," Cassandra said. "The weather will not hold and I wish to visit some who have been taken ill during the winter." With that she abruptly rose and gathered the basket of herbs and powders she'd been sorting through. Refusing to look at either Meg or Stephen, she asked Amber to join her.

The wind had cooled since morning, bringing with it the smell of more snow and reminding them that the respite was brief. They called on several cottages, leaving pouches of soothing herbs and powders in different mixtures according to the complaint.

Clouds filled the sky as they left the last cottage with rounds of warm bread in payment tucked inside the basket. Large, fat snow flakes drifted down on ground that was already white. It had been snowing for some time.

They returned to the main hall, dispensing the bread to the kitchens and shaking snow from their boots and mantles. Amber's cheeks glowed. She was an intelligent girl and a quick study of the different combinations of herbs and powders that brought relief to different maladies. It pleased her to be able to help others. As she hung her mantle on a peg near the main hall, she saw Meg anxiously hovering nearby in the arched doorway.

She knew Stephen and Sir Gavin had decided to ride

out earlier. He was determined to send patrols beyond the walls of Camelot to determine if Malagraine's army had yet advanced through the northern passes with the break in the weather. Fear closed an icy fist around her heart, even as she sensed that the trouble was not with him.

"What is it?" she asked taking the old woman's hand in her own. She immediately felt the connection of thought. Margeaux!

"She has been gone since just past midday. I did not discover it until I took a soothing tea to her chamber. It was then I discovered her gone. She took warm clothes."

"And a horse from the stables," Truan added as he joined them. He had remained behind

"The fool!" Cassandra groaned. "She knows the weather cannot be trusted."

But even as she said it aloud she knew the weather was what had decided her. The brief respite was all Margeaux needed to make her escape in an unguarded moment when others thought she slept, the gates of Camelot opened as Stephen and his men left. How easy it must have been to slip outside along with the column or the residents who sought to hunt in the nearby forest to replenish meat for the kitchens.

"Which direction? Did anyone see her leave?"

"A set of tracks leads into the forest," Truan answered. "No hunters rode astride."

Cassandra immediately seized her mantle and tied it about her shoulders. When Meg tired to stop her Cass shook her head adamantly.

"She is my responsibility. She can't have gone far. The storm will slow her."

"I'm going with you," Truan said with a finality that accepted no argument. Then he smiled. "Perhaps in this way I can redeem myself."

"Or not!" Meg snorted, thinking aloud what each of them had thought at least to themselves—that things had been far more peaceful of late without Margeaux's presence.

"We must think of the child," Cass told them firmly, pulling her hood up over her head. "If she has been hurt, she will need care."

"And what of the child you carry, going out on this foolish errand?" Meg's hand closed over her arm.

"No harm will come to me. Besides, I do not go alone. I have all the faith in the world that Truan can wield a sword as truly as he wields an apple."

At first snow fell lightly as they followed those tracks through the snow, and Cassandra's hopes remained high that they might soon overtake Margeaux. Then anger at her stepsister's foolishness at risking herself and her unborn child turned to a deeper concern as one hour became two and they were forced deeper into the forest.

Here though, shrouded by the canopy of tree branches overhead, the snow did not fall as heavily. But as they rode on the wind came up, swirling the branches overhead against a leaden sky. When they stopped next, snow had begun to fall much harder, making it difficult to see tracks that rapidly disappeared beneath the newly fallen snow.

Truan walked back to her, leading his horse. "It is not wise to continue," he said with an uncharacteristic frown.

"There is still light. I can discern her tracks."

His gaze met hers. "I will not endanger you."

"There is no danger here. Besides Margeaux, the only creature we are likely to encounter is a rabbit seeking its lair."

She laid a hand on his shoulder and felt the warmth there in spite of the cold, which did not bother her in the least. Her concern had been for him, for he wore only a tunic and breeches tucked inside his boots. She need not have been concerned.

"She can be sharp-tongued, but we must think of the child."

"It is the child I think of. I do not like the sounds in the forest."

She listened with her mortal sense of hearing, trying to hear what he heard. "I hear nothing."

"Precisely," he said, the frown at his mouth disappearing into the dark silk of his beard. "We see the wind blowing in the trees yet we do not hear or feel it. 'Tis unnatural."

So intent had she been on following those elusive tracks through the snow that she had closed her other senses to their surroundings. She frowned as she realized his meaning.

"We have come this far," she said with a sudden, growing uneasiness. "We cannot turn back now."

As light faded from the sky overhead, darkness descending upon darkness, the storm grew about them. Snow whipped at their faces and stung at the eyes. The horses continued onward, heads down, guided by Cassandra's inner sight of those tracks she could not see in the mortal way but sensed nonetheless. Then just ahead, a dark shape loomed in the gathering whiteness of snow.

Truan rode on ahead. Cass quickly joined him.

"What is it? Is she hurt?"

Truan strode back toward her, his face set with an unreadable expression. "She is not here. 'Tis her horse."

"Then she must be nearby."

"Perhaps."

"What is it? Have you found something else?" But he said nothing as he guided her past the fallen horse. Cass glanced down at the poor creature, thinking it had succumbed to a broken leg or exhaustion. It was neither. All that remained of Margeaux's horse was a shriveled and wasted carcass as if it had lain there for months wasting away, the only means by which she knew it had not was the torn piece of fabric that clung to the buckle at the saddle. She recognized it as the same fabric in the gown Margeaux had worn that morning.

"We return." Truan said.

"We do not! She is out here. I will not return until she is found." She glanced to the sky, needing no light to find her way, but needed it for her argument. There was still some gray in the sky.

"A few minutes more. She can't have gone far afoot. If we have not found her soon, then I will agree to return."

There was no arguing with her. Truan saw it in the stubborn set of her slender jaw.

"Only till last light," he told her in a voice that tolerated no argument. "And even then, Lord Stephen will be ready to flay me alive."

"It is my decision."

"Somehow I do not think he will be entirely convinced of that."

They rode on, the storm stunning as the freezing cold whipped about them, making it all but impossible to see, even to breathe so that they were forced to cover the lower part of their faces.

Cassandra cast her thoughts afar, searching the vast darkness of the forest that loomed before them, trying to find some essence of Margeaux that would tell which direction she had gone.

"There!" she pointed through the blinding snow. "She is near." She slipped from her horse and plunged through the whiteness, guided by her inner sight, closing her eyes to the storm, letting the power become her eyes, seeing as surely as if the snow ceased and the sun shone bright overhead.

Then fear welled inside her as she found what she sought. Not a hundred yards ahead, she saw Margeaux lying in the snow. She plunged on ahead, Truan close behind, his voice reaching through her vision of inner sight as he called a warning.

She found Margeaux just as she had seen her in her vision. She lay crumpled in the snow. Cass called out as she went to her, gathering her in her arms, guilt welling inside her for all the sharp words between them. Margeaux's head rolled back against her shoulder, her eyes wide, staring, stricken.

"Help me!" Cass cried out as Truan broke into the clearing behind her. As she lifted Margeaux against her, she seemed somehow unbearably light. Then she saw the bloodied snow beneath her.

"She's hurt. The baby." But even as she pulled at the folds of Margeaux's mantle, searching with a healer's hands, trying to find some essence of the child. Truan's hand closed over her shoulder.

"Leave her!"

Her stunned gaze met his. "What sort of monster are you?"

"She is already dead! You cannot help her!"

"The child!"

"Now!" Truan pulled her away with a strength that stunned her. It defied her own as she fought him.

"Look at her!" he said fiercely, turning her toward Margeaux's crumbled body and sightless staring eyes. The mantle lay open across her prostrate body. Her gown was soaked and bloodied, but not what Cassandra would have expected from the recent birth of her child.

Her gown had been torn open, and the flesh beneath

it as well, blood pouring from the womb still warm from the child that had recently laid there. But no more.

Cass stumbled and almost went to her knees. The child had been violently taken from her, the surrounding flesh torn as if she had been attacked by some creature.

"The baby," she whispered, beginning to tremble inside as her thoughts turned to the child that rested within her. Truan did not answer, but pulled her toward the horses.

"The baby!" she repeated fiercely, trying to break his hold on her arm, but she could not. When she willed him to release her, there was no response. Fear began to grow inside her.

"What happened to the baby?" For no matter how her thoughts searched for some essence of the child, she sensed only darkness.

"It is as good as dead!"

"No! There is a chance it might be alive!"

He spun her around, his fingers bruising at her arms. "Better off dead! Than what awaits!"

"What are you talking about?"

As if in answer the wind suddenly came alive around them, howling through the tops of the trees, then plummeting down on the floor of the forest, dragging at them, whipping their clothes about them, sucking the very air from their lungs. Terrified, the horses bolted, disappearing into the swirling miasma of darkness and bitter cold that rapidly closed round them like some violent beast that attacked the forest.

Truan pulled her against him, turning her head into his shoulder.

"We must find shelter," he shouted over the roaring of the wind that pulled at them from all directions as though trying to tear them apart. But there was no shelter to be found. It was as if they had been cast adrift in a bitter cold world of unearthly wind and darkness.

Cass turned her thoughts inward, summoning the power of the Light, drawing upon it as she held his hand in hers, giving him warmth that would sustain them. Weakness poured through her and she gasped at the pain low inside her as if the coldness reached inside for the child that lay there.

Truan felt the unusual strength that wavered within her, then the shiver that spasmed through her slender body. Wordlessly, he stripped the mantle from her shoulders, even as the darkness closed round them as though with powerful hands.

He pulled her to the ground, sheltering her with his body. As he lowered the mantle over them both, she glimpsed the Darkness beyond, a pervasive evil of despair, death, and destruction so vast and encompassing that she knew in her soul mankind could not survive it. And it reached out to her.

As he drew the mantle tight about them, Truan glanced out across the clearing into the storm. He saw a figure huddled in the snow. It slowly stood, half formed, naked, a darkness of shadow. And as it stood, it grew from the size of a child to that of a man. As the snow and wind swirled about it, the creature looked back.

For several long moments that might have been no more than a heartbeat, Truan and the creature stared at one another. Then it turned and fled into the storm, swallowed within the darkness as if it had never been there at all.

He pulled the mantle tight about them, certain in his heart that he had just seen Margeaux's child.

It was as if invisible hands tucked the edges about them, sealing out the cold, protecting them, giving them warmth that glowed about them with the power of light and hope. A golden, protective cocoon that held the darkness at bay, a place where it could not enter, a safe place that sheltered them both, and her unborn child.

She had no idea how much time passed. Only that the wind ceased to roar about them. Slowly the light within their protective shelter faded until it seemed to escape beneath the edges of the mantle. Wordlessly, Truan leapt to his feet, his stance that of a warrior as he gazed about the still clearing, but the look in his eyes different than she had ever seen.

Wordlessly, he pulled her to her feet, securing the mantle about her shoulders once more, and they left the forest. They found their horses, wild-eyed and trembling at the edge of the greensward.

In the distance the lights of the watchtowers winked across the battlements. Huge bonfires had been lit in the outer courtyard. Against the glow of those fires they saw the open gates and the mounted warriors that amassed.

She sensed that Stephen returned. But any sense of relief that accompanied it was smothered by a new and more desperate urgency. He and his men gathered to ride against Malagraine.

With a single touch, Truan quieted the horses and helped her astride. Neither spoke as they rode toward the gates of Camelot.

The call went out along the battlements as they returned. Old Meg met them at the doors of the main hall, her wise sightless eyes watching Cass intently.

"Lady Margeaux?" she asked.

"She is dead." In her connection with the old woman's thoughts she learned what she feared most.

"Aye," Meg said gravely. "They ride against Malagraine."

She immediately climbed the stairs to the starchamber. At the entrance to the chamber, alive with a fierce urgency, as Stephen and his men planned their strategy, she told Truan, "Say nothing of what we have seen."

She slowly descended the steps into the grand chamber once ruled by an ancient king, feeling the darkness of events she could not stop or alter weighting her down with each step.

As in those ancient times, Stephen's knights had taken their places about the table, swords laid with gleaming blades converging on the center point of the table. As Truan joined them, Stephen's head lifted from the crudely drawn maps laid out before him. His gaze met hers in silent communication of love and passion, and something she had never seen in his eyes before—fear.

Then it was gone and he was bending over the round table once more, his thoughts consumed with what lay before them. He had no time for her, yet she remained for a time, listening to their talks of battle, watching their grim faces, but most of all watching him, committing every feature to memory as a sense of something inevitable slowly wrapped around her.

Then she left, knowing that they would share a few brief hours before he and his men left, knowing as well what she must do.

She found the old woman sitting before the hearth in the lord's chamber. Cass sat across from her, extending her hands to the fire against the cold that seemed to have settled deep inside her after the encounter in the forest. A cold she could not seem to escape. Her hand curled protectively over the slight roundness beneath her gown.

Meg watched her with blind old eyes. She sensed there was an acceptance now that had not been there before. The anger and defiance were gone, as well as the stubborn resistance to the legacy she had been born to. She needed no power of insight to know Cassandra's thoughts were of the child that grew inside her. A child for whom there might be no future if she did not accept her legacy.

Cass stared down at the tapestry, spread across the table, those dark images uncertain and as terrifying as those encountered in the forest, the slender form barely visible there woven through with threads that caught the light and shimmered blue one moment, brilliant violet the next. Herself. Her fate in the threads not yet woven.

"Tell me what I must know."

When it was done she sat back in the chair. "Is there any hope?"

"There is always hope."

Cassandra stroked her fingers across the images of the tapestry, woven there by a young woman whose blood flowed through her veins. She had no idea if there would be an answer.

"You have only to reach out to her," Meg said in reply to the unasked question.

Cass turned her thoughts inward, drawing on the power reaching out through time and place as she had those many months ago, on a single word—*sister.*

And in the coldness of the chamber, she felt the warmth of love from a kindred spirit, that reached out in reply.

That night as she and Stephen lay upon the pallet of furs, there was a poignancy to their lovemaking, a new urgency that seemed to flow through her and into him, communicating itself in the almost frenzied way they came together. His from the certainty of the battle that lay ahead, hers from the destiny that awaited her but of which she could not tell him. She came to him, the sleek strength of her body arching above his as she straddled him, her eyes bright with love and tears amid the cries of her release.

Afterward, Stephen held her tight, feeling the strength in her, feeling his life in her in the roundness of his child at her belly and he drew comfort from knowing that whatever awaited, what they had shared would live on in the child.

When dawn came, he rose to dress. She clung to him, her eyes bright with tears. Still there were no words. Finally he left her arms, dressing in the pale darkness, the sword gleaming at his side. She gathered warm furs and left the bed.

"I have a gift for you." She moved to the table near the hearth and retrieved something there. It was a rune stone, half formed, with the image of a woman carved into the flat surface.

"It is the other half of the one you stole from me," she told him, pressing it into his hand.

"If a warrior carries it, 'tis said he carries the one he loves with him."

His fingers lovingly stroked the stone. Then he removed the one from about his neck and placed it about hers. "Until the two pieces of the stone are rejoined."

Her face was pale and drawn, filled with a heartbreaking sadness at thoughts he could only guess. He pulled her into his arms with almost desperate strength, his hands stroking and caressing every feature of her face as if he now memorized her. Yet his mouth was incredibly tender as he kissed her one last time.

"Do not follow me to the courtyard. I wish to remember you just as you are, warm with my loving of you," he whispered against the salty sweetness of her lips as her passion mingled with her tears. His hand lovingly caressed her belly.

"Take care of my son." Then he was gone.

It was only a short while later that the outer courtyard was unearthly silent. Stephen and his men were gone, and Truan with them.

Cassandra settled the mantle about her shoulders and tied it. On a last thought she took the smooth polished rune stone she had once worn about her neck and which Stephen had stolen from her when first they met.

He had worn it since, the unusual flat pale stone with the image of the warrior still warm from his touch. She tied it about her neck, the stone dipping low against her heart. The other half, the one Stephen now wore, was the perfect piece that joined with it—that of a woman in all her naked glory. When the two halves were joined, it was as if lovers entwined. She smiled, for he could not have known the fate that awaited him when he had first seized the stone.

She wanted only to stay in that chamber and await his return. To spend all of her days here with Stephen, to feel their child growing strong within her, and then experience that sweet pain as she brought his son forth and laid him in his father's arms. But she could not.

"Forgive me for what I must do," she whispered, sending her thoughts to him.

The wolf padded beside her, nails clicking on the smooth stones as she left and went to the starchamber.

There in that place where an ancient king had once ruled a legendary kingdom of hope and light, she summoned the power. The portal opened and she stepped through it, Fallon following at her side, on a quest to fulfill the legacy she had been born to.

Sixteen

Light surrounded Cassandra, moved through her, and then exploded with a white-hot intensity that was almost blinding.

Images streaked past in a brilliant blur of color, light, and time, impossible to discern. Voices, like a multitude of souls, called out, whispering, laughing, weeping, tender words spoken, dreams lost, and dreams found.

Remember . . .

Five hundred years swept past her, generations of time, a multitude of lifetimes lived and then only remembered, then passing away beyond memory into legend. Only a single step from the time and place she had been born to, into a world that for some existed *only* in legend.

Then the light slowly receded, fading as she stepped through the portal into the starchamber. Not as she'd left it, but as it had once been with the round table in the center of the great room, the wood rich and gleaming, carved with those panels of Latin words—honor, bravery, courage, and truth.

She slowly walked around it, fingers lightly touching each of the twelve places with a medallion inlaid in the wood. Each of the medallions carried a crest. One was slightly larger than the others and bore the royal crest of the regent—Arthur—and his knights of the round table.

"We have been waiting for you."

Startled, Cassandra whirled around. The man who had spoken stood at the top of the stairs.

He was tall and lean. The blue tunic he wore fell to his knees just above his boots, molding long thighs. His hair was dark and fell to his shoulders. Above the full, dark beard, his eyes were an intense shade of blue.

He was young, no older than Stephen and moved with that same intensity. He might have been a warrior, a scholar, or a king. He was none of those but instead wore the medallion of royal high counselor.

For a moment she was too stunned to speak. Emotions swept through her—surprise, disbelief, anger—and other emotions buried deep for so long she could not even name them, as she confronted King Arthur's counselor. Merlin. Her father!

She finally found her voice. "You do not understand. I have come because . . .

"I know why you have come," he told her. As he turned, he seized her by the arm.

"There is little time. Even now we may be too late." He opened the door. She had no choice but to follow.

The starchamber had been quiet, a place frozen in time. What had been and was again. By contrast, the rest of Camelot exploded in frantic activity over which hung an air of desperation. Camelot was under siege.

He took her to the royal chamber. She drew up at the door, caught by her own memories shared with Stephen in this very same chamber, in that other time. Then she saw the king.

Legend and myth entwined with the reality in the man who lay on the pallet of thick furs. He was handsome with closely cropped russet hair, in the full of his manhood, his long body filling the bed. Above the blanket spread over him, she saw bare shoulders and chest. The massive chest rose and fell with great effort, in shallow struggling breaths.

His knights surrounded him, their features gray and haggard. The blood of battle stained their tunics. All carried swords. In their taut, expectant gazes she saw that she was their last best hope for the man who lay so near death.

Merlin's firm hand at her back gently guided her forward. But it was compassion and awakening sorrow that drew her hand to the fallen king. There was no fever, only the coolness of death that waited.

"You must do all that you can, mistress," one of his knights implored her as they stood by his bed in a protective ring, their swords gleaming in the light of the oil lamps.

A tear-stained face looked back at her from across the pallet. The drawn, delicate features, the fall of golden hair that fell about her shoulders in unkempt disarray, the torment in soft gray eyes, of the queen who had betrayed him. But Cassandra saw only misery in her eyes, and in the softly whispered word at her lips.

"Please."

She nodded, even as she sensed the futility of it.

"I will do what I can." She moved to the side of the pallet and lifted the edge of the blanket. One of his knights held a lamp overhead.

The king had been gravely injured. He had taken three deep sword wounds which were thickly bandaged to staunch the flow of blood. Each of the wounds by itself might be survived, but the whole of them could not.

Even now as she laid her hand at his heaving chest and opened her thoughts, she sensed death already upon him and heard it in the rattle at his lungs as he fought for every breath he took. Still, she fought to save his life, to hold onto that precious life force with the silent thought—Might I be able to change it all, if only he lives?

She closed the gaping wounds, and rejoined muscle and tendon. She joined the life force within herself with that last fierce strength with which he clung to this world.

In that bond through those long hours, she learned of his dreams as a boy, his ambitions as a warrior and king, his greatest joys and greatest sorrows, and of his love for the woman who kept her tearful vigil at his side.

Very near dawn, many hours after she had stepped through the portal, the king slowly opened his eyes and looked upon his knights. His breathing had eased. The pain of struggle was gone from his face.

One by one, he called out the names of his knights. One by one they raised their swords to him as the queen softly wept. He touched her hand, his fingers lacing through hers—a touch that somehow reached deep inside Cassandra and made her want to look away at the tenderness of it. As if she had seen something intimate that should only be shared by two people.

"Forgive me," he whispered. The queen raised her tear-stained face, her expression grief-stricken, filled with anguish.

"Forgive me for not believing in you, as you believed in me." His breathing grew shallow, he struggled for the next words with his last dying breath. His next words might have been for her or his knights.

"Remember, what once was, can be again."

His chest rose and fell once more, then rose no more. His hand lay slack in the queen's, his eyes looking upon the last thing he chose to see in this life—the woman he had loved.

Tears filled Cassandra's eyes. In all the legends, in all the stories told and retold round fires at night down through the centuries, none had told of these last moments. When the king became the man once more, his body bound by human frailties, vulnerable to the sword and the wounds of the human heart.

The king was laid in his finest raiment, dressed in death by those who had served him in life—his knights. Then his sword was laid at his side. While in the hills and mountains beyond, a great army gathered, an army of Darkness, and as in the time she had left, Camelot prepared for the end as history and the legend played themselves out.

The streets soon became deserted, inhabited only by armed warriors and knights, the last of Arthur's once mighty army, all but destroyed at a place called the "broad moor," the king betrayed by one of his trusted knights. In another time it would be called Brodmir where another battle was fought. *What once was would be again.*

The leaden sky lowered over the dark mountains. A cold wind filled the courtyard and halls, darkening the sandstone walls and filling the corners of the castle with waiting shadows.

She sensed a presence in the chamber, an essence that was part of the past and the future, deeply bonded to her through the blood they shared. Her father.

"What of the queen?" she asked.

"Taken to a place of safety, even as we speak," Merlin replied. There, she knew, to live out the rest of her days in the silent seclusion, according to legend closing herself off from the world, living on dreams and memories.

"You must leave as well," he told her, urgency filling his words. "Only his knights remain. They will stay until the end."

"What of you?"

He smiled sadly. "I have my own fate to play out."

"A fate that need not be," she hurriedly told him. "I have come here because . . ."

"I know why you have come, Cassandra," he said with such tenderness that she suddenly could find no words. Startled, she looked up at him through the wavering light of the dying flames at the hearth. She had not yet even told him her name.

And again he said, "I have been waiting for you."

"You know why I have come here?"

"It was foreseen," he replied stoically. Then his voice broke faintly. "When I learned of it, I tried to prevent it so that none of this might ever touch you."

He reached out, a young man born with immortal powers, who had already glimpsed his own destiny, and having glimpsed it had summoned a vision of the future beyond. That future stood before him.

He longed to touch her, this beautiful young woman, his child of the future. His daughter.

But she did not know him as he knew her. As he had seen her in his visions, this daughter whose powers were almost as great as his own, who had journeyed back through time to reclaim the hope for the future.

His fingers curled into a fist of emptiness. There was no time to heal the pain and anger. That could only come in the future. There was only time enough to help her.

She felt his thoughts reaching out to hers and resisted them. The choice she had made to come here was not for him, but for the child she carried.

"Just as I tried to protect you and your sisters in the only way I could," he replied in answer, reading her thoughts.

She didn't want to believe it. She'd spent a lifetime hating him for it.

From outside the walls of Camelot a great wind came. It rattled the windows and doors, then smothered the flames at the oil lamps, bringing with it the smell of battle and death.

It suddenly became cold in the chamber. As cold as it had been in the forest that last morning when she and Truan had followed Margeaux. As cold as death.

He sensed it, too. "There is no more time," he said urgently. He seized her by the wrist. "You must go. Leave before it is too late. Before the Darkness finds you here as well."

They fled through darkened hallways, Fallon loping beside her. They met Arthur's knights at the entrance to the starchamber and retreated inside, throwing the massive bar across the large double doors. There Sir Bors, Melodor, and the other knights drew their swords and prepared to make their final stand as the Darkness found them and hurled itself against the massive doors.

The doors were battered relentlessly, timbers creaking and groaning. They splintered under several more blows then began to give way. Smoke purled under the doors, as fires were laid. Soon the Darkness would be upon them.

Merlin pushed her into the farthest corner of the chamber, at the back wall where Arthur's crest was carved into the stone, a circular crest repeated in the pattern of the round table—the circle of life and the promise that what was would be again.

He drew his sword as more blows fell against the doors, smoke filling the chamber. As the doors finally gave way and the Darkness swarmed in on them, he raised his sword high overhead and struck a blow against the center of the crest set in stone.

Sparks flew as steel struck stone at the wall. The center of the stone circle shifted and opened. In the small niche at the center of the crest was a crystal orb suspended within a golden ring.

It was the size of a man's hand and perfectly round, a magnificent crystal, suspended in that golden orb, slowly turning, reflecting millions of lights like the stars in the heavens. If the Darkness claimed it, there would be no hope for the future.

"Take it," Merlin said. "It is what you came for. It is the only hope for the future."

Her gaze met his as those dark warriors with death behind their faceplates fought their way through the chamber.

"Come with me," she said fiercely. "You've seen the future. If you stay, you'll be banished to the mist."

He shook his head. "If I were to join you in your time, then you will not exist. This is my destiny, Cassandra. You must fulfill yours."

One-by-one Arthur's valiant knights fell under the swords of Darkness, in the same places where they were found five centuries in the future their weapons still clasped in hands that crumbled to dust.

"You must go now!" Merlin told her, pushing her toward the back wall of the chamber. Then he smiled at her gently.

"Your future is my future." Then he turned to face the Darkness that seemed to reach for him with outstretched hands in the forms of those horrible dark warriors with death at their helms.

"Father!"

At the sound of that word, Merlin turned and looked at her, his blue eyes intense. When she still hesitated, he joined his powers with hers, summoning the Light, opening the portal, sending her from him as he had in that other time to protect her. Fallon leapt through the portal with her.

As it closed behind her, she heard those distant sounds of battle. The fierce cries of those brave knights as they fought and died, and the tender, loving thought that connected with hers.

"I will always be with you, my daughter."

* * *

She stepped through the portal from one world into the next, sight and sound sweeping past her, images appearing then disappearing, powerful forces pulling her toward the light.

She clutched the Oracle of Light in her hand as her other hand closed over the rune stone, like a talisman that guided her home.

Then she was stepping through, returning, and through the opening ahead she saw the starchamber, reaching out to her. She stepped through and immediately knew that something was very wrong.

It was the same, and yet it was not. It was changed, somehow altered, not the world she had just left nor the one she had journeyed from, but a world between the two worlds, where there was no light, only darkness.

She turned back, trying to return through the portal, drawing on the power deep within her to keep the portal open.

She felt unseen forces pulling at her and knew the powers of Darkness were there. She had not left soon enough. The Darkness had followed her through the portal as she escaped. She thrust her hand into the portal, trying to hold onto the power but it grew more faint with each passing moment, closing in on itself. As it closed, she saw Fallon running toward her.

"Go back!" she cried out in warning as the opening collapsed. She felt the coarse brush of fur against her hand, the velvet warmth of Fallon's tongue, then the portal closed and Fallon was gone.

As she turned back to the star chamber she felt the sudden cold that closed around her. When she tried to leave the chamber she discovered she could not. Some sort of invisible wall prevented it.

No matter which direction she tried to escape, she

found herself stopped by that wall—a wall of ice that slowly closed round her until she could no longer move.

She tried to summon her powers but found she could not. Then her thoughts no longer seemed clear to her. And always there was the coldness, moving through her blood, reaching deep inside as though it reached for the child.

She turned her thoughts inward surrounding the child with the last glow of warmth within her, protecting it with the last ray of light that struggled feebly within. And her last thought as a single tear spilled down her cheek and joined with the ice that enclosed her was of Stephen.

"Remember . . ."

The portal opened from one world into the next, a narrow ribbon of light that briefly glowed, then wavered and slowly grew fainter. The wolf clawed its way through the fading opening, and collapsed on the other side. Tangled in its white coat was the rune stone.

Seventeen

Stephen and his men sat astride their horses on the muddied field near Brodmir, where once before they had met in battle with Malagraine. But with prophetic truth, he had known that Malagraine would not again be lured into the forest. And so they met on that small, wide plain confronting an enemy met twice before.

Many thoughts ran through his mind. All of them came back to one. Cassandra and the child she carried. His child.

There had been no words between them in the hours before he left. Only that communication of touch as they made love as though it might be for the last time. Now there was so much he wanted to say to her.

That he loved her, that he honored her above all, that he would not make a bastard of the child she carried, that he would speak vows with her wherever and whenever she chose, so long as the joy and passion he had found with her could go on forever.

Forever. A word that held different meanings for both of them.

She was not truly mortal. For her, forever was forever, as long as he could imagine. For him, forever were the moments he spent in her arms, and if the ones past were the last he would ever know then she was his forever.

Then he turned his thoughts to the coming battle and all else was forgotten.

On the distant slopes, Malagraine's army massed. A dark, seething serpentine creature of death and destruction. For days they had gathered there, growing in number, until the slopes of the hills blackened with them.

"So many," Gavin said softly, not with fear but with that resoluteness of having faced many enemies in battle, and seeing a formidable one now facing them.

"It reminds me of Hastings when we fought beside King William."

"Aye," Stephen replied, his narrowed gaze fixed on that distant slope as his men flanked to the left and right in a wedge.

"Only now, we are a bit outnumbered."

When the battle came, they would ride into the enemy, driving that wedge into the heart of the beast.

For a moment he thought of his father, and in that thought, hoped that he would die well. In his death perhaps the king would at last find some small pride he could not show him in life.

Truan's sharp blue gaze met his. Stephen could have sworn he saw laughter there.

"Perhaps a bit," Truan acknowledged as his gaze then scanned the distant slope. "I put it at twenty to one odds."

"Is that all?" Gavin replied incredulously, joining in the game, needing the moment of play to ease the tension of waiting. He scoffed. "Then we've nothing to worry about." His gaze met Stephen's. Both knew the odds were closer to thirty to one.

"We faced that number at Antioch, when first you earned your spurs. It was a good day. And this is a good day."

Stephen nodded as his gaze searched the sky overhead and the feeble sun that finally broke through. "It is a good day."

Across the valley, a loud roar went up, as the beast seemed to stir. Stephen drew his battle sword.

"You are a fine warrior," he told Truan. "You may guard my back any day."

Truan fixed him with that piercing look that was both laughter and fierceness. "*You* may guard my back, English. And do not fail. I have no desire to feel the beast's blade taking my head from my shoulders."

Then he spurred his horse forward and let loose a powerful war cry. It was answered from that distant slope.

As the beast quivered and then rolled down that distant hillside, Stephen raised his battle sword, sending them charging deep into the heart of the beast.

In an explosion of steel, crashing bodies, and blood they met on that small wide plain. The beast was clearly stunned. Malagraine had not expected them to countercharge so few were their numbers, so great the odds of defeat. Having miscalculated once, he did not miscalculate again as he closed his army round them.

In the center of the battle, Stephen abandoned his horse and took to the ground, cutting his way through the dark-helmed warriors who closed round him, slicing, cutting, sinking down to his knees in mud that quickly ran with the blood of his men, then driving back to his feet.

He and Truan fought back to back, while a few feet away Sir Gavin and the rest of his men formed a defensive circle that slowly grew tighter and tighter. Then, he sensed a change in the warrior he confronted, a hesitation that had not been there before. And over the sounds of battle, he heard a familiar battle cry.

Over the crest of the hill atop the slopes where Malagraine had begun his charge, a vivid line of brilliant purple and gold appeared, shimmering in the midday sun.

Battle standards whipped in the wind as mounted warriors charged down the hill, the sun glinting across the crests on their tunics—the crests of Normandy, Poitoirs, and Anjou—along with the royal standard of a lion rampant on a field of blue. They swept down the hill, closing at Malagraine's back.

When it was over, Stephen and his men stood in a sea of fallen warriors. Faceplates pushed back revealed the faces of Saxon rebels, mercenaries, but in some there were no faces. Truan kicked aside one of the helms, his face a hard, lined mask. Nearby Gavin supported John de Lacey. With the amount of blood that covered both it was impossible to tell whose was the most injured.

Stephen leaned heavily on the handle of his sword, as the mounted warriors who had swarmed down the hill and attacked Malagraine from the back, slowly picked their way through the fallen. They reined in their horses and pushed back their helms.

Stephen nodded his acknowledgment as he stared at the fierce warriors before him.

"What took you so long? I thought we might have them beaten before you could join us."

Tarek al Sharif, swung a leg over the front of his saddle and dismounted in the easy, graceful manner of the desert tribes he had been born to. With his arm resting over the handle of the bloodied curved sword belted at his waist, he slowly strode forward.

"Our friend here wanted to see how you fared in command of your own army?"

Stephen squinted through his helm up at the man still astride, who had been brother, father, and mentor to him. Rorke FitzWarren, high chancellor to King William. He slowly dismounted, pushing back the faceplate of his helm.

"You did well, my friend," Rorke said, reaching out to embrace Stephen. "Foolish, but well. You ignored the basic rule of battle. Never let an enemy know your true strength."

Stephen cocked a brow and glanced past his friend to the army of the king now encamped on the battle-field.

"The enemy did not know my true strength." Then he added, "Nor did I. How is it you knew where to find us?" A lone rider threaded through the line of gathered warriors.

Beneath the midday sun, the bright cap of her hair was like a brilliant flame. Rorke FitzWarren reached up and lifted down the slender young woman with a possessive tenderness, setting her to the ground at his side.

"My sister," she replied. "Cassandra."

"Where is she?" Stephen demanded furiously as he slammed his fist down upon the table in the main hall at Camelot, rattling the platters and sending a pitcher over the edge. It exploded as it hit the stone floor.

Truan gently pulled Amber behind him, protecting her from the anger and flying shards of pottery while Pippen scrambled for cover under an overturned basket.

Rorke FitzWarren and his knights watched with growing uneasiness.

"Where has she gone?" Stephen again demanded. "Is there no one who will tell me?"

Finally old Meg approached, unafraid, her sightless eyes guided by the sound of his voice, and the anger.

"To fulfill her destiny as you knew she must."

"What are you talking about old woman?"

She laid the rolled tapestry on the table before him. With a wave of her thin hand, the tapestry unrolled, the brilliant shimmering images of battles, of knights and warriors, dark and mysterious powers seemingly alive in the glowing threads.

"It is her destiny. You carried it to her in the images of the tapestry."

"Where?" he demanded. "How?"

"She has gone to find the Oracle of Truth."

"She did not believe in it. She would not even speak of it."

"Stubbornness and anger," Meg replied. "Until I feared all might be lost."

Stephen braced his hands at the table, refusing to look at the tapestry, struggling not to believe even after confronting the Darkness twice before, and then again on that recent battlefield, where so many had died and Malagraine had escaped. He knew its power, but he also did not trust the old woman.

"How did you convince her of it? What dark power did you use to turn her heart?"

Meg felt his pain. She ached for him, because she knew he had lost his heart and soul to the Daughter of the Light, those images first glimpsed in the tapestry fulfilled in the entwined figures of the lovers whose hands clasped in the design of the threads, and were now torn apart.

"I could not have convinced her in a thousand years," she answered truthfully. "For I have never possessed the power." Then she stunned him. "You are the one who convinced her of it."

"Me?" he asked incredulously, then angrily, "I think perhaps you have become the fool, old woman. I would never convince her to do this." His voice broke, part anger, part helplessness, "I would never send her to her death."

"It is because of the passion and love she found with you," Meg said gently. "And the child that grows within her."

"Explain yourself!"

Meg's thin hand stroked across the tapestry, the threads strong and sure where they securely wove the fabric and told a story.

"Events that have already come to pass." Her hand passed over the lovers—the warrior and the Daughter of the Light, their images woven there as well, and the images of their separated hands. Then across the shadowy darkness that loomed beyond.

"What was, what is, and what will be," she said. "The future of mankind. Lost if the Darkness cannot be stopped. No future at all for the child she carries." Meg sensed the question that still plagued him.

"It is because of what she found in the forest," she said. "What she saw there convinced her as nothing I could tell her. When she returned, she demanded to know what she must do. If I had not told her, she would have taken the knowledge from me in the old way. I could not have stopped her."

He remembered that day, learning later that she had been to the forest.

"You were with her that day," he said, turning on Truan. "What *did* you find in the forest?"

Anguish tore through him as he listened and learned of Margeaux's brutal death, the storm that had very nearly killed them both, and their encounter with the Darkness.

"The Darkness came to claim its spawn," Meg whispered prophetically. "Born of flesh but with powers that can only be imagined, and feared."

"That was not woven in your tapestry, old woman," Stephen said bitterly.

"A child," Meg acknowledged, tilting her head at the

memory. "It was foretold in the threads. A life for a life."

"But which child?" he demanded. "Margeaux's, or Cassandra's?"

She did not answer, and he knew that she could not.

"There is more," she told him when she sensed that he would listen. She held out her hand. From her fingers dangled a flat smooth stone, only half formed, as though the other half was missing.

On it was engraved the figure of a warrior. It was the stone Cassandra had taken back.

"It was found on the floor of the starchamber," Meg explained. "At the base of the great crest, when the wolf returned alone very near death."

Eighteen

Stephen knelt beside the white wolf. The beast regarded him with great wise silver eyes, then licked his hand. In the days since the wolf had been found in the starchamber, it had greatly recovered from the journey through the portal though it was still weak. Only Fallon knew what had happened beyond the portal. Through the wolf, there might be a chance of finding Cassandra.

"Can it be done?"

Lady Vivian, too, knelt beside the wolf, in that way of those with special powers who have no fear of wild creatures. The wolf accepted her scent as if he knew her, and perhaps he did in the shared bond with his mistress.

Her hair spilled over her shoulder in a fire fall of color. She reminded him of another, in that same tilt of her nose, the same curve of her cheek, stubborn chin, and eyes that were several shades lighter but held that same inner light of the power that burned within all Merlin's daughters.

She rubbed her cheek against the coarse white fur, eyes closing as though she pulled the essence of the creature within her.

"Perhaps," she whispered. "He holds her essence, that last moment when she touched him. Through it there might be a way."

"There must be a way!" Stephen said fiercely. "I will

not accept that she is lost to me." The words were like a memory of another warrior who had been willing to face the Darkness to find her.

She laid a hand on his arm. They were friends and had shared much. He had risked his life once for her. She knew he would gladly give it for the young woman who had claimed his heart.

She stood, her hand resting on the wolf's thick mane of fur in much the way he had seen Cassandra touch the creature.

"The memory of the journey is within Fallon," she said gravely. "If the journey is to be made he must guide the way back."

Stephen anxiously rose to his feet. There was more to it than this. He sensed it. "What else?"

"I do not know if I can open the portal. The power that originally opened it was hers. But it is true that once opened a gateway from one world into the next leaves a signpost."

He looked wildly about. "What signpost?"

"An essence of the energy left behind. The same essence that still clings to the wolf's coat." Closing her eyes, she concentrated her power, drawing on the power. Then holding her hand before her, she slowly blew across her fingers. Her skin suddenly glittered with traces of light, as if she held a thousand stars in her hand.

She walked toward the back wall of the chamber where that ancient crest was carved in stone and slowly passed her hand over every inch of surface. Finally, she exclaimed, "I have found it."

A ribbon of glittering light appeared at the stone as she ran her hand down the length of the wall, the light sparkling in reflection of the light that glittered at her hand.

"It is faint," she told Stephen. Then her gaze lifted to his.

"She sent the wolf back with, even as the portal closed, the last of her power."

Coldness settled inside him. "Is she dead?"

"Death is not the same for us as it is for true mortals." She shook her head. "She is not dead. But, neither is she truly alive."

"Send me through now!" Stephen demanded. "Before the essence is gone and there is no way to find her."

Vivian started to protest. She started to tell him of the risk of such an uncertain journey that he could not even be certain would lead back to Cassandra, much less what he might find if he was able to go back. And then there was the much greater possibility that he would not find her at all, but enter a dimension, a world within a world, where he might be lost forever. Then her gaze met that of her husband, who had come to stand beside her.

"Do what you can," he told her. "His fate is his to choose."

Vivian placed her hand against the stone crest and concentrated all of her powers. This was very different from entering the world where she had been born, and where Merlin had been banished.

That way was as familiar to her as breathing, like stepping into a familiar room through the standing stones. But this was like reaching for the unknown, opening one world and traveling through time and space into another. It required enormous concentration and elements of power she had never possessed.

The power wavered within her. Too hard. She could not do it! Through the pain of concentration she heard those beloved voices. Her mother and father reaching out to her each from the world they now occupied, joining their powers with hers. Then she felt a hand beside hers. A strong, powerful hand. A warrior's hand.

"Perhaps we can open it together," Truan said, closing his hand over hers at the wall. The faint glitter of light at the wall suddenly glowed and expanded. It ran the entire length of the wall and then opened.

Stephen was already beside him, Fallon following at his heel. "I think there is a great deal you have not told me," he told the friend who had fought so well at his back at the battle on the Brodmir plain. Surprisingly well. Or perhaps not so surprising after what he had just seen.

"I will tell you of it when you return, for I cannot go with you on this journey. It is not my destiny. Mine is yet to be."

Vivian stood with them, staring up at the handsome young warrior, trying to delve into his thoughts in the old way so that she might learn the truth. He looked at her.

"Do not play games with me, Vivian. You cannot win."

She glared at him, peeved that she could not see into his thoughts.

"Leave it alone, wife," Rorke told her. "At least let there be some man on this earth who may keep secrets from you." As he approached Stephen, he handed him the sword he had carried in battle against Malagraine's army.

It was an ornate sword, with an elegant carved handle, set with a single, gleaming blue jewel in the crest at the hilt. Excalibur.

"I but carried it to you," he explained. "It was sent by another who entrusts you with both the sword and the life of his daughter."

"I will bring both back with me."

"Remember," Rorke warned. "Nothing is as it seems

in the world where you go. You cannot trust what you see or believe."

"Then what can I trust?"

"Only in what you feel."

"I will remember." With the sword in one hand he knelt beside Fallon.

"You must find her for me. You must be my eyes in the darkness." When he released the wolf, Fallon leapt through the portal. Stephen followed him, stepping through into the light. With his hand buried in the wolf's thick rough, they began the journey.

Once before he had traveled through the portal with Cassandra, but then she had been there, the gentle strength of her hand closed around his, guiding him, protecting him through a world of sight and sound where it was dangerous to be mortal.

It seemed an eternity, but probably no more than a heartbeat, when he felt the wolf's sudden urgency. A tension of energy that communicated itself in the sudden, powerful bunching of muscles beneath his hand, and then he was leaving the light, being cast out of it with a force that doubled him over in pain.

His hold on Fallon was broken. It was all he could do to hold onto the sword. Air was sucked out of his lungs, pain tore through him, then burned at his skin as if it were being peeled from his body. Then he was clear of the portal, plunging into the cold darkness, like plunging into a cold dark lake, the surface of light disappearing above him, while he was dragged deeper and deeper into the cold darkness.

At first he could see and feel nothing but that incredible coldness. Then slowly, he felt the coarse fur beneath his hand and heard a faint whimpering. He could not see. There was no light. He tried moving and felt the shift of Fallon's weight beside him. Then a glimmer of light as his hand eased over the handle of the sword.

He saw it again as he again moved the sword, a reflection of light off the blade. He rolled to his feet and felt the wolf's solid presence against his leg.

"We are here," he whispered. But where was *here?* Was Cassandra here also, or had they emerged from an uncertain journey into an unknown world?

He held the sword before him, in a warrior's stance. Again he picked up that reflection of light. It was stationary, looming just ahead, a pindot of light that might have been a star, or a distant door someone had opened. He took a tentative step but could not determine if he had moved any distance.

"The cursed darkness! It takes away my ability to even crawl like a baby."

Think! he told himself. There must be a way out of this darkness that smothered over him and surrounded him.

Twice before he had confronted the Darkness. He knew its illusions and tricks. Things that appeared one way and were not. He remembered Rorke's warning that he could not trust what he could see. Only what he felt.

In the far eastern empires he had heard of men who felt and saw with eyes closed, touching nothing. His friend Tarek knew of these ways, the letting go of the known world, closing off the senses one usually relied upon allowing others to open. Was it that much different from learning a lover's presence?

To become so much a part of another person through shared thoughts and feelings that it seemed you actually became that person. That you might feel them, feel their pain, their joy, their happiness, their passion without touching or seeing.

He quit straining to see the light and instead closed his eyes. He let his other senses expand, reach out, imagined them drifting outward seeing for him.

Once he let go of the real world he was used to and opened himself to experience what was actually around him, he became aware of many things.

The cold against his skin; air that moved across his face, bringing with it the damp smell of dark places plucked from his childhood. Then the air became a specific movement as if something passed close by him. He instinctively turned and felt the brush of air again, subtle as the stirring of a wing, guiding him in a new direction.

He was climbing, moving steadily upward, his hand in Fallon's thick fur beside him. Then his shoulder scraped against something sharp and damp. He felt the trickle of water at his fingers, then heard the rush of water. He followed the sound, moving toward it, always climbing higher. And above, that distant light grew steadily closer as if he was climbing a mountain. Or up through the inside of a mountain.

The wolf scrambled up after him, scrabbling for a foothold, then clamoring for another. Eventually that light was no more than a hundred yards away. He kept climbing, the scabbard of the sword shifted over his shoulder so that it lay against his back, freeing both hands to climb.

It seemed as if that last hundred yards would never end, but even as he continued on two tortured thoughts turned over and over in his mind. What would he find when he reached the top? How had Cassandra endured this climb, if indeed she was even here?

Finally, he reached the top, that light only a short distance above him. Fallon scrambled on ahead.

"Wait!"

But the wolf was gone. Stephen crawled after him. Even in that meager light, he squinted against the sudden brightness compared to the dark passage he'd crawled out of. He looked around and realized that he was on top of a mountain. He immediately recognized it. Only days before he had looked upon that same mountain, Malagraine's army spread across the slopes below.

But on the slopes that now spread below him, there was no sign of that battle. Then he realized there would not be. He had traveled into another time through the portal, a time where the battle had not taken place. Or perhaps had taken place long ago.

It was a chilling thought.

Down the slope he saw Fallon, the wolf's gleaming coat like a beacon in the pall of gray that hung over the land. Stephen crawled over the rocks and started down the slope after him.

He crossed the Brodmir plain, pausing only to glance at the place where so many had died, their blood soaking the earth. Then he was moving on, running with the wolf, following where the creature led, a journey that took them back to that small valley.

The land he passed through was barren and dead, far more than after the winter thaw. It was a place where nothing had ever lived. A place of death, where faceless creatures lurked in the shadows, appearing then disappearing.

Hunger gnawed at him. How many hours had passed? He could not judge from the sky for it was that relentless, waiting gray that never changed.

He paused only long enough to scoop water from a dark pool, then immediately spat it out for it reeked of death and stagnation. Then they moved on. The wolf settled into a ground-eating lope. He was forced to stay with him or be left behind. He seemed to sense something, perhaps drawn on by that essence of Cassandra that he had carried back with him through the portal. Stephen prayed it was so. But he could not shake off the feeling that they were being led to something.

They encountered no enemies, no creatures of Darkness with human bodies and souls of Darkness like on the battlefield. No dragon appeared, no evil winged creature to pluck out his eyes.

Eventually they reached the valley. In the distance he saw the spires of Camelot, and the dark ribbon of water that surrounded it.

Camelot.

It was where Cassandra had stepped through the portal. It was also the place she had gone to find the Oracle. The Camelot they had shared, and the one that existed five hundred years earlier.

He ran across a barren field, so dry and frozen that not a stock of grass grew there. He glanced to the watchtowers and felt relief at the sight of the guards. The gates opened and Fallon leapt on ahead.

Inside the gates, the city was as he remembered it. Huts and cottages lined the street. A smithy's hammer rang out. A horse cart passed by. Nearby a woman tossed food to chickens who pecked it from the dirt in the outer courtyard. Across the courtyard he saw tethered horses and the banners of warriors.

He recognized those as well as the voices of his men came from the armory. He crossed the courtyard in long strides, seeking the gate of the inner courtyard. Fallon ran on ahead.

Hope growing in his heart, Stephen pushed open the gate. Light glowed at amber-colored glass at the windows high at the main hall.

Was it possible that Cassandra had returned after all? And that in following her journey, he had also returned? If he had ever even left.

The doors of the great hall stood open. Fallon ran through them and disappeared, no doubt in search of her. A fire burned at the hearth. Food had been laid out in preparation for the evening meal. He saw his men sitting as he had seen them countless times, including Gavin. His friend looked up, recognized him, and quickly crossed the room.

"Gavin! It is you!"

Gavin looked at him strangely. "Of course it is me. Who else would it be?"

Stephen shook his head. "I had thought perhaps . . ." Then his gaze turned toward the steps that climbed to the second floor chambers.

"Lady Cassandra?"

Gavin nodded. "She is safe and well. She returned a short while ago."

Relief poured through Stephen. "The others?"

"Everyone is safe and well. Join us in a game at the board, and then supper."

Stephen looked past his friend, reassuring himself that everything indeed was all right. Everything was as it had been. The only one he did not see was Truan. It seemed odd that his friends enjoyed games and Truan was not in the thick of it. Then it was forgotten. He shook his head, his gaze going once more to those stairs.

"Perhaps later."

Gavin laughed and winked knowingly. "Your lady is most anxious to see you."

"Then you can understand my preference to her company over yours."

His friend nodded. "Will we expect you at the evening meal? Or do you dine elsewhere?"

Stephen ignored the crude jest. "Later, my friend." Then he turned and vaulted up those steps, taking them three at a time.

He passed a servant in the hall outside his chamber. She quickly moved past as he lifted the latch of the door and stepped into the chamber.

A fire burned low in the brazier, steeping the room

in soft shadows. A platter of food had been laid out as if Cassandra had anticipated his return. Wine glistened in a goblet. A soft fragrance drifted to him, a sweetness of lavender and sandalwood as she stirred at the pallet where she had been resting.

"Milord?"

Relief poured through him at the sound of her voice, remembered from that last morning when he had left there, the taste and feel of her strong in his senses so that he wanted that for his last memory of her. Soft and yielding.

He watched as she rose from the bed, bathed in shadows, the light from the fire catching briefly at the gleaming dark satin of her hair. She did not come to him, but waited until he went to her.

"I have been waiting for you," she said, as he joined her there, pulling her into his arms. Her body was silken and warm, gloriously naked beneath his seeking hands.

Her hands slipped about his neck, drawing him closer until her full breasts pressed against his chest and lower the stunning fullness of her belly grown much larger with the child. His hands glided down over that fullness to clasp over her hips and she moaned softly as her lips sought his.

Incredible sweetness, unbelievable heat seduced him. In the longing wetness of her mouth clinging to his, in the burgeoning flesh at her breasts, heavily veined, ripe, the dark nipples thick and engorged. Her nails scraped the skin at his shoulders as she eagerly opened his tunic and pressed her mouth against the curve of hard muscle at his chest. Then her hands moved to his belt, his head going back at the wondrous feel of her hands caressing him through cloth.

He pulled her against him, her breasts hot against his bare chest. His mouth in her hair.

"The child?" he asked huskily, concerned for her and

the baby, lest their lovemaking hurt either of them. But she seemed not to hear him as she struggled to free his burgeoning flesh that ached for the feel of her.

"Cassandra?" he whispered. "We can wait."

"No! It must be now."

"I do not wish to hurt you."

"You will not."

"But the child has grown so much."

"No!" she insisted, going down on her knees before him,

"I must have you inside me," she whispered desperately. "You must love me." There was an edge in her voice that added to the frenzy.

He tried to calm her. "I do love you. More than life itself."

Something was wrong. He had never known her to be like this before. Not even that last morning when they parted not knowing if they might ever see each other again. There had always been such strength in her.

Fear knifed through him that there was something she was not telling him. Fear for her and for their unborn child overrode any desire to make love. He gently grabbed her by the wrists, pulling her away from him.

"What is it? Has something happened? Is it the baby?"

He tried to gently lift her to her feet but she jerked away.

"Cass! You must tell me."

She shuddered as he held her away from him, her face hidden by the fall of her hair. Then she seemed to be weeping. Softly at first, then much deeper.

"Cass, for the love of God. What is it?"

Her head came up suddenly. She tried to twist free of his hands. When she could not, she began to laugh.

Wildly. Her head went back and her hair fell back from the sides of her face, no longer hiding her features.

The eyes he looked into were not Cass's deep violet eyes. The mouth that gaped wide with maddened laughter was not Cass's sweet mouth. The features at that horrible distorted face were not hers.

When Stephen tried to push the creature away, she clung to him. When he fought her off she came at him, turning toward him in the full light of the fire in the brazier. A creature that was neither human or alive, but had been once. Lady Margeaux.

Not as she once was, but as she had been in death. He knew she was dead. Meg spoke of what Cass and Truan had found in the forest, Margeaux's mutilated body, the child torn from her. In another time and place. Not this time and place.

The illusion had been so perfect. But as he gazed at her, her form changed and shifted. She was no longer burdened by a child full at her belly. Nor was her figure slender and softly curved. But now slack-breasted and hollow hipped, her hair matted and streak. Dead, lifeless. As dead and lifeless as she.

All of it had been an illusion. It explained why he had not found Fallon here. The wolf had not been fooled.

"You cannot have her," she whispered almost frantically now, her features like a mask of death. Then she laughed, a horrible, evil sound that seemed to strangle at her throat. Nothing at all about her any longer resembled Lady Margeaux who had bargained her soul to the Darkness and lost all.

"She is lost to you. She and the child."

Her sudden movement was like that of an animal, quick and darting as she swept the carving knife from the table and came at him.

The creature was unbelievably strong, sinewy arms

slipping through his hands as he deflected a blow and tried to take the knife away from her. She lunged at him again, slicing him at his forearm. He outmaneuvered her, sidestepping, turning, seizing the sword where he'd carelessly set it aside, wanting so desperately to believe the illusion.

He tried to stun the creature with a blow, but it kept coming at him, like a maddened dog, the madness in her eyes. She struck again, screamed her madness when she failed to connect with the knife then struck again. He shoved her away, torn between the illusion before him, and the images of what she had been.

She leapt at his back, claws raking his shoulder, sinking in deep. All trace of Margeaux was gone. She had never been there. Fighting back to his feet, he threw off the creature. With the snap of a wrist he turned the sword, clasping the butt of the handle with both hands, the blade angled back along his side. When the creature came at him again, throwing itself at his back he thrust the tip of the blade impaling the creature in midair.

He fell to his knees, gasping for breath. Blood ran down the side of his head, mingled with the saltiness of sweat and stung at his eyes. He wiped it away as he pushed back to his feet, in one move freeing the sword from the creature and stepping back as safe distance lest it was not yet dead.

Pain tore through his shoulder where the creature had slashed him. He wiped blood and sweat from the side of his face. Still the creature did not move. He prodded it with toe of his boot, Excalibur angled high overhead to strike if the creature was not yet dead.

It did not move. When he kicked it over with the toe of his boot, it stared back with lifeless eyes shrunken back into its head. A creature that was neither human nor beast.

He doused his face and shoulders with water. That

much seemed real. Then he seized his tunic, pulled it over his shoulder and left the chamber.

The first thing he noticed was that the flames of the oil lamps guttered low, sputtering feebly as if a great length of time had passed. With both hands clasped about the sword, he slowly descended the stairs.

It was changed. All changed. No fire burned on the hearth. No torches burned. He saw no one. Not Gavin nor any of his men. Not the servant he had seen earlier. In spite of the sweat that soaked the tunic, a cold chill ran down his spine. It had all been an illusion.

He backed slowly down the passage that linked the main hall to other chambers, finally reaching the passage that led to the star chamber. There he found Fallon, standing at the chamber door, ears cocked forward, whistling softly in his throat.

Nothing is at is seems.

He laid his hand on the huge iron latch and slowly pushed the door of the starchamber open.

Like the rest of Camelot it seemed exactly as it should be, a perfect, exact illusion as he slowly made his way through the gray shadows. Then Fallon darted past him. Stephen warily turned, holding Excalibur before him as he passed the great round table. Then when he turned again, he saw what had drawn the wolf.

At the back wall of the chamber, in front of the royal crest, where Cassandra had opened the portal and traveled back in time, was an enormous crystal.

It was at least twelve feet high, a crystal orb no less than an equal number of feet in diameter. It seemed to be suspended in air and glittered as it slowly turned as though moved on some invisible current of air.

The facets of the crystal reflected light from the blade of the sword as he slowly approached. The air grew steadily colder, his breath pluming in the air suddenly frigid as winter. He tentatively reached out, wondering what he would find. Another illusion? But when he touched the wall of the crystal orb he discovered it was not crystal at all, but ice!

Then it slowly turned, glittering and reflecting the faint gray light that streaked through the chamber. And as it turned, he discovered something within the icy orb, like a beautiful, delicate creature caught in the liquid flow of amber as a tree pours forth its lifeblood, an image frozen in time. Frozen within the heart of the ice crystal.

The perfect curve of her cheek, the angle of her stubborn chin, thick dark lashes that lay against pale frozen cheeks, the midnight satin of her hair spilling over her shoulders, one slender arm crossed low across the swell of the child she carried inside her as if to protect it, her other arm curved over her heart. And clutched tight in her hand was the mythical Oracle. A much smaller crystal that fit her palm, suspended in a golden orb.

The wolf whined softly as it lay down at the base of the crystal.

Stephen had found her.

Nineteen

"No!"

He was too late to save her. Beautiful, delicate, perfect in every way. She was forever frozen in time, one arm clasped over the place where the child lay within her, the other holding the orb she had risked her life to find.

She had found it. But too late. And then could not return. But she had sent the wolf back.

The animal seemed to sense his agony, coming to him, thrusting its nose against his leg. Stephen knelt beside the wolf, burying his hands in the thick, coarse coat that was the last thing she had touched, leaving some of her essence on the wolf's fur. Perhaps in the hope that he could come for her. Too late!

Then he buried his face in the fur, pouring out his agony and pain, raging against his feeble mortal strength that had been no match for the Darkness. Now it had claimed her. And the Oracle was entombed with her. Forever.

He pressed his hand against the wall of ice that encased her, screaming his rage into the darkness, pressing even as his skin grew numb. If only he could touch her. If only he could hold her. If only he could look again into those soft violet eyes that glowed with love and the strength of the power within her.

"There must be a way." But even as he searched for it, he saw no way to release her from the ice.

Then sorrow turned once more to anger. He clasped the sword tight in both hands and began hacking away at the ice. Striking and slicing, chips of ice flying through the air, hitting him, tiny ice crystals melting, water running like tears at his face.

He refused to let the Darkness have her, forever suspended in time, neither dead or alive. As he brought the sword up for another blow, light reflected at the blade. Light in a darkened chamber.

He spun about wondering what new trick this was. But there was nothing but shadows. He swung the sword back around and saw it again, a reflection of light that gleamed on the sword, slid along the blade as he turned away, then returned as he turned back. The light came from within the ice crystal, from the very heart of it, clasped in her hand. The Oracle.

It pulsed, a tiny, fragile glow of light, like a beating heart.

Her power joined with that of the Oracle. The power was strongest in her.

Not dead, but alive. Cassandra was alive inside the crystal of ice. He knew it. If only he could reach her, free her and return her to the mortal world. He raised the sword again, then slowly lowered it. If he shattered the ice, it might kill her.

There had to be a way. . . .

He had to think, remember what it had been like those other times, those other encounters with the Darkness. Tricks and illusions. He could not cut the ice and risk harming her. But it could be melted.

Seizing the sword he returned to the exact place he had stood when the light of the Oracle reflected off the blade of Excalibur. He angled the blade in exactly the same position. The light of the Oracle glowed white hot off the blade, then reflected back at the icy surface.

He angled the blade slightly and the glow intensified. He changed the angle and reflected the light off the blade. It burned brighter, glowing almost blue white. Droplets of water began to form on the surface of the ice. They beaded and slowly ran down the sides like ancient tears.

The light within the Oracle intensified, growing hotter and brighter, reflecting a shimmering heat off Excalibur. The shape of the crystal began to change as it melted, runnels of water pouring from it like the last cold of winter before the blessed warmth of spring.

Renewal, rebirth, life itself emerging, as she began to emerge. A silken strand of hair, the length of slender leg, the curve of her shoulder. Then her features as ice melted away, the pale curve of her cheek, the fullness of her mouth, and still it melted away. The curve of her arm, a rounded breast, the hem of her gown.

A slender hand was exposed, ice melting away at the curve of her back, her neck and her hair. The Oracle emerged, the light within it pulsing brighter like an awakening heartbeat. Ice melted from her eyelids, cheek, and throat. The fingers clasped around the Oracle moved. The curve of her breast rose and fell on a drawn breath. Feebly at first, then as if she had been under water for a very long time and suddenly broke the surface. Her eyes fluttered open, and she gasped. A soft cry of pain as she returned to the world of the living.

Her other hand fluttered, then clasped protectively over the child. Even now, in that place between living and dying, her first thought was for the child. The ice crystal continued to melt, pieces falling away, until she slipped from what remained of her icy prison.

Stephen caught her, easing her to the floor of the

chamber. She was pale as death, her skin icy cold, her
hand slightly warmer where she still clasped the Oracle.

She shuddered with every painful breath she took,
dragging air back into her frozen lungs, her wet hair
spilling over his shoulder.

He stripped off his tunic and wrapped her in it. Cradling her against him, he rubbed her hands and arms,
across her shoulders and down her legs, willing life into
her with every stroke of his hands that forced the blood
through her veins and color back to her skin.

She seemed unchanged, the slender curves beneath
her gown as familiar as if he had touched her only yes-
terday. Then his hand stroked over the child. The curve
of slender waist was gone, the slight roundness now full
and taut, swelling up to her breasts.

How long? How much time had passed? It seemed
only days since he had ridden out with his men to meet
Malagraine. Yet the fullness of the child within her
spoke of the passage of weeks, months, and seasons in
this place where time moved out of itself.

Then he felt the child move, a slow, stretching of
movement like awakening. His child, alive within her.

She reached up, her fingers brushing his cheek. His
hand closed over hers. He kissed the tips of her fingers,
still cool against his lips. Yet through the lethargy of
the long sleep, Cassandra felt a new urgency.

"We must leave this place," she whispered.

"Can you stand?"

She nodded, her jaw clenching as she slowly sat up.
Then fell back again. It had taken all her strength to
sustain her own life and that of their child. Superhuman
strength that the powers of Darkness could not kill or
vanquish. And so, unable to destroy her, they had imprisoned her. As Merlin had been imprisoned.

Holding her against him, Stephen slipped the sword

into the scabbard at his back. Then he guided her arm up around his neck.

"Hold onto me," he whispered against her damp hair as he lifted her in his arms and turned toward the portal.

"No," she cried out weakly. "The power of the Darkness is too strong here. And mine not strong enough to assure the journey. If we open the portal again and fail, we may leave a path open into our own world through which the Darkness will follow."

"Then we will find another way," Stephen replied as he called to Fallon, the wolf falling into step at his heel as he carried her from the star chamber.

He carried her through the darkened halls of Camelot—a Camelot that never was—and across the courtyard. Fallon ran on ahead. They crossed the main courtyard. When he had passed through only a short while before, the city seemed alive.

Now the courtyard was empty, the building crumbling to dust. The gates gaped open. No guard stood at the tower. No lights glittered along the walls. No conversations or laughter reached them. Only that strange foreboding of silence. Of something waiting and watching.

The sky overhead was leaden. It might have been those last few moments before dawn, or the last before night fell. That pall of grayness hung over everything. He gently set Cassandra on her feet as they reached the stables.

They were empty. Without a horse there was no hope of reaching the mountains. He turned back to her, wondering if he had released her from frozen sleep for his own selfishness only to lose her now. For she could not travel afoot the distance he had.

There in the yard, with the evil of Darkness closing around them, she knelt beside the white wolf, laying her head against his shoulder. The creature's wise silver eyes gleamed. Her eyes closed.

Her thoughts reached out, connecting with Fallon's, in that bond that was old and familiar between them as the power of the Light moved within her, slowly at first, then painfully as she stroked that strong shoulder.

Where the wolf had been now stood a white horse. The white horse tossed its head as Stephen approached. Silver eyes gleamed.

"We must go now."

Stephen swung astride the horse, then lifted Cass before him. A length of rope provided a halter and reins.

Stephen pushed them as hard as he dared. The ride was long and grueling. It seemed to stretch on for hours, perhaps days. It was impossible to know. Cass rode silently before him, wrapped in his tunic, the Oracle held tight in her hand.

They stopped briefly to rest at the river where he had passed before, but he dare not let the horse drink from the brackish water. Then moving on, climbing through the hills, toward a distant mountain he was not even certain he could find again without the wolf to guide them.

He felt the moment when the horse was spent beneath them, yet drove him on.

"Stop!" Cassandra cried out. "You must stop. You're killing him."

But Stephen forced the horse on, slipping to the ground and leading when the animal could no longer bear both their weight. Until he heard the creature groan painfully. The horse stumbled, yanking the reins from his hands as those long legs buckled and it collapsed, rolling Cassandra to the ground.

She pushed to her knees and crawled to the horse. Its great sides heaved. Bloodied foam appeared at its mouth. She lifted that massive head and cradled it in her arms.

She was weeping softly when Stephen reached her, the creature transformed, the wolf laying with its head in her lap. Eyes bright with tears lifted to his.

"There is nothing you can do," Stephen told her gently. "We must go."

She nodded, stroked the white head tenderly, and then slowly stood. As they began the last, long climb through the rocks, she glanced back. The wolf's silvery white fur glistened. Then mist slowly began to rise, surrounding it, fading, until it disappeared completely.

They continued climbing up through the rocks, like the spires of a castle.

"It is here," Cassandra said, moving with certainty through rocks only he had seen before and was not at all certain he could find again. Then he saw the glow of residue on the rocks as she passed her hand over them—the essence of their earlier passage through this place.

They found the opening and slowly began the descent into the passage. As it grew darker within, the light of the Oracle glowed brighter, guiding them.

Her breath caught as the pain moved through her again, this time without warning. It seized like a fist, driving the air from her lungs on a startled sound.

Stephen was immediately beside her.

" 'Tis nothing," she lied, setting her jaw stubbornly. "We must go on." But even as she defied the pain, it returned, drawing her belly tight, twisting inside, until she cried out. Stephen's arm went round her, a strong, fierce strength to hold onto as the pain moved through her.

Even now, her thoughts turned inward, toward the child, communicating in the rhythm of a beating heart and the lifeblood that flowed between them.

Not yet. Not in this dark lost place.

His hand low at her belly, Stephen felt the sudden clenching of her slender muscles, and the powerful surge of the child as it moved within her.

He swung her up into his arms. Ahead, a ribbon of light glowed. He concentrated on that glow of light, moving steadily toward it, away from the darkness that had tried to claim her.

The Oracle glowed brighter in her hand, reaching out toward that distant light, connecting them, glowing around them.

Then they were stepping through, light surrounding them, brilliant colors and images blurring past as Stephen held her tight against him, reaching for the other side, praying that the world that waited on the other side was the same world they had left behind.

Twenty

Pine oil lamps burned about the chamber, their pungence filling the air. A fire glowed in the brazier, creating halos of gold light across pale sandstone walls and the girl who lay on the pallet of furs.

Perspiration beaded across her forehead, the midnight satin of her hair damp against her cheek. A soft woolen bed cloth covered her breasts and swollen belly, the edge pulled up over her bent knees.

As another pain took hold, her body convulsed. Her head went back, slender arms stretched overhead, knuckles white as she clasped the stout wood pole that had been tied across the posts of the bed.

The pain receded and another immediately began. When she again reached for the birthing post, Stephen's strong hands closed over hers instead.

He slipped down onto the pallet beside her, his arm going round her shoulders. He held her as the pain rolled through her and then peaked, until she lay spent, her head against his shoulder.

Almost immediately another pain began, coming almost on top of the last one so that she could hardly gather her strength to meet it.

When Lady Vivian brought a cool cloth, he took it from her. With great tenderness, he stroked it across Cassandra's forehead and down her neck, across her breasts and down the length of each arm. Then her breath caught and the next pain was upon her.

Stephen held her tight, feeling the pain peak and twist within her as she struggled to bring forth his son. Another pain and Lady Vivian was drawing back the cloth, exposing Cassandra's slender bent legs.

"Is there nothing you can do to ease the pain?" Stephen asked.

"If I were to take it from her," Vivian explained, "she would not know when to push. Have faith, she is strong."

But in his anguished eyes, she saw the deep and profound love he felt for her sister and felt a wave of pity. It was so difficult for men. And she thought of her own husband when their child had been born, a brave warrior reduced to tears as he swore he would never allow her to bear another child for he could not bear her suffering of it. Yet even now a new life stirred inside her. She must remember to tell him of it.

"It will be soon," she said, her clear blue eyes watching the young warrior who cradled her sister, giving him the opportunity to leave if he so chose it. A tumult of emotions lined his face not the least of which was fear. But there was no hesitation in his decision.

"I will stay."

As the next pain began, Cassandra clung to his hand, straining, trying to push the child from her body. The pain immediately rolled into another, her muscles cramping and spasming. She cried out, dragging deep gulps of air into her lungs, gasping as another pain took hold.

The cloth was drawn back. She lay naked on the bed, knees drawn up, body straining. A cry broke from her lips, followed by a startled gasp. Over the taut roundness of her belly, Stephen saw a tiny head emerge.

Her body convulsed with another pain and she clung to his hand. As Stephen watched, both terrified and humbled, a small shoulder appeared. One more push and his son slipped into the world.

He was small and perfect, crying lustily as Vivian cleaned and then wrapped him in a blanket. Rounding the bed she handed the baby to Cassandra.

Stephen stared down in awe at the small new life that lay against her breast. A cap of dark hair molded the baby's head, blue eyes squinting back at them, the small stubborn chin quivering as his mouth opened and closed.

Cassandra brought him to her breast, a child that was both mortal and immortal, the wisdom of the ages flowing through his veins, a legacy of love and power.

Stephen tenderly stroked his son's small hand. Fingers opened then closed over his, taking hold of his heart. He stared down in wonder of this fragile new life that was part of them both, and part of a legacy that wove their lives together in the threads of a tapestry.

"What do you see?" Cassandra asked.

As his mouth sought hers with aching tenderness, Stephen said, "I see the future."

Epilogue

Light glowed in the starchamber from a dozen torch lamps that lined the walls. They spread a glow across pale, sandstone walls, gleamed across the ancient embossed crest on the wall and across the gleaming dark wood of the round table.

Here, all of Stephen's warriors gathered. Sir Kay, Gavin, and de Lacey. Eleven in all. At a nod from Stephen, they all laid their swords upon the table, so that those gleaming, deadly tips all converged on the center of the table in a gleaming circle of steel. Including the sword Excalibur, carried from the place in the mist into battle. All except one.

"Your sword, Truan Monroe," Stephen insisted, reminding him of the place he had earned among them.

"You must join us. Twelve places about the round table. Twelve warriors with brave swords who faced the darkness of Malagraine."

Truan hesitated, feeling the weighted stare of the one who waited in the softly steeped shadows.

"The place is yours," Stephen told him. "I would have no other lay his sword beside mine."

Finally, Truan nodded. Slowly and with great care he laid his sword in the twelfth place at the legendary table, taking his place with Stephen and his warriors. When it was done, there was a movement in the shadows.

Cassandra carefully handed her son to old Meg. A strange expression crossed the old woman's face as she took the small, warm bundle, as though through her blindness she saw into a distant future.

A tiny fist waved above the curve of blanket, with a warrior's strength, and wise old eyes stared back from the baby's face. The light of the torches gleamed in the baby's eyes, the power of the Light strong within his blood.

Cassandra carefully unwrapped the small crystal orb. It seemed to glow with a fire of its own. Fire that joined with the power of Excalibur had been enough to melt the icy cocoon that encased her, freeing her from the world of Darkness into the world of the Light.

It was suspended within a gleaming golden orb and seemed to float within her cupped hands. She approached the round table where another ancient king had once sat in counsel with his warriors. In another time and place.

She thought of Arthur and the poignant sadness of the betrayal that had torn him from the woman he loved and destroyed his kingdom. Her gaze sought Stephen's and in their golden amber depths, she saw the bearing of a king, the fierce passion of a warrior brave enough to face the Darkness, and the deep, tenderness of love he'd shown when he had first held his son, only minutes old and still wet with her blood. A warrior-king not unlike Arthur.

She slowly approached the table, the light of the orb spilling through her fingers. As she leaned over the edge, the light glowed brighter and expanded. Then she set the Oracle at the center of the round table.

It slipped into place, like a brilliant jewel set in a ring, the light spreading the length of each gleaming sword so that it looked like a sunburst and the Oracle was the bright sun at the center of the universe.

Light expanded throughout the chamber, like a star

exploding, bathing the walls with light, a white-hot intensity brighter than a hundred suns. At the center of the light very near the ancient crest, a portal slowly opened.

Stephen squinted against the light. At first he saw nothing. Then, eventually he saw a man, as though seen from a very great distance, slowly walking toward them. Then he seemed to step through the light, streamers of mist clinging to his long blue tunic that winked with the light of a thousand stars.

He was dressed all in blue, except for his black leather boots that molded his long legs. He had the leanness and the stance of a warrior, his silver capped head held high, his unusual blue gaze above a full close-cropped silver beard, sweeping the length and breadth of the starchamber with a sort of awestruck wonder and fierce possessiveness.

He had patrician features, sharp cheekbones, strong chin, and a firm mouth. But his eyes were the eyes of a sorcerer, wise, older than time itself, filled with enormous sadness of things lost and things he could only imagine—the touch of a child's hand in his, small and fragile, the warm sweetness of a child's kiss against his cheek.

Those wise, old eyes met Cassandra's in silent, tentative communication. Tears pooled in her eyes as she held out a hand hesitantly and said, "Father?"

He was older than when they had last met in that other time and place. She remembered the young man he had been when he had tried to send her back to fulfill her destiny, knowing what it meant for him—banishment to the world between the worlds. A nonworld that existed only in myth and legend, until she returned the Oracle to its rightful place, at the center of the round table at Camelot where a much younger man had once been counselor to a king.

So many feelings. So many things she had not understood before.

"Daughter," he whispered fiercely as he reached out and pulled her into his arms.

The great hall at Camelot was once more alive with laughter and conversation, as it had not been for five hundred years.

Stephen's knights and warriors joined in the celebration. An abundance of food was spread across the tables. They joined in games and contests of physical prowess. Stephen saluted Truan across the long table.

"You still have much to account for, my friend. How is it you were able to open the portal?"

Truan shrugged. "I did not open it. It was the Lady Vivian."

"You opened the portal. I saw it."

"Did you?" Truan asked, his eyes glinting with laughter. "Or do you merely believe you saw it. Illusions can have that effect."

"Several saw it."

"Or perhaps saw the same illusion."

"Yet, I was able to pass through the portal and return with Cassandra."

"Did you?"

"Here," Stephen invited, "have another goblet of wine. Then we shall speak of this again."

Only Amber held herself apart from the celebration. She moved about the edge of the great hall, silently refilling wine goblets, seeing that food was replenished. But always her gaze came back to Truan.

The priest also drank deeply of the wine brought from England, after christening the newborn son of the new lord of Camelot, proclaimed by King William himself. Only Cassandra knew that Stephen accepted it with mixed feelings—feelings that were still unresolved between father and son. But he had made a solemn vow to Cassandra as they lay together after their son was born.

I will never set our son from me as my father did. Upon my life, he will know that he is loved.

His fierce vow had moved her to tears—tears that joined his as they looked down upon their son, the legacy for the future.

Now, another gazed down upon the child, his grandson, and saw something of himself in blue eyes that stared back at him with undisguised curiosity.

"You risked much, daughter," Merlin said, lovingly stroking his hand against her cheek.

Cassandra laid her hand over his. Closing her eyes, she tried to capture all the missed love of a lifetime and hold it to her.

"You made it possible."

Merlin leaned forward. "Then you do remember your journey back through time."

She nodded. "And that you saved my life."

"You saved your own life and that of my grandson."

"But you lost so much," she protested.

"And much was gained."

"What of Arthur and everything that went before? Will it happen again?" For they both knew that the threads of the tapestry were not complete. Many lay unwoven, the images unformed. Images of a future that was not yet determined.

Merlin understood the fear in her heart—the fear for her child, just as he had feared for his children in an uncertain world.

"The future is in your hands," he said prophetically. "Yours and your sisters'. It is for you to determine what it holds."

"And the Darkness?" she asked, desperately wanting

him to tell her that it was over—that she need not fear for her son's future.

"It waits at the edge of the Light."

She shivered as she remembered that terrifying trip into the forest and Margeaux's brutal death. A child of Darkness that waited at the edge of the light.

"Are you cold?" Stephen asked, later that night as they lay together on the pallet of furs. He felt the quiver pass through her. Between them, curled in the curve of Cassandra's body lay their son.

She shook her head. " 'Tis only that I had hoped . . ." her voice faded as the thought went unspoken.

Stephen's fingers slipped beneath her chin, lifting it. "What had you hoped for?"

"That we might have more time," she whispered softly. "I have waited a lifetime for my parents and now he has gone to London."

"I promise we will see them both soon," Stephen assured her. "He could not bear to be parted from Ninian. She is his life."

Between them, their son awakened. He made soft, squeaking sounds at first, but then turned his head in search of her. When he did not immediately find Cassandra's warmth, he made stronger sounds. She lifted the blanket and brought him to her breast.

Stephen watched as that tiny mouth latched on to her engorged nipple, a tiny droplet of milk appearing at the corner of the baby's mouth. Then the babe's eyes closed and he settled to suckling contentedly.

He reached out, tenderly stroking that small round cheek and the powerful connection that drew life from her breast, and he felt humility he had never known before. He was a warrior, like the figure etched into the surface of the rune stone she wore around her neck.

He took lives, but she alone had the power to create life. He lifted her chin and tenderly kissed her.

"As you are my life, my heart, my soul."

In October, 1997 Zebra Books will publish MERLIN'S LEGACY: SHADOWS OF CAMELOT, the fourth book in Quinn Taylor Evans' wonderful, mystical series. Here is a taste of the passion and adventure to come.

MERLIN'S LEGACY:
SHADOWS OF CAMELOT

Amber followed the tracks through the snow out to the newly built stables. The scent of fresh-hewn lumber blended with the clean pungency of dried grasses and leather harness.

She called out as she entered the stables, but there was no answer. There was only the sound of the horses. They snorted and moved restlessly in their stalls, darting this way and that, as if trying to escape. As if some creature darted amongst them.

She had followed him, hoping to catch some moment alone with him. But as she walked through the long, low building her uneasiness grew.

He watched her as she came closer. The way the late afternoon sunlight slanted through the door opening behind her, slipping through her golden hair like fingers of fire, framing her in light, glowing around her like a brilliant sun.

He sensed her fear and the wild urgency, one overriding the other as she bravely walked farther into the stables, tiny clouds of dust exploding into the air underfoot with each step she took, the blood fierce in his veins with needs that terrified him and should have terrified her.

Amber thought she saw something. A horrifying beast

that rose out of the shadows, like a creature of the night. It moved along the wall, stalking her, backing her to the doorway.

Then she was bathed with sudden warmth. It washed across her face then down along the curve of her neck. Almost like a lover's caress. A seduction of the senses in those dark shadows so complete, so fierce and passionate that it stole the air from her lungs and built a fire along every nerve ending.

"Truan?" Still there was no answer, only the certainty that she was not alone.

Then he was upon her, pinning her against the wall. Hands plunging back through her hair, molding her head as he held her for his kiss, then plundering her mouth until she cried out softly.

"You should not have come here." His voice was harsh, a snarl torn from somewhere deep inside.

"I had to," she whispered, struggling between fear and a raw naked desire like a wild creature clawing inside her, trying to get out.

"I could not bear to let you go. I was afraid I might never see you again." Her slender hands lay against his chest, fingers gently curling into the fabric of his tunic as she lifted her mouth to his.

"I love you. I have always loved you."

The words were sweet from her lips, she who had spoken no words after the terrors she had seen, and now spoke them to him from her heart.

"You do not know what you say. 'Tis impossible. There are things you do not know." His hands trembled as he stroked her cheeks, fingers tangling in her hair with a longing that came from that hidden place inside him.

"I know only that I love you, and I cannot bear to let you go."

Truan groaned, a sound that was part agony, part fear,

and then all desire as he kissed her again, plundering her mouth, hating himself with every breath he took.

He cursed the fates that had made him what he was with every stroke of his tongue; tasted her sweetness with a sort of wild, desperate hopelessness; and prayed with every part of his soul that she had not seen the creature for he could not bear to see in her eyes the look of passion and desire turned to fear.

ROMANCE FROM JANELLE TAYLOR

ANYTHING FOR LOVE   (0-8217-4992-7, $5.99)

DESTINY MINE   (0-8217-5185-9, $5.99)

CHASE THE WIND   (0-8217-4740-1, $5.99)

MIDNIGHT SECRETS   (0-8217-5280-4, $5.99)

MOONBEAMS AND MAGIC   (0-8217-0184-4, $5.99)

SWEET SAVAGE HEART   (0-8217-5276-6, $5.99)